The Sands of Time

Book 4 of the Kate Mallory Chronicles

Cover design by Bernard Pearson using
elements from
Solomandra Dreamstime.com

DEDICATION
***

This book is dedicated to fellow ancient Egypt lover, Laurie Palmer – our escapades in Cairo, Luxor and along the Nile live on here, dear friend.

And to the memory of the great Siberian Baritone Dmitri Hvorostovsky, whose beautiful voice has formed the background to my writing.

ACKNOWLEDGEMENTS

The talents of the incomparable
Bernard Pearson, whom Sir Terry
dubbed the Cunning Artificer, who has
urged me on in my writing and designed all the
fabulous covers.

The Discworld Community, fans of the great Sir
Terry Pratchett worldwide, and all the good and
helpful friends within it, who have encouraged and
helped in so many
ways. Without you there would never have been four
books, and certainly not the unimaginable magical
thing that put
amazing characters into my head and got
them going where all I had to do was try to
keep up with them. I'm as amazed by these people and
their activities as any reader. It's a wonderful ride.

Also by Nancy Wolff

The Kate Mallory Chronicles

The Dragons of Wyvern Hall
Book One

A Wedding in Venice
Book Two

Chen Shi's Children
Book Three

Prologue

"Apep, wake up! Wake up!"

The huge coils of the snake that was the ancient Egyptian God of Chaos Apep or Apophis, moved slightly. A mighty head appeared from under a coil. What was unnerving was that this enormous reptile was semi-transparent. This didn't stop it from reacting with rage.

"What? How dare you disturb my slumbers you wretched demon. I sleep now as a dead god because no one believes in me. No one fears me. There are no more Egyptian gods, evil or good. Get thee gone, foul demon, or I will make of you a snack. A snake snack, ha!"

The demon in service to the great Apep, backed away in fear, dropping to his belly he mumbled into the sand, "I wake you, oh Great One, because there is news. Finally, there is news of rebirth."

Apep hissed. "Not my rebirth, oh foul smelling one, I would have known."

"No, Lord of All Evil, but there is an awakening of belief in the Cat Goddess Bastet, and her power increases. There has been a festival for her in Bubastis, and it is said thousands attended."

Apophis felt something like a faint stirring in his long, long body, something that felt like…life. There was a rebirth of belief, was there? And in a cat goddess. He remembered with extreme distaste the battle between himself and Mau, another cat god, closely linked to the Sun God Ra. Mau who protected the Persea Tree, the Egyptian Tree of Life that gave knowledge of the divine plan.

Apep, as God of Chaos, battled the Sun God every night to keep him from rising again. He always lost. So he had tried another tack — taking control of the Persea Tree of Life and thus the fate of the world and Ra. But the Cat God Mau (that some called another facet of Ra) had done battle with Apep, and finally cut off the serpent's head. Although Apep was entirely immortal, this had stopped that attempt to control the world. His head, of course, had regrown, or been replaced by magic. Even he was not privy to all the laws that governed the immortal.

And then came the Romans, the Ptolemies and finally the Christians and the Muslims, and the old Egyptian Gods were to all intents and purposes no more. Just hieroglyphs and stories, souvenirs and museum exhibits. And in his long sleep as a 'dead' god, Apep sometimes dreamed of his hatred of cat gods and his desire to, if not destroy, at least be the equal of these fiends in fur. And able to torment them. Unlike any other Egyptian god, Apep had an army, small demons like the one now grovelling before him. And he had something else. Unlike so many of the gods and goddesses, who could be very human in their ability to do now goo and now bad, to be kind and loving and the be tormented bo jealousy and anger and lust—Apep was simply—evil. Unalloyed pure evil. No redeeming features whatsoever. Also, unlike the other gods, Apep never changed his for or identity. It was probably what made him so strong, so truly immortal.

"A reawakening of real belief? This is news indeed. And what can happen for one could happen for all. Or if not all, at least many," mused Apep.

"And the scales must balance. So Evil must also rise," ventured the demon, looking up with hope in his eyes.

"As you say, as you say, this could happen. What is your name, demon, I don't remember?"

"I am Decay, oh Mighty One," said the demon, venturing to stand once more. Several bits of him dropped off.

It made Apep laugh. "Decay, you are, decay you do! But you bring important, possibly good news. I will not therefore devour you."

"Oh, the Evil Apep is merciful," cried Decay.

"I..eh…actually now go by initials. You know, like rap stars? I'm the Demon D K!" He stood straight and puffed out what passed for his chest. If possible, it made him even uglier than before.

"What, you excrescence upon the earth, is a 'rap star'?" growled Apep.

The demon who, along with small horns had upon his head a growth, which wasn't unusual. Apep's demon army were essentially small, painfully thin brown to black beings with horns and tails. But each possessed many distinguishing features. D K had skin that both flaked and oozed, and he left a trail of bits when he moved, plus having an assortment of warts and sores, some rudimentary scales and spikes of a lighter brown than his body, a matted hairy coat but with beetle wings also, and this extra headdress. Except now he removed this, leaving just his horns and some strands of oily hair that he'd done in a comb-over. He held out the thing to Apep—who literally recoiled.

"Oh, my Lord Apep, just allow me to move this closer to your ear," cried D K eagerly, "and you will understand what Rap Music is."

Apep lowered his great head nearer the object and shot back as something like a car crash erupted from the thing. It was followed by a mix of rapid-fire words and something like an orchestra with St Vitus dance. "That's R J and the Frogs, that is!" announced D K who was vibrating his body and shuffling his misshapen feet to the intrusive beat.

"It's   vile! Vile! But strangely compelling." His coils were vibrating, his head nodding to the beat and his enormous body seemed to be gaining substance and was less transparent. "I like it."

Chapter 1

That evening back in Devon Chauncey was in a celebratory mood.

"I'm sending out announcements. I'm going to visit Egypt, the Egyptian Dragon Principality, first to thank them for cooperating so quickly and so well to eliminate Wyvern-Proteus. And see how Mirabelle and Gently are getting on there. I won't try to contact Feral or Elvira at this point, but I do need to express my deep gratitude to Prince Faisal and his court. Maybe they will give me a 'coming out' party. What do you think?"

"I think you deserve every bit of pomp and fun they can arrange for you," said Kate. "And it's lovely that your first real free outing will be to thank them."

"And after that I will do a quiet visit to the Chinese Dragons. I'm very fond of my brother, the Vizier. They will want to brag that I came to them, but I can make sure they don't. No splendid banquets, no parades, just me and my brother. And if anyone else gets to know about it, they also know to keep their mouths shut.

"But what about you two? Are you going on to university now?"

Kate and Robin looked at each other, slightly

embarrassed.

"Actually, no," said Kate. "Although I haven't figured out a good reason to tell Uncle Hugh. He's taking it for granted that I will. But maybe I can put it off another year and get Perry to back me up that I haven't quite got all the courses I need for what I want to study."

"Or a gap year to travel," said Robin.

"Maybe, maybe…but maybe we might actually go travelling like ordinary humans."

"Oh, of course! Just as I have had to go around like a thief in the night, you have been living a very unusual life as well," said Chauncey.

"We've come to think of it as just our lives," said Kate. "And honestly, although you've been half a prisoner, we've been, well, set free. I don't think that we are going to follow a more ordinary path now."

"I don't think we could, really," said Robin. "My mother has lived a double life, or maybe triple — antique expert, forensic accountant and powerful witch.

"Or quadruple or something," laughed Kate. "Married to a Faerie Prince and the job of being your mother."

"The thing is…" said Robin, "the thing is, we don't quite know what we want to pursue besides being magical. There's still so much to learn there. And we both want to help or just be friends with dragons."

"There is so much I'd like to learn about so many things," said Kate. "A lot of Egyptology, and also, believe it or not, marine biology and astrophysics, and geology, plate tectonics, that kind of thing. But I don't think a degree from a university in any of those is what I want, especially when I can call on you, Chauncey, to tell me about the Earth 'way back when, or use magic to study the stars or the earth, to ask the Egyptian dragons what it was like centuries ago, well that's more than I can learn from a university or a lot of text books. History as it's taught seems so often to be dates of battles and who was born or married or died when. That's important, but I want to know how people lived, what it was like to experience ancient things.

"Plus, I feel like we should—witches should—be using their powers to help. Bunged up in a university it would be difficult to just suddenly disappear on a mission of some sort. So having thought it through we've decided that universities aren't for us. But how I convince Uncle Hugh of that I don't quite know.

"One thing I do know. My mother had a friend, in so far as she had friends, who'd been a prima ballerina and later on took advanced degrees and taught at university. She saw that I was bright, but had no focus, so she tried to get me to seriously consider being a university professor as a career. I remember two feelings. One was I probably wasn't bright enough, even though I was beginning to show I was. But the other was that I felt she—this now famous woman—had trapped herself in two very narrow areas. I never said anything, because ballet and academic brilliance were both a big deal in New York, but to me it seemed she'd locked herself into such specialist areas, both, by the way, full of back-biting and politics, that I felt if I went that way I'd suffocate. So, I drifted, as my mother would have said. But as it happened, I drifted into something much bigger and more exciting, and not so constrained. Plus really no politics. And plenty of acceptance and love."

"There has been danger though," said Robin. "You were in real danger more than once."

"But I had people on my side, and I got out. Honestly, if I had to choose, I'd rather danger than back-biting and gossip and narrow confines to what is acceptable."

"We'll figure that out, my daughter," rumbled Chauncey. "Perry will have ideas, and Maggie and Julien. Hugh wants you to be happy. And at his age I think he might especially love to have you stay around Ashley. Plus you should tell him the story about the famous ballerina and college professor, and how you saw it as taking raw talent and putting it into a suffocating world, or worlds. So long as you see him often, and can also share new things you're learning, no matter how, he should be happy you have stayed."

"Oh, Ashley is my home for as long as Uncle Hugh is there...or maybe forever. Devon is also Robin's home, with the Cottage Over The Stream. We love it around here, even if it is getting so crowded — I guess the rest of the world loves the West Country too. But I dearly want to see more of Egypt, so maybe we could come with you there?"

"You've given me an idea," said Chauncey. "Remember I promised you to take you flying and also diving? Well, I'm much too big for you to ride me like you do Lilac Moon and Dark Moon. And it goes without saying you couldn't survive the stratosphere or the ocean depths."

Never one to hide his enthusiasm about his own cleverness, Chauncey continued, "I had a really fine idea! You know those clear glass or whatever deep-sea rovers, where you sit in comfort and have an unimpeded view of everything around you? I thought with a bit of modification something like that would be perfect to seat two or possibly even four, shaped at the bottom like the saddles you use when you ride, to fit comfortably over my neck in front of my wings. It would be equipped with sufficient air and pressurised for both deep sea and high atmosphere flying. I'd fly, and you'd sit in comfort, and we could talk and I could show you both the wonders of the earth from space and the incredible diversity of what lies under the sea. You'd be quite safe, and we could finally go adventuring together."

Both Kate and Robin were literally gasping with wonder and delight at the very thought of what might be available to them, plus the sheer joy of going adventuring with Chauncey.

"And since you are longing to return to Egypt, that could be our first trip. I will fly you high, where there is almost no atmosphere, over Europe and when we reach the Mediterranean, I will dive and show you the wonders of the deep sea. Then I can drop you off near Luxor where you have your dahabeeyah and you can spend time with Elvira and Feral. Perhaps you can discuss the possibilities of them helping to teach Dawn, or perhaps I should say, give Dawn a sense of family and a sense of purpose. A few weeks ago, when their extended trip up the Nile was over, the Magical Misfits and the Dragons had persuaded Elvira (Feral didn't need any persuading, he'd have inhabited a palace if offered one) to accept a helping hand in the shape of a nice small villa near the Nile with a garden big enough to contain trees and arbors and pools that could conceal a few young dragons such as Peony Moon.

In return Elvira and Feral gave their promise that if she and Feral could help in any future adventures they would jump at the chance. They'd also been supplied with a computer and a tablet and mobile phone service. Now, given the similarity of parts of their childhoods, Kate and Elvira emailed at least once a week. Kate was quick to tell her Egyptian friends of Chauncey's plans to have a deep-sea rover modified for their use and their wish to finish off that adventure with a visit to see Elvira and Feral while Chauncey went to visit his Egyptian Principality. Elvira responded that Bastet (the Egyptian Cat Goddess who had been instrumental in destroying WP) was often a visitor and she and Elvira and Feral sometimes went riding on Peony Moon, sister to Kate and Robin's special dragon friends Lilac and Dark Moon.

"And you'll never guess," Elvira added on one of their FaceTime chats. "They've persuaded their sister Blue Moon to leave her semi-isolation and come to meet Bastet. Peony is convinced Blue and Bastet might really hit it off. You know how eager Bastet is to have a special dragon friend. And even though dragons are always their own people and never a pet, you know that to please a Goddess such as Bastet can make all the difference. We are hopeful. Maybe you can be here when Blue arrives?"

"It would seem a natural match, wouldn't it?" said Kate. "Since each wants to guard their privacy and I know Bastet prefers to keep her 'normal' life out of the public eye, even when she is involved in increasing her power by increasing the people's belief in her. Rather like a rock star or famous actor — the secret private life and the public persona. Blue Moon will certainly be helpful in protecting her privacy, since she knows so much about protecting her own. But I doubt she, Blue that is, would ever agree to helping Bastet's quest for power by letting her appear flying on a dragon."

"It wouldn't fit with the image Bastet has created over the millennia, anyway," said Elvira. "Bastet doesn't wish to become a modern superhero. The last thing she would wish is to be the inspiration for films or manga or any sort of world-wide fame that has little or nothing to do with her real role. She may wish to have a dragon for a friend and hopes to ride and take part in private adventures, but her role as a Goddess, although it evolves, evolves within certain limits and the culture of ancient Egypt. And we have no dragons in that pantheon."

"That's good. As I understand it," said Kate, "Blue, although not a recluse, also regards her privacy as paramount. She would never agree to some kind of cult accruing around herself and a goddess. But, yes, maybe we can arrange to be with you when Bastet and later Blue arrive. I'd love that, so long as we didn't overwhelm what should be a quiet meeting.

"Meanwhile, I'll keep you up to date on how Chauncey gets on with finding and modifying a deep-sea rover, or possibility having one built from scratch, and then when after that you can expect to see us again."

"Don't think of arriving in your summer, Egypt then is impossibly hot if you're not a native. Plan for October perhaps or later if your transport isn't ready."

Chapter 2

It turned out that a deep-sea submersible required a lot more careful crafting to resist the immense pressure deep under the sea than was required to build a space craft, which faced none of the hazards of great pressure. Quite the opposite in fact. Sufficient breathable air and protection from radiation were about all that was required for a spaceship such as the International Space Station. So there seemed to be no reason why a deep-sea going submersible shouldn't also provide air and more than enough shelter for dragon-back journeys into space up to about the level of the International Space Station or even out as far as the Hubble Space Telescope whose orbit was some 350 miles above the Earth and 150 miles above the ISS.

That was about the limit of Chen Shi's power to fly above the atmosphere anyway. But it was going to allow him to show his beloved adopted daughter and her partner wonders they would never otherwise get to see. He was full of plans and excitement.

"I feel much like your Santa Claus must feel shortly before he takes his magic sleigh each year—such excited happiness to know I am going to show you things no one human being has ever seen, and even make some of it up close and personal. I have loved the freedom to fly high and dive deep, unhindered by pressures or need to breathe [except occasionally], free to experience so much more of Earth that you can only imagine. Now I get to make my dream real—to take you to see these things too, so we can share the wonder." Chen Shi, Dragon King, was awash with shifting colours, all portraying his happiness.

Kate was almost bouncing with delight. Chauncey's colour display always enchanted her, and knowing that it was one of the ways dragons communicated (rather like cephalopods or some lizards) and that she now could understand the meaning behind some of those colours and the way they flashed (like Morse code) gave her the thrill that mastering any new knowledge could do. She remembered when her beloved Grandmother Lucinda had introduced her to the wonders of flowers and how their Latin names were interestingly descriptive—but the real excitement was the day when, looking at a plant, its name was there in her head. It was as if, after many hours looking at books and visiting gardens, she suddenly went from needing to read a label to just 'knowing'. It was thrilling.

"I remember when you first told me about diving deep into the perpetual black of the sea where the sun never penetrated. You said you discovered so many creatures that were bioluminescent and also that flashed their colours in various ways.

"Have you yet found any who can communicate as dragons and squid and octopuses do? That can send actual messages? Can you talk to any using your bioluminescence?"

Chen Shi pondered before answering. "You know I and a few of my children and some of the Japanese Principality dragons can converse with cephalopods, so when I dive really deep sometimes there is a giant squid or one of those rare deep-sea octopuses that can speak with me in a limited way. Bioluminescence isn't good for complex conversations! But along with 'Go away' or 'I am dangerous, poisonous' sort of thing I have met with 'Hello, who are you?' and 'Can we be friends?' or occasionally 'I haven't seen anything like you before.' which indicates a fair degree of intelligence. But just like humans have different languages, creatures of the deep may use their colours and codes to indicate something different than those living nearer the surface, so it can be complicated. Which is a very long way of saying, we don't communicate very well yet."

Kate laughed. "Thank all the gods that you could gather the dolphins and cephalopods to rescue me from WP's plan to have me drown in the Venetian lagoon. And that they could talk to me inside my head to reassure me. Now that you are free, Robin and I can hardly wait for this modified deepsea submersible to be ready so that we can fly with you—it will be the thrill of a lifetime."

"I've bought one of the four-seater ones and am having it modified by some very special craftspeople so that a new bottom is being made and fitted, one that perfectly suits the contours of my neck just above my shoulders where my wings start. So, you guys will sit in the submersible just as those aquanauts do, within a viewing bubble that enables you to see all around and above. I've even had it modified slightly so there is more breathable air available for longer trips, and protection against too much sunlight and radiation when we fly high above the earth, plus—ahem—snacks. Of course, you will be able to film and photograph just as the aquanauts do."

"What is it made of, to do all these things?" asked Robin.

"I'm afraid I'm not so scientifically minded that I went into that in detail. The brochure says it's made of composites, which I understand are carbon fibre stuff apparently similar to what Formula 1 racing cars are made of, and titanium, and the viewing bubble where you will sit is acrylic or Plexiglas—this can all withstand pressures over seven-thousand feet below sea level. That's about

2000 metres, or almost a mile and a half. Mostly I only dive to about 1500 metres at most, although I have gone deeper. The saddle will be positioned under where you will sit. There's a bit of a problem in that you enter from the top, but I figure if I lie my neck down flat and we have a ladder, or I'll get them to make a set of mobile steps, like those used when you board an airliner from the ground, then you can climb up and in without any trouble."

"What about flying up into space? Is it safe to do that?" queried Kate.

"With the addition of the filter against radiation, and the fact that even if I fly you to the height above Earth of the International Space Station or even the Hubble Space Telescope, we are still within the Earth's own field of protection against solar radiation, you shouldn't be in any danger at all," said Chauncey confidently. "I rarely fly even as high as the Space Station anyway, as I am much more interested in seeing the earth itself in more detail than up that high. Theoretically it would be fun to fly high enough so you could see other galaxies and nebula and stars as they are seen and photographed by Hubble—but those photos are telescopic and that means thousands, even millions or billions of miles further than Hubble itself, and that isn't a possibility for any of us, ever. However, I will call you attention to the amazing similarities between the deep-sea creatures we will see and some, even many, of the pictures of deep space objects Hubble has photographed. I find that endlessly fascinating."

"Oh, that makes this all the more exciting," said Robin and Kate was nodding her agreement enthusiastically. "We not only get to fly on the back of the Dragon King but explore things we've always wanted to see."

Kate ventured, "Chauncey, could we possibly have a few smaller flights and deep ocean descents before we use the trip to Egypt to see both? I'm looking forward so much to getting back to Egypt, but I really would love just to take our time exploring the seas and the earth for a few times before we make that trip."

"Splendid idea!" said Chauncey, beaming. "A few trial runs and we can go some special places that aren't on the way over Europe and the Med to Egypt. I'll take you to see some things I find really interesting. And we can sort out any little hiccups we might encounter."

"Let's just not do any hiccups under the sea," muttered Robin, but Chauncey heard him.

"Do you think I would risk you or Kate?" he demanded. "Never. There are back up air containers, and the whole thing is built to close off any kind of leak immediately. I was thinking more along the lines of any kind of water claustrophobia or fear that you are in a see-through bubble with apparently nothing between you and space. Or that you won't be as interested in what I can show you as I hope you will."

"Ah," said Robin. "I apologise. And remembering my fear when I went cliff climbing with Perry, I won't automatically say I will be fearless about height or depth."

"When will it be ready?" asked Kate, full of anticipation.

"In about a month, I reckon," said Chauncey.

"My stars, that's August already. This year has flown by. So if we do our 'test flights' for a month or two, amongst all the other stuff we'll be doing, we can be ready to go to Egypt in November, when the weather is pleasant for people like us, and stay on until about April."

Chapter 3

July in England, even in Devon, certainly wasn't like the hot, sunny weather Kate had once known in the USA. Here it might be warm, even sometimes quite warm, but hardly ever actually hot. And the skies were as often grey as they were blue with the sun beating down. But the fact was, she liked it. And for some reason, there were no insects intent on biting her. In America, Kate had been plagued with mosquitoes and sometimes flies. Here at Ashley Manor, unless she went to the pasture to talk to Uncle Hugh's horse and her own filly, Foxfire, or occasionally rode bareback round the field, she hardly even saw a fly. She occasionally came across mosquitoes, but for reasons unknown, they didn't bite her. She had an idea that somehow Devon, at least around Ashley, was so tied to her or she to it, that the area itself protected her from these irritations.

All in all, she much preferred England to anywhere with blazing sun and biting flies. But of course that was partially down to her red hair and pale skin. She knew the English preferred to take off for hot climates and come back sunburnt and tired, or, if they were lucky, suntanned and with some beautiful new romance beside them. She still needed sunscreen in blazing hot climates, but she already had her beautiful romance.

There was once again some work going on at Wyvern Hall. Without the risk of harm from his former nemesis, Ivor Wyvern empowered with the magic of the Chimera Proteus, Chauncey (with some urging from Kate and Perry as to their beauty and uniqueness) had decided that necessary repairs to the fabric of the building and restoration of some of the frescos and furnishings would make this a perfect aboveground resting place for him and some of his favourite children. It was close to Ashley and had the perfect outbuildings for housing the uniquely modified undersea rover that would shortly allow Chauncey to take Kate and Robin, along with Perry and Maggie or Julien, diving deep into the seas or high into the stratosphere.

Meanwhile, Maggie was once again busy in her office at Ashley Manor, keeping Sir Hugh's estate running smoothly, with no red entries in the ledgers.

"I insist," rumbled Sir Hugh, "that all my work on Save Our Seas with Julien be free, gratis— the world can't afford money-grubbing salaried people taking from what is planet-saving work."

"Lord Julien Reinhardt-Foxx can well afford to give his time and expertise," stated Maggie acerbically. "You, Sir Hugh, cannot. Your income from the estate is adequate now to run the estate, but to afford me, and support Kate and have the nice extras of life, you need to draw a proper salary. And," she added, raising a hand to stop the objections that he was about to voice, "I am here to see that it happens. Julien won't mind, believe me he is making money in lots of other ways. And don't you dare give me any of that codswallop about no owner of Ashley Manor has had to do salaried work, that's blatant Edwardian nonsense, and you know it. You're a child of the 1960s Sir Hugh, not of the 1860's."

Which made Hugh laugh and brought him down off his high horse with only minor damage to his pride.

"I suppose I should be proud to be making a living trying to save our oceans," he acknowledged. "Lord knows I was proud enough to make a wage as a seaman and a captain, then an admiral in Her Majesty's Navy. I guess this is no different."

"Exactly," said Maggie. "Particularly when your niece is about to cost you some more money taking her gap year before deciding upon university."

"Why does everybody know these things before I do?" grumbled Hugh. "But then I didn't expect Kate not to go haring off with Robin, probably to places I've never heard of. Do you know what they're up to, Maggie?"

"No more than you," lied Maggie with ease.

"Robin is much more forthcoming than when he was in his teens, but they have a whole life I know little about. At least, my friend, we know we can trust them these days. They've proved themselves to be intelligent and responsible and I've no doubt any plans they might have will probably be useful as well as exciting."

"I still worry sometimes about 'exciting'," mumbled Sir Hugh.

"Don't we all!" laughed Maggie. And that, thank goodness was the end of that.

Meanwhile, Kate and Robin were in the Cottage by the Stream redecorating the kitchen with magic. "I know they appreciate the modern look here, so much of the rest is fantasy land but I just thought it would be fun to keep the mod cons but make the kitchen a festival of colour," said Kate So they arched the ceiling and painted it with flowing designs incorporating fantasy animals, frescoed the walls with bucolic scenes of food and harvest, interspersed with some of their favourite recipes in various flowing scripts, changed the grey granite worktops for rose red granite and made embroidered pillows for the kitchen chairs. Tiles around a fireplace were decorated with animals and flowers, and cabinets were painted with clever artwork depicting what was inside. It was a feast of colour and pattern, but no modern piece of kit had been disposed of, just 'enhanced'. It gave them a day of honing different magic skills and looking forward to enjoying the surprised looks (possibly of horror) when Maggie and Kailen got home.

Kate was also taking a cram course via the internet on reading ancient Egyptian hieroglyphics. She'd figured out some time back that names always appeared within cartouches (ovals containing the pictograms spelling out the name). Now she was seriously studying the language itself.

"Look Robin," she said showing him her tablet. "Once you know that each tiny 'picture' is either a word or a syllable, things fall into place. Plus, although hieroglyphs were written in rows or columns and could be read from left to right or from right to left, the direction in which the text is to be read is obvious because the human or animal figures always face towards the beginning of the line. Also the upper symbols are read before the lower. So it's easy really. Well, sort of easy."

"For you maybe," said Robin. "For me it is total gobbledegook, nonsense."

"Well to get beyond the pictogram as a word and have it become a syllable you do have to learn to pronounce each one," admitted Kate. "I'm only at the beginning with that."

"And just why are you so involved in

reading ancient Egyptian?" he queried.

"Because I love Egypt, and we will be spending a lot of time there at the end of the year and into next year."

"But nobody we know there will be speaking in ancient Egyptian, or reading it either," said Robin.

"Bastet does," said Kate. "And the other gods."

"But she speaks English to us," countered Robin.

"Think a minute, if we want to really get on with her, and any other ancient Egyptian gods, speaking their language will be the finest compliment we can give them— it shows how much they mean to us."

"How much they mean to *you,* you mean," said Robin. "We might not even see Bastet again. Let alone any other old gods."

"Okay, so I'm just doing it because I'm really intrigued. But, Robin, I get this kind of tingly feeling when I think about the old gods and a sort of supernatural 'push' toward learning hieroglyphics. So I think my magic is telling me that learning how to do this could become important."

"In that case, I hope your magic is also going to help you to do it, because it looks awfully complicated to me."

"Actually, I think it is, I learn certain rules of the language and then things are falling into place much faster than I would expect. For instance, I get how to pronounce the words so fast, the pronunciation just sort of flies into my head once I can read a bit. That never happened before. I had an awful time learning how to pronounce *English* properly when I was a little kid. Never thought I was good at languages. So I'm guessing there is some bit of magical help going on here because this might become important."

"Well, since we're going to be hoping to convince Elvira and Feral to take on the unexploded bomb that is Dawn and are charged with helping with that—plus hoping Blue Moon might become Bastet's special dragon friend—I suppose learning ancient Egyptian can't go to waste," said Robin. "I'll give it a go if you'll help me."

Then they heard Maggie opening the front door, and, giggling, hid behind the centre workstation of the kitchen to see her reaction.

As people do, Maggie came first into the kitchen...and stopped, looking stunned. Then she slowly turned, taking it all in. Everything was in its usual place, but now scintillating with colour and pattern.

"I could change this back you know," she

spoke with a certain ominous tone. Kate and Robin froze, expecting the worst.

"But I'm not going to. I think it's fabulous! You've outdone yourselves, plus I see that those lovely pictures actually tell me where everything is. And I love the red granite. You're right, the other was much too sterile."

Kate and Robin appeared and embraced her just as Kailen appeared.

"What the ….?" he fairly bellowed. Kailen didn't take as quickly to change unless he was in charge of it. *Typical male, even if he is a faerie,* Kate had thought more than once.

But also because he was one of the Fae and they did love colour and decoration, plus seeing Maggie's brilliant smile and Kate and Robin's proud looks, he melted into approval. "About time the kitchen got a makeover," he said.

"You're lucky it isn't all Egyptian," commented Robin. "Kate is getting so fascinated by hieroglyphics that she's learning to read them."

Maggie laughed, "We'll give you a bedroom and a sitting room you can cover with all those lovely scenes of Egyptian afterlife if you want."

"Oh, that's sweet of you," said Kate. "But this is my English fairyland. I will wait for being in Egypt to create my beautiful ancient Egyptian decorative schemes."

Chapter 4

Chen Shi appeared on Kate's tablet as she settled for the night. Their nightly chats were ritual and a precious way of staying in close touch. They could also speak mind to mind but that lacked the extra of a picture of each other as they chatted.

"It's ready!" his grin was huge and toothy, but dear to Kate. "They're delivering it here tomorrow. Shall we go flying?"

"And diving?" asking Kate.

"And diving, yes, definitely. I won't go too high or too deep just in case the module isn't entirely airtight, we will test for that, but I can't put you at risk. It will, however, be a start."

"Can't wait," said Kate. "Thank goodness we're used to being invisible already. But...wait! That will mean the module is invisible too, so we can't manage any of its controls should we need to."

"Not a problem, there aren't any controls you have to manage—for you it will be just a comfortable bubble. I will manage any controls that might be necessary, a minimum I assure you. After all, once the undersea rovers are deployed and under the water, the only controls the pilot has are for steering, all the pressure and other things are out of his hands. We won't be pressurising it this time anyway, we are staying within easily breathable air both above ground and under sea. No difference in pressure. And plenty of air to breathe."

"And, of course, you're steering!" added Kate.

"Of course, exactly, as modified, it's really just a cabin for you and I'm the plane or the submarine!"

"I'll tell Robin. What time should we be at Wyvern Hall?"

"Mid-afternoon, I think. We'll have some sort of lunch or early tea, and then we can dive. Then some invisible flying to enjoy Britain from the air, and then back for some dinner and we'll fly again to enjoy the night sky. How does that sound? I've checked, the weather is supposed to be very clear, we're in luck."

" We'll be there at two pm, ok? Oh, my stars, I can hardly wait."

She explained it all to Robin, who'd been reading, and he was as excited as she was. "Do we need special clothes?"

"Chauncey didn't say, I'm sure he would have, or if not, they will be there waiting for us. You know him, he's always prepared."

"Well, then I'm going to wear something I'll be comfortable sitting in for a few hours, like on a plane. Kate, Sweetheart, are you crying? What's wrong? Everything sounds perfect."

"It's, well it's like the end of a nightmare and the beginning of something incredible—Chauncey is free, and we are going flying and diving," Kate wiped her eyes. "I remember when he told me about how he loved that, it was while he was still magically bound to being the central heating furnace. What I remember most is that he wasn't feeling sorry for himself, he was replaying his memories like a film, and he said he'd lived so long he knew this was just a sort of blip in his life. But I know how delighted he was to be able to go off flying and diving once we freed them all. Tomorrow, we get to do that too, a new chapter."

§ § §

As Robin's Mazda MX5 in brilliant red, that complimented Kate's MX5 which was British Racing Green, rounded the final curve that brought them up the mountain where Wyvern Hall was perched, they could see Chauncey and Lilac, Silver and Dark Moon all basking in the sunshine around a picnic table. There was no sign of the 'bubble'. But a splendid luncheon was laid out. It included an extremely large multi-storied cake, with a slight list.

After they had finished the usual greetings,

Lilac pointed it out and, laughing, admitted she'd been trying her hand at baking. "I got Maggie to give me the recipe for that wonderful cake she made us, and then I multiplied all the ingredients by ten. Luckily the oven here was large enough to hold all the layers, I baked them at the right temperature but for somewhat longer. Maggie said until a skewer or a knife blade came out clean. So I did that. The frosting was difficult, it took four huge mixing bowls to hold everything, and putting it all together, well, you see, it is not quite straight."

"But it tastes good," said Silver.

Although dragons must have a certain amount of coal and oil and even wood and minerals, many like Chen Shi and his children had also developed a taste for many human recipes, and Lilac particularly had a sweet tooth.

Kate went to hug her special dragon friend who was also the one she rode. In fact, everyone hugged everyone, even Chauncey extended a front foot for them to embrace his fingers. And all the dragons showed their happiness with a beautiful display of rippling colours over their scales.

The food was excellent (Chauncey had hired one of the stone people Wyvern had enchanted, who used to be a chef), but Kate and Robin were really just waiting to see the module with its special fittings. In fact, Chauncey decided he wanted them to see it already attached to him, so he disappeared behind the coach house that sheltered farm machinery, a tool shop, cars, even horses and now the module. Here his children brought the contraption out and settled it on his neck where it joined his shoulders and wings, and carefully strapped it in place, making sure it was secure but comfortable.

Then he marched out to show them the result. It was quite beautiful in fact. The 'saddle' that had replaced the pontoons was of some flexible material that shaped itself to his neck and cradled the Plexiglas viewing bubble. What was surprising (although knowing Chauncey, it probably shouldn't have been), was the splendid colours and decorative detail that blended beautifully with his gorgeous colours and the detail as of scales and a suggestion of wings that blending back over the beginning of his own.

"Oh gods! You look like a kind of gigantic modernist carousel horse!" cried Robin. He and Kate were both clapping. The clear Plexiglas bubble it cradled was about three metres (almost 10 feet) in diameter, with the entry not at the top but on one side, which was a relief to Kate. Since Chauncey himself was some 20 metres (about 65 feet) long, the bubble with its saddle was hardly a huge extra appendage. In fact, it blended in very well.

"But I thought we'd have to enter from the top," said Kate.

"Only because this is based upon those submersibles that float on pontoons and people have to be lowered in off the sides of boats," explained Robin. "Here we climb up a few steps to enter on dry land. And there's no extra space needed around the insides for equipment used to manoeuvre the thing."   "Exactly, Robin, exactly." said Chauncey grinning. "This is just the Plexiglas shell created before everything else was added to make it drivable. The extra air needed is built into the 'saddle'. Instead of all that instrumentation I've had them add extra seat padding and some containers for food and drink, plus cameras and a viewing camera that magnifies.   And look, here are the steps."

Dark Moon came around the corner of the building carrying the set of steps, also carved and painted to match the saddle. It did make Kate think of a carousel just a bit. There were only five steps to the door of the module.

"So, are we ready?" asked Chauncey, every scale glistening with his eagerness.

"Err, loo break!" declared Kate. "I don't care how well I know you all, I prefer not to use the 'facilities' in that bubble where every star and planet has a ringside view." So she and Robin retired to what in days past had actually been called 'the retiring room', and came back ready to go.

Chen Shi had lowered himself to the ground and laid his neck out flat, and the steps had been positioned up to the open door of the Plexiglas bubble. Kate paused at the foot of the steps for a moment, then saying "wait here," to Robin she turned and ran up to her dragon father's enormous head, and coming up to the side of his face, she stroked his cheek and kissed him. "Thank you," she breathed.

"Ready now," she called as she jogged back to the steps.

Inside was not much smaller than one of those budget hotel rooms, and she and Robin strapped themselves in and found there was already a bottle of water in the arm rest. The entire thing moved, although the flexible padding made comfortable, as Chauncey's head turned to look at them.

"Strapped in? I'll rise slowly and only gain some speed as we get up to the height of an airliner. Invisible of course, so be ready. The kids are coming too so that they can watch from all angles. Whatever you do, don't get out of your seat while we're invisible, you're sure to trip over things and could get hurt."

Chapter 5

Being a magical creature, the mighty dragon stood up, pushed off with his feet and gave a lazy flap of his wings and they were airborne. Gaining a bit of altitude, where they might be spied from the ground or a plane, all the dragons became invisible. Although the sphere they sat in was clear about three-quarters of the way around, going invisible always made Robin feel queasy for a few minutes. He closed his eyes for a brief period until Kate said, "Okay, should be better now."

They were moving smoothly a few hundred feet in the air over Devon, having left Wyvern Hall behind, Chauncey was taking them for a nice view of Ashley Manor down the valley. Somewhere in the forest in between was the Cottage By The Stream that was Robin's parent's home. Then they were out over the fields and pastures of Ashley, where Sir Hugh's old horse, Beaumont, wasn't fooled by invisibility and was about to rear and have a bit of a panic, except that Kate had anticipated that and sent out a soothing spell that included her presence. Beaumont stamped with his front hooves and raced in a bit of a circle, but aware that no danger was actually present, he settled quickly back to grazing, as did Kate's own horse, Foxfire, a chestnut mare Hugh had surprised her with on her last birthday.

She had only ever ridden Central Park stable horses previously but was getting to enjoy her new and surprising present. She knew Sir Hugh had got the mare as a remembrance of her grandmother, his beloved Lucinda. She was sure that when she was riding, she felt Lucinda's presence, guiding both her and the horse.

Now she felt the same total sense of safety and comfort with the nearness of Chauncey and Robin, plus Chauncey's children keeping watch over this maiden voyage. Keeping his turns wide and gentle, the great dragon took them for a leisurely tour over both Devon and Cornwall. East toward Exeter the checker-board pattern of tilled fields and pastureland looked like a quilt with what might be an embroidered village here and there that could be covering a giant taking a snooze.

Then along a bit of the Jurassic coast in Dorset, famous for the discovery of the fossil remains of creatures that had lived eons ago, some of which had first been discovered by the intrepid Victorian self-taught fossil collector and palaeontologist, Mary Anning.

Robin had become very interested in fossils since meeting the dragons and knew a lot about the findings of the fossilised skeletons of giant marine air breathing reptiles such as the ichthyosaurs, plesiosaurs and giant pliosaurs. He knew the dragons had made their way from their own version of Earth some centuries after the great asteroid strike that wiped out the huge dinosaurs and made way for mammals. But partly because of his fascination with the dragons and his living so close to the Jurassic coast his fascination with those ancient relatives of 'his' dragons had grown.

When his mother Maggie complained a bit about the great chunks of stone that he brought home (with permission from the authorities) to try to dig out a particularly interesting specimen, Perry reminded her that antiquities (their mutual passion and source of income) were known to include many things besides art works. Wonders such as the great alabaster sarcophagus of Seti the first, and, yes, often fossils. But it was easy enough to assign a large room in the underground habitat of the stone statues and equip it as a laboratory for whoever might want to have a go at liberating a fossil from the surrounding stone.

Then Chauncey swung back to fly along the coast of Devon and then Cornwall where they got splendid views of the English Channel and the coastal towns, cliffs and small fishing villages with tiny beaches. or picturesque harbors. Fishing was still a way of life for some, but tourism had taken over as a money-spinner, and many of these coastal towns drew tourists searching for a picture-postcard view of an England that no longer existed, sadly to Kate's mind. Although could she have seen the beautiful cob and thatch cottages when they belonged to poor farm laborer's, she knew she'd have changed her mind. That was before Sir Hugh's time as well, but he told her stories of when he was a young man back from the wars, how the smell of coal smoke was part of winter and quite large families would be crammed into the tiny low-ceilinged sitting room looking at the first black and white tellies, while inhaling smoke and fumes. The lanes, with high hedges on either side were mostly for people riding their bikes, and a fair number on horseback, because they couldn't afford a car. Once the coal smoke went away, and the cars came, it made the lanes a dangerous place for bicycles or horses. Always the trade-off between one kind of discomfort and another, thought Kate.

But mostly she was just enchanted by the beauties of these two western-most counties of England. The sea, the extraordinarily varied landscapes. including a number of stately homes with beautiful gardens, some of which along the southern coast of Cornwall were home to otherwise tropical plants. The two gigantic moors, Dartmoor and Exmoor, each with its own breed of wild horse (or ponies as they were called) and each giving rise to the areas two largest rivers, the Dart and the Ex.

The Mayflower had stopped over in Dartmouth for some emergency refitting before undertaking that perilous journey across to the new country of America. Painters, poets, pirates, scientists and smugglers had taken the situation and landscape of these areas to their hearts. As had a dragon from another Earth, where there were places still wild enough to house him and some of his children, because even now when it was so crowded with people, there were wild areas where a fabulous beast could make a home.

Speeding up, the invisible dragons flew north up the middle of England so that Robin and Kate could get glimpses of Wales to their left and the home counties and then the beginnings of the 'industrial' north. Not so industrial now that so much manufacturing, particularly of cloth, was happening in countries where wages were lower. In fact, many mills had become tourist attractions or even hotels. But there was the beautiful Lake Country to the west and to the east the beauty of Cathedral towns like Lincoln and then Durham.

Then over the border into Scotland and a brief tour that took in Loch Ness where Chauncey repeated how some of his offspring swimming and diving in the Loch had started the legend of the Loch Ness monster a few hundred years back. They were told off and didn't swim there now. *What he doesn't know won't hurt him,* came Lilac Moon's voice in Kate's head and she got a fit of the giggles.

The tour now took them back south over areas they hadn't viewed before, including Edinburgh, Manchester and finally London, where they could see how it had grown outward, taking in forests and parkland, views of the Thames and the Royal palaces and, just to the west, of Windsor Castle. "You know the story about the American tourists and Windsor, don't you?" asked Robin. When Kate indicated she didn't, he said, "They were impressed by the Castle, but wondered why on earth Her Majesty would have had it built so close to Heathrow Airport!"

Kate laughed, "Unfortunately, that sounds like a number of my mother's friends. Not just a joke."

Now they flew east over Kent, then back over the Sussexes and then Hampshire and the Isle of Wight and finally were back in their home territory of Dorset and Devon. The entire tour had taken about two hours, with commentary on various bits by all of them as they recognised something or asked a question. They came into land at Wyvern Hall, and all were once more visible.

"I hope you've had a good time. I've waiting so long to be able to show you some of how I see the world."

"Oh, Chauncey, it was truly fabulous," said Kate. "I never saw the world like this except occasional bits of TV, but this—we lived it, there was nothing between us and the incredible things to see. Thank you, it's been a huge present."

Robin too was full of praise for what they'd seen, and how like being a bird and comfortable at the same time was a marvel.

"I kind of expected to feel queasy, with a lot of wing flapping and turns and going up and down, but you flew so beautifully it was like sitting in a wonderful easy chair and having the earth move under us. I rarely felt that we were moving. I knew we were, of course, but it was so comfortable I could put my entire attention on what we were seeing.

Chauncey felt his heart was full to bursting, he'd dreamed of being able to take Kate and her friends on adventures to see their world as he was privileged to see it, especially his dearly loved Kate. And now it was possible, now it was happening, and it made him feel like he could finally share with her and thank her for her courage and love.

Chapter 6

"Dinner will be ready in about an hour, so have a rest or a walk, and then as it gets dark we will go diving. We'll head along the Cornish coast where there are occasionally basking sharks—nearly as big as me, but very gentle—and out into the Atlantic where we'll go deep enough to see some of the phosphorescent creatures. And maybe we'll find some whales. I even know some of them. I'll pressurise the cabin a bit for you, but we won't be going all that deep. In future hopefully we can dive in day light along some of the beautiful reefs in the southern oceans, and really deep in some areas that abound in amazing 'creatures of the night'."

"Night diving," breathed Robin with a kind of suppressed excitement that surprised Kate. "I've always thought that was the be all and end all of undersea exploration, but dangerous. Only with Chauncey, it won't be dangerous at all."

"Plus once we're sufficiently deep we won't have to be invisible. I will enjoy that. I know there won't be lights on in our module, but we should be able to see each other at least a bit. I think there are little lights on our chair arms so we can see our drinks, and on the headrests so we can point them at things outside that aren't florescent, plus outside lights to see creatures."

Kate too was enthralled by diving without any of the dangers. Obviously, from what he'd told her in the past, diving, even deep diving for hours, was a great pleasure of his, so it couldn't be fraught with the dangers human divers had to cope with. "Just so long as our module is really up to the job."

"It's been tested to the limit that all those spheres are," said Robin. "Anyway, Chauncey and the others wouldn't put us into any danger, they'll have run their own tests. And he won't dive so deep that he can't just explode back up to the surface without worrying about us getting the bends."

"With the pressurised module, you wouldn't get the bends anyway," remarked Chauncey. "So far, I've met nothing down there that is dangerous— to me anyway. A giant squid—they are huge by the way— made a pass at me once, thinking I might be a new food source, but I told him off, having mastered a fair amount of cephalopod language, mostly light signals and now occasionally we meet and exchange news of the deeps. Also the big whales, we speak to each other differently, no light shows, but I have learned some of their vocalisations and again we exchange news. Did you know that, with all the huge animals that have inhibited the earth, the largest animal known to have ever existed swims in our oceans today? One of them, fully grown, makes even me feel rather small, much like you must feel standing by an elephant."

"A blue whale," exclaimed Kate, "the largest animal ever known to exist—and it's a mammal."

"Proof that once the asteroid destroyed the large dinosaurs, those insignificant furry beasts that were beginning to take a hold on the land could expand in size and shape and begin to conquer our Earth." said Robin.

"But mammals, reptiles, everything first crawled out of the seas," said Kate.

"Not all of them, and even some that became land dwelling air-breathing mammals decided to give up the land and return to the water. Whales and dolphins were among them." said Robin.

"I imagine that it was their sheer size that enticed them back to the sea, that, and the relative ease of getting a meal." said Chauncey. "Dolphins may have developed later, or possibly it was their intelligence and, if you will, sense of fun, that enticed them back to the oceans. The only dinosaurs left on this earth are birds, and many show every indication of loving their chosen biosphere, the air, the freedom. Similarly many mammals, having crawled out of the sea, found it more salubrious to return.

"Now I get to take your down to see for yourselves. Not just mammals such as whales and dolphins of course, they make up only a fraction of life in the oceans, but a variety of marine life that is still mostly undiscovered by man."

So having finished dinner, and with several of Chauncey's children again putting on the module that would allow Kate and Robin the freedom to join their adventures, Kate and Robin mounted the steps and settled themselves within. Already the skies were black and for once cloudless, sparkling with stars. So invisibility wasn't an issue. Joining them to fly and swim along with their father were their special dragon friends, Lilac and Dark and Silver Moon.

Kate felt a shiver of pleasure mixed with nervous excitement as Chauncey took to the air and flew gently over the fields of Devon and out over the ocean.

A few miles offshore still in the English Channel but headed toward the Atlantic, he let them know he was about to dive.

"Ready when you are, Captain," said Robin, which made Chauncey laugh. And then he slipped gently down and through the restless surface of the ocean and into the world under the water. Down they went, gently but at a steeper angle that they'd taken when flying. Each seat had a screen set up at about chest height, and there were readouts, which showed that they were already some 500 metres below the surface. Other parts of the screen were set up to show close-ups of what they might see, or extra information if they desired it.

Soon there were other large creatures swimming along with them, dolphins and "Oh, my stars, Robin look—a whale shark." Kate's voice was almost trembling with excitement. The great spotted animal was about two thirds the size of Chauncey and larger than his children. It appeared to ignore them, but also swam quite happily along with them for some time. "It's seen us before," remarked Chauncey, "and of course it's a plankton feeder, so perfectly harmless."

"What exactly is plankton?" asked Robin. "I know it's very small and the diet of many sea creatures, but that's about it.

"You're in good company there," said Chauncey "The name is from the Greek, and means 'drifter', so anything living in the ocean that isn't much of a swimmer and depends upon currents to move it about is plankton. But basically, it's either plant or animal, usually very small, so good food for other just slightly larger animals, or sometimes huge animals like our friend there, the whale shark. Plankton is either this very small size its entire life or is the eggs or larvae of larger animals. But its importance is as the large and absolutely essential bottom layer of the food chain. If you like, the foothills and under-pinnings of a mountain."

Now there were phosphorescent glows and patterns appearing. Some were cephalopods and Chen Shi exchanged glowing patterns that he translated for Kate and Robin.

"They were asking about the module, since they haven't seen me with it before, and when they heard you were aboard, some were quite excited. It seems your octopus adventures in Venice have been a story told far and wide, Kate. They are quite thrilled to see you. These will now be telling every other octopus they meet that you are real, and not a story."

Indeed, a number of octopuses had come up to the dome of the module and were examining the interior, and Kate and Robin with their huge eyes. Robin and Kate both waved and Kate made hugging motions, which the dragons 'explained' in flashing images to the cephalopods, who then made hugging and waving motions back.

Lilac Moon's voice came through speakers: "You are one of their myths or folklore stories or bedtime tales you know. As intelligent as they are they only live about two years, and your story has already been passed down several generations."

This left Kate feeling rather strange. She knew from reading that cephalopods didn't live very long and no one so far had figured out how their quite extraordinary intelligence could develop in an animal with such a short lifespan, but it made her feel funny inside to think she'd become a sort of folk hero (or perhaps the octopuses were the heroes and she the classic 'maiden in distress') already passing into legend.

But she forgot all this when, out of the black loomed something even blacker, visible only because it obscured the fluorescent life around them. It was big, as big as Chen Shi or bigger. He could seemingly sense her tension, because his voice came soothingly. "Relax Kate and Robin, remember I said I knew a few whales? This is Arvik, she's a fin whale, and has adopted the Inuit word for whale as her name. Arvik, I'd like you to meet two of the magic persons I have talked about, Kate and Robin. They are taking their first ever undersea trip and I was hoping I could introduce them to a whale."

Under this automatically translated English, they could feel a faint rumbling in their bones it seemed. It was, Robin knew, the actual speech of Chen Shi to Arvik, at a frequency lower than the human ear could hear.

"Would you mind moving off a little and

allowing us to shine a light on you so my dear friends here can see you in all your magnificence?" asked Chen Shi.

Arvik responded, "Not at all, I'm happy for them to see me properly, and thank you for asking." Her dark shape moved away and then was illuminated by a large light. She was a stunning animal, in shape very similar to the blue whale, a long, beautifully slender shape, 'pointed' at both ends, shades of dark grey on her upper side, and white underneath.

"She's like a racing yacht," remarked Robin.

"She's longer than you are," said Kate to Chauncey. "Arvik, you are beautiful."

"I can swim faster than Chen Shi too," remarked Arvik. "But only for short distances, once he gets going he is faster. Still we enjoy our meetings. May I now come close and observe your friends? Please turn off that light."

And out of the sudden dark the huge shape glided closer until one great eye was positioned about ten feet away from the side of the module.

"You are small and, uh, not at all streamlined. I've seen pictures of humans, Chen Shi shows me, but you are the first I've met. I can see that we must live very different lives, except for family groups. We fin whales also prefer to live with family. Chen Shi, I am grateful for the chance to meet your friends. How clever to overcome the difficulties of our habitats with this sphere."

Kate could just make out that Arvik's fin was resting against Chauncey's wing to keep them aligned.

"I must go now," said Arvik. "My child is calling, and the others. They are not yet accustomed to swimming with dragons. And we are feeding. Enjoy your trip here." And almost like a dream the great shape slid away into the darkness.

"We…we just talked to a whale," breathed Kate. "The   most beautiful whale. Oh, I …" and she reached out for Robin's hand. There were tears on her cheeks. It was that wonderful.

Chapter 7

After recovering herself from the deep emotion stirred by talking to Arvik, Kate asked, "Chauncey, are there any good coral reefs in this area? I know the most colourful are tropical, but wondered if there are any we could see here."

"And are there really deep-water areas where we might see some of those very strange but wonderful bioluminescent creatures we sometimes see on TV?" asked Robin.

"Both, both, but Kate the reefs are, as you say, not so beautifully colourful as in the far south, and most that feature a variety of creatures are rock based. The corals that can start from scratch are again from warmer waters. But, Robin, for the kind of truly deep waters you would like to see it is a trip of several hundred miles before we get a significant drop-off. Even for me, that is a trip some hours long, and I think it better to wait until we have the chance to combine that with perhaps an overnight stop or two— a mini-holiday just to view undersea locations perhaps."

So they went to see a coral reef growing out of a rocky shelf, covered in quite beautiful and exotic plants and animals, and then Chauncey breached and flew airborne back to Devon.

Kate and Robin thanked Chauncey profusely. But it was Chauncey who was really moved by the experience. He had known for several years, while staying safely hidden to protect not just himself but all dragon-kind from the malice of WyvernProteus, how much he wanted to take his Kate to see some of the wonders of the world and had planned out a series of possible adventures where they could fly together. Now, having finally achieved the first of these, he was moved to great, private joy that he had finally be able, because of the efforts of her and her friends fighting for the freedom of the dragons, to begin what he hoped and intended would be an on-going series of adventures. It somehow validated and made real his freedom. And he could not regret the century and a half that he and all his kind spent in slavery as living statues and ornaments since it had brought him the extended family of magical people who now were as dear to him as his own children.

It had opened up the world to Kate as well, giving her a loving family and setting free her abilities as a formidable and talented witch, surrounded by dragons, the fae, and her dearest love, Robin, whose parents had become like the parents she never had.

§ § §

Returning to the Cottage Over the Stream, Kate and Robin slept deeply for the remainder of the night and into the next day. They were awakened by the sound of dragon wings and Maggie and Kailen calling out in alarm.

Lilac Moon with her siblings Silver and Peony were sitting in the large garden, where the Magical Misfits gathered too.

"What's happened?" cried Maggie as Kate asked, "What's wrong?"

They'd thrown on caftans while Kailen and Robin stood barefoot in jeans, all alert to whatever danger might be near.

Peony spoke, "I have come from Egypt, where we were enjoying time with your boat" (The dahabeeyah that the Misfits had taken a long lease on as a holiday home.) Bastet is there with her new dragon friend, our sister, Blue Moon. She is as nearly frantic as one would ever expect a goddess to be. Blue, who as you know is shy and retiring, has amazingly come forward, comforting her and promising aid."

"What, what has happened to upset a powerful goddess like Bastet?" asked Maggie.

"She was taking Blue on a kind of tour through the ancient tombs and temples near Luxor and in the Valley of the Kings. Showing Blue her own history as the protective Cat Goddess as illustrated on the walls in hieroglyphs and paintings," said Peony. "But in the tomb of Ramses the First there is a large wall painting of the ancient God of Chaos, Apep, and apparently it has frightened Bastet badly. She is shaken and Elvira and the others can't get much sense out of her. But she is afraid. Elvira has used her own gifts to search out some of what is happening as it is, she says, virtually unknown for a goddess such as Bastet to be anything but in charge of herself no matter the circumstances. She finds not just some hysterics but a real fear based in the millennia of history. There is history between Bastet and this Chaos God.

"Elvira wants us to come, as many of us as possible, because she says that, except for the recent resurgence of belief in Bastet, the ancient gods sleep, enjoyed as myth and story and history, but without belief. She says that for Bastet to exhibit real fear of this old god is like an extinct volcano to suddenly show signs of life and imminent eruption."

Kate said, "Is Bastet afraid that this Apep is also awakening, that he is coming back into his power? Chaos doesn't sound very promising, but chaos is part of the world, the universe, and woven into the fabric. I have enjoyed studying Egyptian gods and goddesses as well as the pharaohs and the culture of ancient Egypt, but I have not yet read or heard of this one. Is he as ancient as you say? Is he dangerous to Bastet?"

It was Silver, that most elusive and usually quiet of the Moon dragons, who answered, "They have history, Bastet and Apep, eons of history. Apep or Apophis as the Greeks called him, is depicted as a huge snake, and as God of Chaos was the first of all the Gods to—how shall I say?—to gain reality in the Egyptian pantheon. You know how their gods tend to morph into each other, take on various identities and attributes. Bastet has always been herself, but there are a number of other cat gods and the Egyptians have confused her with them. Originally perhaps there was only a fierce lioness warrior goddess, with different names such as Sekhmet, who then became a different god and assumed the warrior aspect, while Bastet emerged as the Cat Goddess, protector of women and childbirth. Those are only a few of the aspects attributed to cat gods and goddesses over the millennia, but Bastet as we know her is associated with hearth and home, as cats are good companions and keep crop destroying rodents under control. In addition, her festival at Bubastis is in a beautiful temple with abundant space, and a particular way of celebrating the Goddess is to drink a lot of alcohol. In what is now a predominantly Muslim country, this departure into drunkenness is actually quite popular. Hence, perhaps, the rise in belief that has brought our beautiful Bastet back to life in her full powers.

"Whereas, so far as I can tell, this Apep is considered so distinct that he or it has never become another god, or had much to do with all the godly goings on, except that he is evil, and once held captive the Tree of Life, and at one point the Cat Goddess Mau killed him. Except being immortal he didn't really die. His main 'job', if you want to call it that, is to try to kill the Sun God Ra every night between sunset and sunrise when Ra the Sun God is in the land of night and many dirty deeds are done and then many heroes defy the evil ones, and the Sun can rise again. Still, somewhere, long before the gods of Egypt became stories and legends, powerless and asleep, Apep virtually disappears from the tales told. Only now, according to Bastet, she saw a change in the painting in the tomb, and it is of Apep rising. You understand, these paintings are four thousand years old, yet today she saw him changed and she said she could feel the power."

"And this has frightened her?" asked Robin. "She wasn't afraid of WP, she was eager to destroy, or help destroy, that evil."

"Yes, true, she was very angry with that abomination, but he or it wasn't an ancient Egyptian god with a long history of clashes between them," said Peony. "She is only recently 'back from the dead' if you will, and found she was the only god or goddess who had achieved this resurrection of belief. It made her feel secure, restful. The ancient Egyptian pantheon of gods and goddesses were always at war and it couldn't have been a secure time to be a god—they killed or were killed, morphed into other gods, lost and regained power. Not a time to feel at peace."

"Sounds just like the human race," murmured Kailen. "Okay, or the Fae for that matter."

"And like every other human group that invented a pantheon of gods, those gods did nothing but make war and kill each other, acting out with all the attributes of humans. Plus they had magic of course." commented Robin.

"Well, since they were created by the Egyptians, they were given most aspects of the human race, weren't they?" commented Kate. "It is beyond my human understanding how belief in all these mythic beings could actually endow them with life, but then I don't understand most of what I now accept and make use of, including my own magic powers, or those of the rest of us. My brain won't really understand the many versions of Earth, and how the dragons got here either, but I accept it. And our interactions with all these beings that, although tempestuous at times, have enriched my life so much."

Robin laughed. "Your brain can't figure out electricity either, you told me so yourself, but you, okay we all, accept it and use it."

"Except the Fae, we use magic instead, we can't use electricity," said Kailen. "You are fortunate, my son, that with a human witch for your mother, you have avoided our inability to tolerate most metals, hence also electricity."

"It would be nice if my Fae magic could fix my computer or phone when they act up, though," said Robin, shaking his head sadly.

"All very well," said Maggie. "But we have strayed from our real subject. We should take this seriously and prepare ourselves to fly to Egypt to stand with Bastet if she is threatened by this ancient snake god. It is the least we can do after she helped us dispose of WP.

Kate, you need to tell Chauncey. I'm sure he will agree. And perhaps he can also offer help."

Chapter 8

Apep had gained substance and felt himself alive. He uncoiled and moved sinuously through the mud. As the embodiment of pure evil, he felt the strength of that vile power returning. And as the possessor of an army of demons, he had what no other Egyptian god had, power to strike without being there himself. A prolonged hiss called a number of his minions to him. He stared at them with his cold reptilian eye. Even to him they were hideous, and so small as to be almost pathetic. But he knew he could infuse them with his wrath and send them to wreak havoc. But first, breakfast. A snake can only go so far without breakfast, he thought. "You, you there, with the bits of fur, come here."

A larger demon with a passing resemblance to a rat, moved reluctantly forward on its belly. "You called, Master?" "Of course, I called, idiot! I am hungry. If I am once more alive, I need to eat. You, I perceive are a possible snack." And Apep struck, his huge head flashing forward so fast the rat-like creature had no chance. It made a squeak and disappeared down the vast throat.

"Um, better," gulped Apep, and belched. "Where is that one, the one that calls himself Decay?"

Decay (or D K as he called himself) was being inconspicuous among some of his fellows, but, because they feared Apep more than they feared him, Slime, Muck and Sludge backed away so that D K was obliged to move forward as if it were his own idea. "Here Lord of Darkness, I am here, awaiting your pleasure," D K announced with a bravado he didn't feel.

"My pleasure would be to have that upstart Cat Goddess within my coils, as I squeeze her oh, so slowly until her yowls of distress are only squeaks, and like that creature I just consumed, she is dead before me. Then I will devour her."

"Ah, My Lord is planning a Comeback. A great Rising Again! We can facilitate that, My Lord, we can arrange for a great festival, with music and dancing and feasting. Err, definitely feasting, and worship to increase your strength."

"And the Cat Goddess? I will then move against her, demonstrate my power, remove her from her position, and Chaos will reign once more."

"Oh, yes, Lord, certainly." D K's mind was running for cover, but found none. Apep, in his powerful coils, was clever in his way, but being used to having his own way, in fact his mind was as chaotic as his title. It really did depend upon D K and a few of the more intelligent of the demons to guide him to achieve his ends. And D K didn't much like the odds. He was beginning to regret that he had brought the news of awakening belief to his master.

Because in the millennia since Apep had been a power in the land of Egypt so much had changed. Some of the other gods, like Bastet the Cat Goddess, and Hathor, popular and powerful, were endowed with many things, love, beauty, music, fertility and pleasure, plus being a protector of women. Ma'at above all, the embodiment of truth, order, balance, harmony, and justice, was everything opposite to Chaos, and always there to restore the balance.

It was this fear that, following Bastet's awakening due to a resurgence of belief, these other powerful ancient gods and goddesses might also gain in belief and awaken, that had prompted D K's decision to prod Apep into wakefulness before the odds were stacked against him. He might indeed overcome, with the help of his demon army, one strong Goddess, but he stood little chance of succeeding if the others were to stand against him.

All of these, due to their varying talents and aspects, had the ability to morph and change to adjust to the passage of time, and the profound differences in how the world perceived itself. Apep, unchanging, unaware, self-involved and sleeping away for over four thousand years, was simply…Chaos. Chaos in various forms had indeed grasped parts of the planet over and over again, but always as part of the great ineffable plan. Apep was not part of any plan but his own and was not flexible.

D K and the other demons, who had remained somewhat aware, if stuporous, during this long period, knew that to guide him to the victory he demanded would take all their skill. D K, who had developed a liking for both modern music and television, thought they might be like the god Steve Irwin, called the Crocodile Hunter, who could and did handle these giant prehistoric reptiles with cunning and care for their welfare. The crocodiles themselves had no friendship or trust of him, but still he had managed. But even he, the invincible, had been cruelly slain by an accidental collision with another ancient denizen of the oceans, the lethal sting of a sting ray. So, they, if they were to avoid Apep's stupidity and lack of ability to change to suit the times, must learn to handle him with care and cunning.

Chapter 9

"Okay, we need to plan this out a bit," said Maggie.

"That's what you always say," laughed Robin.

"Because it's always true," Maggie grinned back. "We need to tie up loose ends here, I've put in a call to Parry, and we need a little more information before we go in mob-handed."

"She's been watching too much television again," murmured Robin. "But right with you, Mum. Tie up loose ends, get info, don't go off half-cocked."

"Oh, no," cried Kate, 'It's the battle of the out-dated TV cop show sayings again."

"Okay, who's going and what do we need to do to get ready," asked Kailen.

"Well, we're all going," said Kate. "I mean all the Misfits and the dragons of course, and maybe a few Fae if Ariane and Dmitri are available. Oh, and Chauncey! Chauncey is free to come. My stars! Chauncey is free to do whatever he chooses. I'm not sure I entirely took that in before. We can have Chauncey. If he wants to, of course."

Parry's face appeared on Maggie's laptop. "A new problem, a new quest? What have we got going on?"

They filled him in with what Silver Moon had told them.

"Oh, ancient Egyptian gods. A particular interest of mine," said Parry excitedly. "Apep? You know he's supposed to be huge? The great snake who guards the Tree of Life, or more likely holds it prisoner. The first and still most undisputedly evil of all the gods. Makes Seth or Set look like an upstart. Although, interestingly, he isn't 'invented' or mentioned in all the god stories until after the first dynasty has been and gone, but then although he appeared rather late in the writings, they say he was the first one and had always been there.

"No wonder Bastet is upset," he continued, "her 'risen again' surge in belief appears to have aroused flickers of life in some of the other gods and goddesses, or at least this one. I suppose it's not surprising, Egypt itself is enjoying a resurgence in popularity, and tourism, which includes lots of ordinary folk who are excited by all of ancient Egypt, and would in theory love to see the ancient gods come back. TV is deluged with programs on archaeology where they are digging up the past there." Parry was metaphorically rubbing his hands with glee. "Did you know he has an army of minions, of demons, some of them smaller snakes, and when a dead person descends into the nether world to fight his way to, well, paradise using a copy of the Book of the Dead to out-fox the gods and spirits that would keep him from winning through, he is faced by some of these and they have incredible names. So the dead one says 'rescue me from those snakes that live on men's flesh and sip of their blood, because I know their names. Slobberer Living on His Fellow is the name of one; He Whose Face is in His Coils is the name of another; He Who Lives on Maggots is the name of another; He Who devours Bones is the name of another…' In other words, these snake demons and other demons who follow Apep are there to meet the newly dead and devour him before he gets a chance at redemption. But by saying their names, he gains power over them. That's a quote from a Book of the Dead I read back a few years, somehow this bit stayed with me."

"I can see why," said Kate. "And it's almost the opposite of most modern religions, where they don't say the names of evil, they instead keep saying the name or names of god, whatever god means to them. Interesting. Perry, I hope we can spend some time on this. I'm fascinated by Egypt, but I'm not nearly as deeply into the gods as you are. I'd love to know more."

"Absolutely," he replied. "I'm always happy to talk about my enthusiasms. And do I understand we are heading for Egypt? I'm coming, of course."

"Huge snake god?" queried Robin. "Maybe

Chauncey will find that an interesting challenge. We have Bastet to thank for a lot, and he is always so ready to respond to those who have helped him."

"One question. Anyone here afraid of snakes?" asked Kailen. "Really big snakes? And there are cobras of course. But Apep isn't a cobra, more perhaps like an anaconda or a python."

Kate answered, "I've never been afraid of snakes, per se, but I would be quite nervous of a really huge one, or poisonous ones. I had a grass snake for a pet once, they like being warm so it was quite tame. And I've held a python, but it was only about nine feet long. So afraid generally, no, but if this thing is enormous, ah, well it depends on how magical it is too of course."

"You never fail to surprise me," murmured Robin, slipping is arm around her waist and whispering in her ear.

"I'm afraid of snakes," offered Peony Moon. "I stepped on one when I was quite a small dragon, and it reared up and hissed and I've never felt quite safe about them since." "Ah, well, dear one, you can always fly so as not to be too near any," offered Maggie to Peony, her personal dragon friend. "Don't let Kailen worry you, we aren't going to be besieged by snakes. You've been in Egypt already, and we never saw one. Now, do we still have our Egyptian clothes?"

"Oh crumbs, it's packing again," muttered Kate.

"We've got our Chen Shi gear from taking the Rain clutch to their new homes, and that includes some lightweight clothes and sun stuff," said Perry. "And I'm sure we all bought some things. Or did we leave those on the dahabeeyah? I'm really longing to see her again, what a beautiful modern built replica of those splendid old sailing boats that used to take tourists and the well-to-do sailing on the Nile to view the ruins and enjoy the beauties of Egypt. She's like a dream come true, faithful to the old, but with everything built in that our modern selves enjoy and demand."

"We'll be going to a dahabeeyah, all right. But Perry, this is our new, larger, and very own dahabeeyah," said Lilac. "The other—our lovely *King Arthur*—was one we found and rented and paid for it to be renovated. But when Elvira and Feral decided to live on board as keepers and with Bastet there as well, the owners wanted to start making money from it by taking it cruising with tourists, and it would have been cramped if you all showed up anyway. So Chauncey decided that the Misfits and the Fae and the smaller dragons needed a larger boat—and now we have it. It's still everything you love, built as a replica of the old ones, but with all mod cons and enough cabins for everyone plus that upper deck space for gatherings is large enough for us younger dragons.

"It's where Blue brought Bastet when she had her panic in Ramses tomb," Lilac continued. "And I would imagine they have named her by now. We'll find out when we get there. A surprise for us."

"We can all get more suitable clothing if needed in Luxor while we are docked there," said Robin. "And we'll probably be based there unless this Apep has temples or other bases of operations elsewhere."

"Do we fly or go through Faerie?" asked Kate.

"Kate, if Chauncey wants to come, maybe we could fly with him?" asked Robin. "In the module, so that will be available too."

"If not, I think we should go through Faerie, if you think Queen Elowen will be okay with that, Kailen?" asked Kate.

"I don't think we've worn out our welcome, my mother is quite taken with our adventures, so much more real and interesting than the fantasies they concoct in Faerie," smiled Kailen. "She'll just want to be kept up to date on what we're doing. And if we're to deal with an ancient evil god who is just reincarnating, or rising from the dead, or whatever, then she will have Fae magic and Fae, erm, 'army' that might be even more useful that we will be. It's a shame really that she is queen, because I think she would love to be able to come with us to share things that mean more than keeping a bunch of slightly mad Fae within bounds."

"But why go through Faerie?" asked Robin. "Even if Chauncey doesn't come, we could fly on Lilac and Dark Moon."

"For about six hours or more, maybe overnight, is that right, Lilac? And invisible all the way. I'm not comfortable doing long invisible flights and also getting the wind or the rain. And I imagine the Moon dragons get tired too, it takes more energy to be invisible plus carrying passengers," said Maggie.

Lilac replied, "It's true, we would be glad to do it if it were necessary, but it is a long flight with passengers for dragons our size and gets quite tiring, we have to be so aware of air currents and weather and trying to keep you all comfortable while making good time. Maggie is right, Egypt is a long way."

"Oh, crap, I'm sorry," said Robin. "I hadn't thought it through. So Faerie it is. My grandmother I'm sure can make it a short journey and keep us out of any tricksy 'fun' the Fae might think up."

"And she always enjoys the chance to see you, Robin," said Maggie. "She's clearly very fond of you, and I'm relieved to say that seems to have had a good effect on her attitude toward me. She wasn't best pleased when her favourite son ran off with a human, perhaps especially a human who is a witch."

"So when do we leave," asked Perry from the computer. "If you don't mind, I need a day, preferably two, to tie up loose ends, and let Julien know what's up. He may want to join us at some point."

"And we need to ask Chauncey." said Kate. "It could be his first real adventure since he has his entire freedom."

"Or he may have other plans," said Maggie. "Don't be too disappointed if he declines the invitation."

But Kate thought she knew what Chauncey would say, he'd be eager to accompany his friends on an adventure that didn't include real risk to himself, and he could make sure of protecting Kate and all of them. Perhaps, with all those mountains and cliffs peppered with tombs, he could find himself a large and comfortable abode not too far from the Valley of the Kings. But that wouldn't solve the problem of what to do if they wanted to actually be face to face with him easily, as they could with his much smaller children, the Moon Dragons who were the friends and cohorts of the Misfits.

"We can't all stay in that villa we rented before," she said. "Although the garden is large enough that some of the Moon Dragons can visit, it's not large enough to conceal Chauncey. I propose that we find an estate near Luxor where the grounds are large enough and have tall trees and walls that mean Chauncey can visit and be visible without endangering us. I really, really want to have him able to spend time with us in comfort now that it is safe. Maybe even a great hall that would accommodate him when he visits. I imagine he will either want to fly back and forth from Devon, or I did think that perhaps somewhere in the area some miles from the Valley of the Kings he could find a cave system large enough for him to set up temporary housekeeping."

Chapter 10

A day later Maggie met up with Kate and Robin and they put in a call via Kate's tablet to Chauncey. His great head appeared on the screen smiling. Chauncey's smile showed some formidable teeth, but they were accustomed to that, and were smiling back at him. Kate had already told him the night before about plans to go to Egypt in a few days. They would, if possible, help Bastet, and hopefully also enjoy some of the sightseeing they'd missed when dealing with the stone Egyptologist gone rogue and how he, not the Misfits or the dragons, had torn Ivor Wyvern-Proteus limb from limb and then into smaller pieces. Or how in the end the dragons had flamed those pieces to ash, ash from fire so hot that no DNA or other life could survive it. It was this that freed Chauncey, the final complete destruction of his powerful enemy.

Now Kate explained what they hoped to do. "I thought you'd like the chance to come with us, now that you're truly free to roam the world as you used to do. But even the new dahabeeyah you got for us—and thank you so very much, it's a splendid present—or the villa we rented in Luxor aren't big enough to accommodate you, and we so want to spend some real time with you. Our first thought was that you could probably find a cave system somewhere a fair distance from the Valley of the Kings, but that would still mean us making a longish trip to be with you, and I, well we, all of us really, would love to have your company for more than just visits. So we've searched the area for a mansion or palace with large enough grounds that you could be there without anyone knowing."

Chauncey was looking quite moist- eyed at this evidence that his lovely Kate should want to make this possible. Maggie took up the tale. "It wasn't easy, the big mansions are mainly within the centre of Luxor, and the land around is not heavily treed or with a great house that would protect you from being seen. However, I did find one hotel on an island. The Jolie Ville Hotel and Spa, on Kings Island. It's got huge grounds, well landscaped with trees and other features that could more than disguise your presence there, and as it is now run as an hotel, there are plenty of rooms for all of us, humans, goddesses, the fae and the Moon Dragons. There is a drawback, it would be very expensive and maybe hard to rent—it's got 647 rooms plus restaurants and other facilities, it takes up the entire island."

Kate broke in then. "But I told Maggie that if you liked the idea you could afford to rent the entire island, all the facilities and everything. Of course you don't have to at all if you'd prefer not, but I have figured out from our conversations that over these thousands of years you have accumulated enough wealth to rent or buy it without flinching. So it could be a perfect spot where we could all gather and be together. And plot how to help Bastet and go on day trips to all the amazing ancient Egyptian ruins and eat like kings. But mainly we could all be together!"

Chauncey laughed, though a tear trickled out of his eye as well. "You love me that much? You would want my enormous bulk to be with you day in, day out?"

"Well, of course!" said Kate as if it were the most obvious thing in the world. "But you'd have to want it too, because you'd have to pay for it."

"I see. Yes, honourable Chinese gentleman of vast fortune, name of Chen Shi, desires to rent entire island, uproot—how many guests? Over a thousand. Maybe bring in all new staff? We could, yes it could be done."

Kate was whispering to Maggie and Robin, "You see, I told you so."

But then Chauncey held up a talon. "Wait, my lovely girl. It doesn't have to be so complicated. You know the Egyptian Dragon Principality is quite close to Luxor. And of course it is equipped to deal with dragons, hundreds of full-grown dragons. And

I still owe them a visit. Plus after about two days all the fuss will be over, and I can ask for a nice villa—with a garden should I so desire, and you can come every day easily from the vicinity of Luxor. Or with minimal fuss, they would make a villa with rooms big enough for me, and others small enough for you. And you could travel from there as often as you wished to sail the Nile. I do not mind spending the money for this island, but it is the rest of it that becomes a logistical nightmare—uprooting all those people. I personally don't find that acceptable. And it would take a lot of magic to keep the newspapers from getting hold of that story and making it into an international incident. I don't think we want to be responsible for putting China in a bad light either."

Kate had been quite excited about the Jolie Ville on its own island, where they could dock the dahabeeyah and be right on the Nile with enough space for everyone and then some. She looked a little downcast now, but when Chauncey had pointed out the difficulties both as to time, disruption of so many people and the potential of causing a diplomatic incident that put China in a bad light, she could see that it was not actually a workable idea. Enough money could make it happen, but that would put them in the same boat as all the mega-billionaires who ground the working class under their feet. So she was quick to agree that Chauncey's idea was better.

"But how long would it take your half-brother the Prince to arrange for a new villa with quarters for all of us? That's a big project, surely?" she asked.

"My beautiful, magical daughter!" Chen Shi was laughing. "It is all done by magic and can be done very quickly. Our entire existence here is based on magic, we are magical animals, our Principalities, hidden from the world, are created and hidden by magic, just as is Faerie, just as is Maggie and Kailen's Cottage Over the Stream."

And Kate had to laugh too, if a bit ruefully. "I haven't known I was magical for very long really, and now it is part of my life, it seems an ordinary part. I forget just how much it can do, even though Robin and I completely redecorated Maggie's kitchen in less than an hour, and I can change my bedroom there in less time than that."

"Indeed," agreed Chauncey. "And I think we've all got the right hands. So, do you want a garden in our villa — one of those you used to dream about where the house is built around the garden and it all becomes beautifully private and, well, magical?"

Kate and Robin both laughed delightedly. Robin said, "Perfect, it would be perfect. I hate to say it, but along with that being Kate's dream residence, it also will shelter us from having to see and be seen by all your Egyptian dragons. It's not that we don't love dragon-kind. You know we do. But hundreds of them, and so very big. And with the Prince and his court being, well, rather Royal… Will your quarters adjoin ours though? We don't want to be separated from you!"

"I am imagining two of the sides for you and the other Misfits, and your Fae friends, the Free Spirits, and two sides with much larger rooms, higher ceilings, where I and my children can reside. It will be a very big garden you know, because I want to take my ease in it as well. Oh, and we can arrange an entrance/exit that will open right onto where your dahabeeyah is docked, so you will have that right with you as well."

"It sounds like perfection," said Maggie. "I also sometimes forget just how much magic can create, even though I both watched and helped Kailen make our cottage, and we sometimes play with the interiors. Plus of course our more important jobs, like freeing you and helping the stone people to adjust.

So it was decided. And they settled down to designing a beautiful villa, with all the magical mod cons anyone could think of, knowing if they forgot anything, it would be simple to add or remodel. As they talked or sketched or just thought of ideas, there was a sort of tabletop in their minds that quickly manifested all of it. To create the finished design wouldn't have been possible so quickly in the real world, but they were dealing now with the Egyptian Principality, all of which was a manifestation of magic.

Chapter 11

Kate once more bid farewell to her Great Uncle Hugh Mallory, her other dear 'foster father'. He had confided in her that her Grandmother Lucinda, Hugh's lost love, whose death had been the event that brought the frightened and miserable 16-year-old Kate to Devon some years ago, had appeared to Hugh in a dream. Lucinda had assured him not only of her love but that he must let Kate go to live out her own purpose, that it was time, and not to be afraid for her. He even told Kate that Lucinda had then given him the ring he had once given her, and when he woke he was actually holding that ring. It had startled him at the time, but also comforted him to think it wasn't just a dream, but that somehow the wall that separated the living and the dead was not so impenetrable as he had always thought. For Kate it was also a comfort to know Lucinda was somehow still 'there', but even more of a comfort to realise her dear Great Uncle had taken those words to heart. So now she could tell him she was off to Egypt with Robin and he didn't turn a hair.

Hugging her close, he simply said, "Have a lovely time, my dearest girl— and if you have to save any worlds, know you do so with my blessing." That last bit startled her, but then he winked and said, "And if you bring me back one of those horribly tacky King Tut heads I will disinherit you!" she laughed delightedly. Somehow the need to keep Uncle Hugh safely in the dark seemed to have resolved itself.

"I do solemnly swear not to bring anything of the sort. And please take good care of Poppet—and maybe ride Foxfire for me."

"I think you'd find it is Poppet taking care of me, dear heart. And I'm too old and heavy for that filly. But Bates' grandson is training to be a jockey, and he has a lovely way with a horse. Would that do?"

"Oh, yes! You're still one jump ahead of me, aren't you?" Kate said. "Anyway, we'll be back almost before you know it. Although I do want to spend time on the Nile to see some of the ancient wonders."

§ § §

She quickly packed her caftans and the desert clothes, hat and boots she'd got for the last trip when they had tracked down WP buried deep in the Egyptian desert and went to say goodbye to Bates and Mrs Bates and Foxfire and Hugh's old hunter, Beaumont. She cuddled Poppet and told her to be a good dog, to which Poppet seemed to give her one of those looks.

"Ok, ok," she laughed. "I know, you are always the best dog. I love you to bits, Poppet, take care of Uncle Hugh. Yes, I know you will."

She couldn't resist taking her Mazda MX5 to drive to The Cottage Over The Stream. In the garage (newly created now that both Robin and Kate were driving and equally invisible to the ordinary eye) she parked up beside Robin's motorcycle and his own MX5.

Robin had heard the distinctive sound of the Mazda. plus it was rare that a car of any kind would come along the forest track, and came to meet her, taking the duffle bag from the boot and hugging her with his other arm.

"We're going to be leaving via Faerie just after lunch," he announced. "And Mum says we really need to stop off to chat with my grandmother, because she understands now just how difficult it is for Queen Elowen to be stuck in that 'playpretend' world with most of her subjects little better than spoilt children, and she — Elowen that is—really appreciates knowing about our adventures."

Kate was nodding agreement. "Yes, she's like your dad, her son, really—and like Ariane and Dmitri—grownups. And wanting to live in a world where real things happen. Hey, I've got an idea! You know how Bastet has stand-ins that are made up, or magicked, to look like her when she wants to be away from her followers and doing more interesting things?"

"Like exploring today's Egypt with Elvira and Feral and taking to the air on a dragon?" Robin's grin was wide.

Kate elbowed him in the ribs, but gently. "Exactly like that, doing what she wants in our real—okay, yes, and magical— world. Away from the ancient formalities of her court. Being incognito and having adventures."

"And your idea is for my grandmother to nominate or create a stand-in while she comes with us? I think we need to run that past the parents before we take it any further. There could be difficulties. "

"Like what? It's unlikely the Unseelie Court would pick just that moment to declare war, or her own subjects start something really vile. Anyway, doesn't she have the power to keep in touch in case she's really needed?"

"I was thinking more along the lines that my dad would not enjoy having his mother along. They have a somewhat strained relationship, or haven't you noticed?"

"In the past, yes, and I did notice, but things change and now she welcomes Maggie and you and her son, and just wants to be kept in the loop so to speak. And it has seemed to me that the more she sees of us, the more she approves of Kailen, and I believe, no, I really know, she'd give a lot to be included. After all, she has given us a lot of help over the years, sending the Fae she knew could help us and making sure her more unruly subjects are warned off. I'm not suggesting she become a Misfit or a permanent fixture, and I doubt she'd feel she can spend that much time away from Faerie, but I think it would make her happy."

"Okay by me. We'll talk it over with Mum and Dad. He's the one who has to be comfortable with it or it will put a strain on all of us. Anyway, maybe she can't do it, maybe there's no 'stand-in' that would fool the Fae or maybe she wouldn't really want to."

As Kate half expected, Maggie was enthused, but careful to defer to Kailen on this subject. For years his mother, the Faerie Queen Elowen of the

Seelie Court, and he had been at odds because he had simply refused to take his place as Prince. Who his father was not even he knew, possibly his mother didn't know, that was just how it was with the Fae. There had once been a tradition that the Seelie Queen and the Unseelie King would meet to produce offspring, possibly a way of keeping the two Courts from each other's throats, but as it didn't actually work very well to prevent wars, that tradition had died a death. But mating, like other Faerie fun, was a free and open part of their lives and there was no shame involved. Rather like the 'Summer of Love' Kate's mother had told her about, where lots of pot was smoked openly and in Central Park there were 'Happenings' and a lot of 'free love'. Post birth control and pre-AIDS, a time of indulgence and excess. She wouldn't have been surprised to learn that quite a few of the Fae had taken the opportunity to play along with the human beings in that time.

So Maggie turned her bright and loving eyes to Kailen, a gentle question in them. He had been startled by the suggestion, there was no doubt, and Kate, with her witch's sense had seen the conflicting emotions scrolling through him. Finally he spread his hands out, palms up and said, "So long as it turns out she would enjoy it, and it doesn't become habitual, I see no problem. I have been quite grateful for the better relations we have enjoyed over the past few years, and have come to see that my mother would prefer not to have the job she was born to. So a holiday would seem like a nice thing to offer her."

Maggie embraced him, and he laughed, "Not many women would be so eager to invite their mother-in-law along."   "Well, she's hardly my 'mother-in-law' because there are no laws and we aren't married!" laughed Maggie. "I like her, she does a hard job and does it well.   And after disapproving of me, maybe hating me, as the human who stole her son and gave him a halfling child, she met me and liked me, so she's shown she can overcome preconceived notions. Very like her son, I'd say."

Kailen hugged her close and spoke into her blond curls, "You are a wonder worker that's why. You make the world change."

After which they all sat down to a hearty lunch prepared in equal parts by magic and real cooking. Then, picking up their hand luggage, they gathered in the lovely terrace garden off the small dining room with its wall of flowering vines, and walked into them and through them—and out directly into Faerie.

Chapter 12

With seemingly perfect understanding of their wishes (or a quick spell from Kailen) they were in the antechamber leading to the throne room aka Queen Elowen's office, or perhaps bower. When they were announced by a beautiful young faerie who cast doe-like eyes at Kailen (who somehow dismissed her without moving), they stepped through an archway into what was indeed a bower. Elowen was reclining like Cleopatra upon a chaise longue of spring-green silk in a room that resembled a beautiful glass house hung about with garlands of spring flowers and with grass underfoot. Kate thought it suited her. Elowen's hair was no longer dark leaf green, it was now a gentle white blond, decorated not with jewels, but with violets and miniature daffodils. But her beautiful violet eyes were the same.

"My Lady Mother," said Kailen bowing over her hand. Elowen did what she hadn't done before, she took Kailen's hand for support and rose up to embrace him and kiss him on both cheeks.

"My son," she said warmly, "I am pleased with you. Somehow you have made being Fae something I can be proud of. Unlike most of my silly, occasionally vicious, people. But it seems that hearing of your exploits, several more than before have shown every sign of being truthful and kind. And the Fae Free Spirits have recruited some new members. Most of my people remain as they were, but there are new stirrings, which are also partly involved with the dragons."

Still holding his hand, she reached out toward Maggie. "And you have proved to be a true friend of mine and of the dragons we all care for. But I was already becoming fond of you. All of you. You live a life I would once, as Kailen knows well, have condemned for any Fae. But only a fool or a monster could fail to see that your way of life is a fine example to follow. But I digress, what brings you here—have we another crisis? Is there another threat to us or dragon-kind?"

"We don't know. But a friend has had a nasty shock and talks of an ancient Egyptian god, a god of evil and chaos, stirring and perhaps rising again. We are indebted to her for help in destroying WP last year and are going to Egypt to find out more and offer help if it's needed." said Maggie.

"And what has happened to your friend that she talks of gods rising up? I know that it is true that belief both creates and strengthens gods, but as I have no belief, I've never been bothered by them."

"Ah, that is part of why we came," said

Maggie. "You see, we, that is witches, have a belief in a spirit we often refer to as the Goddess, so perhaps it is not so difficult for us to encompass the idea of various gods. And then when we were first searching for a way to free the dragons, I was teaching and testing the extent of Kate's, Robin's and Perry's magic powers, and Kate actually called up the Muse of History. As a daughter of the ancient Greek god Zeus, she is certainly an ancient goddess. And she helped us with information. To say I was shocked is an understatement, but after that we were not so surprised that later in our quest to end WP we were introduced to a spirit cat who informed us he was a messenger and manifestation of the Egyptian Cat Goddess Bastet. And later still we became acquainted with Bastet herself, who took a personal interest in destroying WP as the start of his monstrous cruelty was torturing cats. She is the friend I spoke of who has been shocked to find that an old adversary, another Egyptian God, but one of evil, is also stirring."

At this point, Elowen interrupted the flow of information. "This Bastet is an ancient Egyptian Goddess who has become a *friend*? Is that even possible?"

"Apparently, based upon the Egyptian belief that their gods and goddesses were very like humans.

Bastet can assume human form, or human form except for a cat's head, depending apparently on her mood. Egyptian gods were almost always depicted as human, but often with animal heads."

"Fascinating," murmured Elowen.

"Historically they also had many human characteristics," Maggie continued, "and in fact Bastet, who was presiding over a huge festival in her honour, nominated one of her handmaidens to take her place while Bastet accompanied us across the desert to do battle with WP. All it required was a slender young woman wearing a cat's head mask and being rewarded to sit on the throne and just be a presence. As a Goddess, Bastet wasn't given to much talking or making of proclamations—her presence was enough for her people. And we found we liked each other quite a lot, plus she was particularly delighted to meet dragons. Egyptian history and religion have no dragons. She got to ride one and was totally enchanted. When we left our dragon friends were introducing her to one of their number they thought might become a friend for her."

Robin came forward at this point. "So we thought, knowing you now as well as we do, that you might enjoy a small holiday away from Faerie and having to be queen day in and day out. Well, Kate thought of it first actually."

Kate found herself blushing, and wished yet again that there was a spell to make that stop. But at least it no longer stopped her from carrying on. "I did think, your Grace, after what you have said about the constraints of dealing with a small kingdom of unruly Faeries, you might, if you could find a suitable substitute, enjoy coming along with us and seeing a little of the world we live in. I hope that wasn't disrespectful."

"No, of course not disrespectful. It's a very kind idea. I…I must say you have totally surprised me. I have sometimes dreamed of such a thing. But other than a few hours here and there, which weren't all that satisfying alone, I had resigned myself to the role I was born to."

"Mother, I know we can shape-shift and take on the aspect of another. Do you have someone you trust who could play this role for you for a few days or weeks even?" asked Kailen.

"Oh, I think I could simply order someone to do it. But it wouldn't make them Queen, and that could be troublesome. I take a more active role than seems to be played by your goddess friend."

"What about Mayleone? She's your favourite daughter and I know you hope she will agree to become Queen," said Kailen. "Maybe you could institute a 'holiday' or 'time off' or 'important state matters that require your absence'—you are Queen after all, your word is law here. If you say you are going to do something important, and also give Mayleone some experience, who would dare to speak against that?"

"Ah, what a good—and devious—advisor you could have made, my son," said Elowen. "I still regret your absence, even though I am reconciled, even pleased, to see the life you have made. This could be a fine idea. If Mayleone is willing."

Several of the Misfits looked about to speak, but she put up a hand to still them.

"Yes I know I could command her—but she is my daughter, Kailen's sister, and has just as strong a will. She would do it, but it could drive a wedge between us if she didn't do it willingly."

Maggie smiled, "I think if we presented it as providing you with a real treat, something you have secretly wanted, she could be convinced. And it would only be for a short time, in fact with how you can bend time here, you could make it only a day or two for her and spend weeks with us if you wanted. I have met her, you know. She is a strong personality, but she really cares for you, and I do think she will, as you did, see that both Faerie and you could benefit."

Queen Elowen smiled back, a real smile. "I

would love to see your world in your company. I am touched that you would want me. I will call Mayleone and we can present the idea to her. But I will assure her she can say she doesn't want to. I have learned a thing or two since I fell out so badly with Kailen. It is not very 'Fae' to respect and care for the feelings of others, but we are obviously an odd family of faeries."

"Very odd indeed, Mother" came a new voice, and Mayleone stepped into Elowen's chamber. She had a look of Kailen about her, tall with tanned skin and long dark hair. Her eyes were like her mother's, violet and sparkling. She looked to be about 40, but could, as the Misfits knew, be any age at all. Unlike Elowen, she was dressed in a simple leather jerkin and leggings, all in different shades of blues and violets. Although clearly made for moving freely, they were also decorated around the neckline and sleeves with jewel-like flowers, a stripe of similar flowers ran down the side of her leggings and decorated the tops of her boots. Flowers were also strung through her hair.

"Please meet our friends, the Magical Misfits," said Elowen. "My friends, this is my daughter and possible heir, Mayleone."

"My mother talks about you, I know all your names. It is a pleasure to meet you last," said

Mayleone And Kailen, my brother, I am so glad to see you again. Mother, you called me. Is it because your friends are visiting?"

"Yes, they have made me a most intriguing proposal," Elowen answered.

Chapter 13

It was Kailen who took his sister aside and explained their idea that Elowen, Queen of the small and fractious kingdom of the Seelie Fae, might want to join the Magical Misfits and their friends on a holiday to have different kinds of adventures. He knew that Mayleone also had wanderlust, and often went off out of Faerie and pursued her own interests in the wider world. He didn't actually know what these were, having been unwelcome amongst his own family and people for so long. But he played upon the sympathy he thought she'd have for their mother's desire to also go walk about and experience a different sort of world and life. He had known Mayleone was the obvious choice to be the next Queen of the Seelie Fae, but now also knew that Elowen wouldn't force the role upon her daughter, but hoped that she would, in time, be prepared to do it.

"Our lady mother would dearly love to experience what you and I have done now for many years—escape the tedium and petty feuding of Faerie and see more of the world, have a few adventures. She has been steadfast in her duty, now we want to offer her this opportunity. But she has said she cannot go in all good conscience unless someone responsible can fill her place. That someone is obviously you, Mayleone, and we are hoping you will agree. It will only be a few days and might give you a real knowledge of what you could be taking on later as Queen."

"Only a few days?" the doubt in Mayleone's voice was apparent. "I'm not yet ready to resign myself to a lifetime of servitude. And your adventures seem to take months, not days. Plus until quite recently I thought our mother Elowen was quite okay with being Queen of the Seelie Court, she was always the complete picture. Only since she's been helping you and your group— what is it you call them? The Magical Misfits? I might have known, you never did fit, did you? Well I don't really either, I'm mostly away as you know. So I never blamed you for wanting what I have wanted and taken. And now it appears you've infected Elowen. Can't say I'm really happy about that."

Kailen was prepared for that. "I thought, yes, we might be weeks or months, but since here in Faerie time is malleable, we could set it up to be only a few days. So you could get a taste of what goes with the job, or even plan how you might change it. And we would be off for a longer time, letting our mother find out what we do."

"I am interested in the potential to change how things work, hopefully for the better, and yes that would mean spending enough time to see how our mother has coped with the daily grind. Although we have made changes, particularly hatching and raising the Rain clutch of dragons. Doing that was a big change to the usual vacuous playacting and indulging in bad behaviour, plus of course, always keeping a watch for trouble from the Unseelie Court. In fact I have done a lot of spying in that area on behalf of Queen Elowen.

"But, as you've explained it, I do see that this could have advantages for me. I may not really desire the position, but I have learned enough in my fairly long life to know that there is no one else presently available who could do as good a job as our Lady Mother. I have not told her this, just in case I find that it is something I cannot pledge myself to, but this will give me some practice and hopefully a lot of knowledge. I'll be better able to make my choice when the time comes."

"Mayleone, I hoped I could count on you. It would seem it is those who see being Queen as a sacrifice and a service who make the best leaders. You probably know our Lady Mother has decided that she will not force the position upon you, or even this short trial period, if you say no. I am exceedingly grateful that you are willing to give it a try. And give Elowen the break she probably needs and would enjoy. Thank you."

§ § §

"So, it all worked out in the end," said Kate to Chauncey via their mind-link that evening. She couldn't use her tablet in Faerie, so it was the magical link, made even easier by the strong magical 'currents' in that place. "We are going via Fae routes to the Egyptian Principality tomorrow. and I'm really looking forward to seeing Elvira, Feral and Bastet again. And find out what has upset the Cat Goddess so much. It is a mystery and appears to be a very ancient one, since it was something in the hieroglyphs or frescos in the Valley of the Kings that upset her so much. I hope we can help. But it's exciting too that there is a mystery involving ancient Egypt, since of all the history I studied in school, Egypt under the Pharaohs was by far my favourite. Even a real passion."

Chauncey laughed, "More fun than battling Wyvern and Proteus and finding out dragons and magic are real?"

"Oh, Chauncey, that's comparing apples and

oranges, there is no comparison," said Kate looking slightly wounded. "You and magic and, well all of it, even fighting WP, even coming up against my mother, but especially you and Robin and Maggie and Kailen, Perry, the Moon dragons—you've made my life what it is, and it's the most fabulous life.

"See, Egypt is an old dream from back when I was a child and was so unhappy and didn't know about any of the wonders that were in store. But it really can't hold a candle to what my life has become…what I have become. It's a new adventure perhaps, but an adventure with all of my crew, the Misfits, the dragons, the fae. And it should be exciting to be involved with ancient Egypt. But it's only because I'm with you all now."

Chauncey nodded seriously. "I was only teasing a little, Daughter, but I understand what you mean. My life too has been enriched and made new because of 'your crew'—I've lived so long, had so many adventures, but never dreamed I'd be saved by a slip of a girl I've come to cherish and have magical human friends who have come to my aide again and again until now I am free to enjoy the world once more. And, just as you say, it is because I am with you all now."

"And are you coming to Egypt?" asked Kate.

"Yes, Kate. Just like we planned, with the big house in the Egyptian Principality and then out into

Egypt itself. The house is now all built you know. Although I've left a lot of the decorating of your part to you all, I thought you'd enjoy that."

"Ah, magic, so much more powerful and easy to do in a magical place," said Kate. "I'm not complaining, I think it's fabulous that here in Faerie and in any of your Principalities we can create not just illusions but realities as easily as we can boil water in the ordinary world."

§ § §

The next morning they met again in the queen's bower, still in its 'Spring dress', but instead of a chaise longue, there was an armchair, throne-like, but comfortable. And sitting in it was Mayleone dressed in a long gown of many shimmering shades of green and violet and with a circlet of amethysts in her hair. Standing beside her was Elowen, dressed in clothes rather like their own.

"As you see," said Elowen, "we are ready."

Mayleone grimaced slightly, but then laughed. "As ready as I'll ever be. Don't be gone too long, Mother, I might develop a taste for this."

"I'm rather hoping so," responded Elowen. "But don't worry, it won't be forever yet."

So the Misfits and the Fae Free Spirits, now including Elowen, which was making Ariane and

Dmitri feel a bit awkward, set off for the door that would lead them into the Egyptian Dragon Principality. An announcement had gone out that Queen Elowen was on a short 'diplomatic mission' and their path was smooth and clear, with luxurious flowers and jewelled trees on both sides, and silver deer glimpsed in faerie glens.

"There are definitely some advantages to being royalty," murmured Robin.

Maggie turned to Kailen and asked, "So why, my darling Prince, did we have such a hard time getting to Venice via Faerie? I mean, look at this," she waved her hand in the direction of all the lush and beautiful planting. "Not a thorn bush, a nettle or a bramble in the lot."

"I know my love, and I was very sorry, but I was definitely out of favour then, and you were the human who had stolen me from the Queen."

"I must apologise also," said Elowen, having overheard the exchange. "Kailen was my favourite son, and I was still hurting and angry. But I had never met you, and I was being selfish. A lot has changed since then."

Chapter 14

And in next to no time they had reached the door. Kailen stepped forward and opened it with a deep bow and an 'after you' gesture to his mother and his wife. Kate and Robin followed and gasped.

They were in a vast courtyard garden with fountains and trickling rills, palm trees and cypresses reached for the sky, and bougainvillea made a riot of peach, pink, red and purple climbing walls, pergolas and arbours. A large ornamental pool hosted white and blue lotus, and papyrus. Roses and jasmine scented the air, and poppies and daisies grew here and there. The walls were terracotta, with beautiful inset tiles, the paths and sitting areas were also tiled and rills of water ran alongside them. Two sides of the building that surrounded the garden were vastly taller, and there was a beautiful mosaic running along just under the roof line featuring multicoloured dragons. They could easily make out most of the dragons they knew with all their splendid differences of colours and wings.

On a large terrace just in front of this part of the house Chauncey was sitting. It was always a bit of a shock to see him in the flesh as opposed to on their tablets or as mind magic, he was so very large. But Elowen made for him like he was an old friend, and he cupped his hand to make a seat for her.

"Faerie Queen and Dragon King can finally meet again," he said. She stroked his finger with its long golden talon, and her violet eyes were moist.

"I mourned you," she said. "I feared you lost forever. It was a great blow. I knew your folk had Principalities, like Faerie invisible to the world, and not available to me either. Did Wyvern get them too?"

"Yes, everyone. A great disadvantage, that by capturing me he could capture all of them. He had no idea at the time how many we were, but he made use of us all. It was the Chimaera, of course, who hated us so much, and found his tool in Wyvern. But he couldn't kill us, so there we were, frozen and mostly unconscious thank goodness, and sold for huge sums making Wyvern richer than he could have ever dreamed. Until Kate arrived, and you know the rest."

"When the Fae found the eggs left by Summer Rain, I thought these were probably the only Noble or Celestial Dragons left," said Elowen.

"And they would have been if Kate hadn't come along."

They both thought of that sad, confused teenage girl from New York who was mourning her grandmother, the only person she had known up until then who'd been genuinely kind and loving to her. Chauncey shook his head gently, in remembrance of this. "But, she was 'the girl who could see dragons'. So she became our saviour. Well, along with Perry, Robin, Maggie and your Kailen of course. And the spirit of her grandmother, Lucinda who appeared when she was most needed."

"I still feel a shiver when I remember hearing all that," said Elowen.

§ § §

"Dragon King and Faerie Queen, together at last," said Perry. "What an amazing sight, what a lovely reunion. I had no idea they were so fond of each other."

"It's a lonely thing, being the King or Queen of a hidden realm of magical beings in a world that doesn't know they exist," said Kailen. "I imagine that once they discovered each other and found they were also similar in their thinking, they were profoundly happy to have found another with whom they could speak and act honestly. The Unseelie Kingdom of Faerie and its King are essentially enemies. As shallow and untrustworthy as the majority of the Seelie Fae are, the Unseelie are downright wicked. My mother could never have made a bond of friendship with their King, any of their Kings."

"Now that I understand things better," said Maggie, "it's probably why she missed you and was so angry with me for, in her mind, seducing you away. Because you had so much in common with her. And as she said, you could have been a trusted councillor, which I'm sure she often felt the need of. Well, thank the goddess now you can be that to her and also my mate and Robin's father."

"I was much younger, and didn't know that," remarked Kailen. "When I was a child she seemed distant and unknowable, and with my budding feelings so unlike the fae I knew, I thought her like them, shallow and sometimes unkind. I was hurt and angry too that she seemed to have cast me out. It took our grouping together to save the dragons that brought us to know each other as people. I'm grateful that has happened.

"She inherited a job she didn't enjoy, but she was making the best of it, knowing what might, nay, what would happen if a weak and uncaring member of our royals took the throne—the Seelie Fae would have been subsumed into the Unseelies and that would have been that for the balance that she worked so hard behind the scenes to maintain. I'm proud of her now, and proud to be her son. But mostly grateful that she has accepted you, my love," hugging Maggie to him.

Robin and Kate were unabashedly listening

in to this and learning a lot about areas of this expanding alliance they'd never even thought about previously. "It's like that pebble dropped into a pool," murmured Kate. "Just a pebble, and if you're the pebble, you think that's the whole of it. But the ripples — all the ripples expanding, touching and changing other people and things."

"My   pebble, "whispered Robin, kissing her ear.

"Oh, I didn't mean me…" Kate started. But Robin put his finger to her lips.

"It was you all right, totally definitely you. And you hadn't a clue, just as you said. And none of us did have a clue, not really. Only now are the puzzle pieces coming together it seems."

"I think you actually mean I'm the chaos butterfly," grinned Kate, but it didn't seem to trouble her. "Let's go explore," she said grabbing Robin's hand. "Chauncey said he's left a lot of the interior decoration of our part of this beautiful villa to us, so we'd better get cracking. I'm glad we've had a lot of experience from changing and redecorating The Cottage Over the Stream."

Existing as it did in a bubble of spacetime, or possibly a bit of a parallel universe, the Egyptian Dragon Principality was entirely constructed with magic, and any magic used here was enhanced. This meant building, renovating and decorating using magic were much easier within its purviews, just as it was in Faerie. So Chauncey had already created the villa with the enormous west side for himself and his various children. The north and south sides were also each tall enough to accommodate dragons until a third of the way along, when the ceiling heights became more human-sized. The east side which faced the Nile outside the magical bit of space-time was as long, but not nearly so high, as the dragon side, to suit the witches and fae. He'd made the garden too, remembering all he knew of Kate and the other's preferences and what the perfect desert paradise garden should be.

Maggie, Kailen and Perry plus Ariane and Dmitri with Queen Elowen joined them. It didn't take them long to choose spaces. The Fae took the south-facing wing, leaving the eastern end of that wing for Perry to be close to the rest of the Misfits in the eastern wing. This was divided in two by the entrance door facing the Nile and a corridor leading into the vast interior garden. Maggie and Kailen had the southern half, and Kate and Robin the northern end. The north facing wing was half large enough for dragons, the rest left for Elvira and Feral and Bastet, should they want to join them, plus any other guests that might appear.

Having decided upon the areas, they all settled in to enjoy the potential of the interiors, choosing bedrooms and expanding bathrooms, enlarging and diminishing windows, adding those carved and pierced marble screens known as Jali screens that allowed looking out but not looking in, plus a magic spell that deterred insects and another to regulate temperature.

Finally they turned their magical artistry to the colours and materials within the rooms. Living areas were rich in the colours of ancient Egypt, and furniture was for comfort. Knowing that they could change these virtually at will led to some rather bizarre decor on Robin's part featuring camels and pyramids and Tuareg tribesmen in murals of a sand-swept landscape where the camels and Tuareg were galloping in and out of the murals and the sand escaped onto the floor (although somehow didn't get spread around or into the bath or bed). Kate also indulged herself with opulent rooms in jewel colours, and brought the verdant gardens indoors, where a bathtub became a pool. Egrets and dragonflies and butterflies and fishes were there in abundance, but magical ones (that didn't poo, greet the dawn with shrill cries, or get in your way). The bedroom she shared with Robin was however just quietly lovely and very comfortable. Perry opted for a sort of 'opium den' effect of low lights and dim niches, with lavish use of silks and velvets in deep rich colours.

Maggie and Kailen, having had many more years of this fun, decided on a big, comfortably furnished set of rooms with several baths and a small kitchen, rich details and colours of ancient Egypt and some wall murals. Elowen decided upon a very human luxury hotel look, just to give herself a change, but Ariane and Dmitri brought details of Faerie into their areas. All agreed upon a long hallway running the outer sides of the building so that they could visit each other without intruding into private areas, and each set of apartments had doors out into the huge central 'paradise garden' Chauncey had made.

Having created their living quarters, they gathered again outside and found that previously unseen staff had set out a feast in the big pavilion near the central pool. Chauncey was already feasting upon varied dishes, including human food and dragon food upon his terrace not too far from them so they could all converse.

The upshot of the conversation was that Kate and Robin with Maggie would go immediately after lunch to the dahabeeyah and bring the Cat Goddess Bastet, Elvira and Feral, and the dragons back to their new villa within the Egyptian Dragon Principality where they could be safely hidden from the ordinary world. It had been difficult for the dragons as the Misfits lovely new dahabeeyah, though big enough for the Moon crew to fit into the large salon, it was a bit crowded and they still had to remain invisible on the open upper deck or lurk under water.

Meanwhile, Chauncey would get the formalities over with at the palace, where he would be welcomed with appropriate pomp. Hopefully he would also be back in time for dinner at Villa Magica, as Ariane had dubbed it. This time the door that led from the Principality into Luxor itself was the door of their villa, and as the three stepped through they found themselves on the road by the river where their new dahabeeyah was moored.

Chapter 15

When they came aboard what they saw surprised them. The Imperial Cat Goddess, Bastet, was sheltered under the protective wing of the dragon Blue Moon. Bastet had her arms around Blue and her head resting against the lovely young dragon's chest. Blue appeared to be humming some gentle song.

"But…that's the Cat Goddess Bastet. And you said Blue Moon was shy. Yet they are like mother and child, only in reverse, Bastet is the child, Blue the protective parent." Robin voiced what they all felt, astonishment and, yes, worry. At least Bastet looked to be settled and feeling protected.

Elvira, witch and seer, with her friend and occasional protector, Feral, the large black cat with his knowing green eyes, were beside them to greet and explain.

Elvira smiled. "We - err - Peony and Lilac Moon, Feral and I—decided not to tell Blue that Bastet was a goddess. And Bastet agreed to that, because we told her that Blue was shy and preferred to live mostly alone. Although one of the Moon dragons, she has never felt at home in company. So Bastet, to help Blue be comfortable around her, just presented herself as an Egyptian spirit who longed to befriend a dragon. Blue still doesn't know that she's a goddess. Although Bastet took her on a tour of the Karnak temples and showed her hieroglyphs and pictures featuring herself, Blue was intrigued but didn't understand that Bastet was 'important' to appear there. To Blue it was like a picture book and could have been about ordinary folk. She had no trouble accepting Bastet as a woman with a cat's head. She took that in her stride. So when Bastet became so frightened, Blue just took over, comforting and protecting her as, we think, she would want to be protected if she were frightened."

"That's amazing, it's wonderful," said Maggie. "Look at them, Bastet with her guard down, able to let go and be comforted. Blue Moon giving what she would hope to receive. It's…well, it's what white magic and witchcraft try to teach. Blue must be an empath. No wonder she has found the world overwhelming." Elvira smiled and Feral looked smug.

"Yes, I believe she is, and she has taken a big step for a very shy and, I also believe lonely, dragon. But it is very healing to be able to give what you know is needed and have it accepted. And Bastet, who really meant it when she begged to be able to befriend a dragon, has got something quite beyond her expectations."

"As in being scared half to death by a

hieroglyph?" mentioned Robin.

"Yeah, that too," said Feral, "enough to make a cat laugh. But you know what my mistress means—Bastet, the Goddess who must always be 'on stage' has been able to be normal…well, normal-ish…and so when she really needed comfort, there was Blue who allowed her instincts to overcome her shyness to give what is needed.

"Oh, and speaking of magic—come look." And Feral strutted away to the stern of the dahabeeyah and pointed down. There in large letters embellished with scrollwork and flowers was the name of their new boat—*Heka*—with the hieroglyphs in ancient Egyptian underneath. "We thought of all sorts," said Feral, "but in the end, Heka, which is ancient Egyptian for Magic, kind of says it all."

"It's perfect," said Kate. "But is that how Magic is, err, spelt in hieroglyphs?"

"Those are the hieroglyphs for Heka, which is ancient Egyptian for magic, also for the God of Magic and healing. Because of course there's a god." said Elvira.

"Of course," murmured Maggie.

"Another one that doesn't change aspect all the time," added Elvira. "So probably an old god."

Bastet had finally noticed that some of the Misfits had arrived. She came forward, shadowed by Blue, and extended her hands. "Please forgive my not noticing you immediately. Elvira has told you what happened? And she has told you who I am?" It was clear to the Misfits that she meant that she wasn't to be acknowledged as a goddess.

"Yes," said Kate, "we are pleased to see you, Bastet. But, distressed that you saw something in Karnak that upset you."

"It was in Ramses tomb in the Valley of the Kings actually. Blue and I went there after I showed her around Karnak. But I'm much better now," said Bastet, "thanks to my new friend Blue here, she told me she knew just how I felt, and has been such a comfort. Do you know her?"

"Only as one of Lilac and Peony's other sisters," responded Maggie. "Blue Moon, you seem to have a real talent for comforting even someone you haven't known long."

Blue's scales flushed with a hint of magenta, and she bowed her head. It was clear that she was still quite shy. "I only did what anyone would."

"We've come with an invitation," said Kate, deciding that much more conversation about Bastet's scare might reveal things better left unsaid for the moment. "We've taken up residence in a really fabulous villa within the grounds of the Egyptian Dragon Principality. It has lots of rooms and two whole wings built big enough for dragons. We thought you'd like to move from *Heka* to a place where you can spread your wings and not be worried about being seen. And Chauncey is there already. He's finally able to travel without worry. And I know he'd love to see you all and catch up just as much as we do. The invitation extends to you, also, Bastet and Blue Moon of course, plus Elvira and Feral if you want to come."

Lilac and Peony raised their heads above the waters of the Nile, where they'd been lazily swimming and staying out of sight of humans. "Yes, please, we'd love that. It's tiring after a while being invisible. And we'd enjoy some proper dragon food and to see our father. Blue will come too, won't you, Blue?"

"We'll go together, yes," replied Bastet. "I can see, my friend, that this vessel is cramped for you, so let's find this place where you can stretch out and I can see something more of dragons and their world." She turned to the Misfits. "Dragons are so beautiful, I am dazzled by them, and Blue has been so kind."

Elvira and Feral were eager also to see something that, even living all their lives in Egypt, first in Cairo and then in Luxor, they had never known existed. "But if it's all right, we'd prefer to keep on living here," said Elvira. "It's extremely comfortable for us, and Feral has much more freedom to roam than from my tiny apartment. Plus we can keep a watch against any possible thieves or other troubles."

"I think, don't you, that it would be best if we go first just to let them know we are bringing guests," murmured Maggie.

"Good idea," responded Feral while Elvira nodded. "The Princes of the Principality might need a little warning of an Egyptian witch and a black cat!"

"Not to mention the Dragon King." laughed Robin. "And the Queen of Faerie, plus my father, a Prince of Faerie. You'll be tripping over Royalty."

"Ah, I believe the phrase is 'a cat may look at a King'," said Feral. "And I bow before no one except my mistress, here," rubbing against Elvira's skirts.

"Don't believe him, he's a shyster and a thief and has never bowed to me in his misbegotten life," laughed Elvira, scooping up the big cat and nuzzling him. "And my dear friend." she added. Feral patted her cheek with his paw and purred.

Chapter 16

Kate, Robin and Maggie led the way up the quay to a space between two buildings that appeared to be an alley, but when they looked closely, it seemed to shimmer as if not quite there. Robin, being half fae, waved his hand and a door appeared, which he opened.

"Apparently I've been given this power now that my grandmother approves of me," he whispered to Kate.

He stepped aside to usher the others through, then closed the door on the view of the Nile and their dahabeeyah *Heka.* A short hallway led through the Nile-facing wing of their new villa. There were audible gasps from their friends at first seeing the beautiful garden within the surrounding villa. But both Bastet and Elvira were stunned into silence by their first sight of Chen Shi, the Dragon King.

Lilac and Peony both laughed at the expression on Elvira's face. "I had no idea," was all she could manage to say.

"That is our father, Chen Shi, King of the Noble or Imperial Dragons," announced Lilac impressively. Then she laughed. "Big, isn't he?"

Bastet, however, had pressed back against Blue. Perhaps the length of Chauncey's tail reminded her of Apep, but she was clearly again shaken. Blue whispered to her, "It's okay, he's our father. Eventually we will all be almost that big. Not as big as he is, but very big. It's all right, he is indeed noble, kind and generous and loving—and protective. You are safe here."

Chauncey meanwhile had stayed quite still, not wanting to startle these new people until they had taken in his size and been reassured. Queen Elowen was sitting beside him in a chair, and now Kate also ran to him, announcing that he was her adoptive father.

"Well," said Elvira. "So that is what a grown-up dragon looks like. I think I'm glad I got to know you younger ones first."

But Lilac and Peony didn't reply, as they were making their way through the garden to bow before their father in that lovely way dragons had, one front foot crossed over the other with their foreheads laid against the top foot and their tails held almost straight up.

Blue also, consigning Bastet to Elvira, crossed the garden and bowed. Chen Shi lowered his own head, and touched each of his daughters, including Kate, tenderly on their heads, saying in a gentle rumble, "I am well pleased with you, my children, and even more pleased that we meet again." Then he turned his hand so Kate could sit in it. "Will you introduce me to these new friends?" he asked, and his daughters beckoned toward Elvira and Bastet.

Elvira started forward, but Bastet hung back. Blue came over and again sheltered the Cat Goddess with her wing. "Come now, he is the best of fathers, the best of friends," said Blue, and Bastet let herself be led across the garden to stand beside Elvira.

Kate made the introductions, "Chauncey, this is our good friend Elvira, who rescued Dawn and helped her escape from Luxor when she was in danger. And there, trying to be inconspicuous, is Feral. He is a cat but also a magician or a mage. He actually flew over the Nile on Dawn's back and hid her in an old tomb!"

Chauncey's rumble of laughter was kept as quiet as he could, but even so the ground trembled slightly.

Kate continued, "And this is our friend Bastet, she has just had a very unsettling experience, and would not ordinarily be so shy I think."

Bastet, who had been looking up at the colourful, beautiful, but huge mass of the biggest dragon on earth in awe tinged with fear, managed to incline her head in recognition of the introduction.

No one apparently had made it clear to Chauncey that Bastet's status was unknown to Blue. "Madame, my homage is to you, Cat Goddess of ancient Egypt, a deity, whereas I am a mere sovereign." A very flexible neck made it possible for him to incline his head in a way suitable to her status. At this she automatically gave a most definitely 'royal' wave of her hand. Blue stepped back. Bastet instantly sensed her surprise. The regal movement of her hand immediately turned to stroke Blue's neck.

"I wanted you to like me for myself, I didn't want to establish any boundaries. Please forgive this deception."

Blue, it seemed, was up to the occasion. "You are my friend, we are friends. I, after all, am a child of the great Dragon King. I have never found that gave me any status I wanted to use. As you know, I am notoriously shy and a loner. It may be part of what drew me to you."

The rest, including Chauncey, who heard this with surprise and delight, were relieved. That tricky part was over.

Kailen stepped forward then and took his mother's hand. "As we appear to be amongst not just witches, faeries, a magical cat and dragons, but a goddess and royalty, let me introduce you to my mother, Elowen, Queen of the Unseelie Fae. Elowen inclined her head. Bastet inclined hers. Elvira looked suitably impressed and dropped a curtsey.

But within moments, Maggie, Elowen, Bastet

and Elvira had gathered together around a table set with tea things and were engaged in conversation. Shortly, Kailen, Perry, Robin and Kate joined them. "All this regal stuff makes me hungry," said Robin—while the Moon Dragons gathered by their father and exchanged news.

Mid-morning snack over, Maggie asked if they'd enjoy a tour around the villa. "You can decide the rooms you want and decorate them to suit your own tastes. The Principality and our villa exist in a bubble of space-time, entirely constructed with magic, so magic here is enhanced. This means decorating or even renovations using magic are much easier. Bastet, if it pleases you, we have delegated most of the north wing that connects to the dragon's side for you, so as to be nearer to Blue Moon."

The idea met with real enthusiasm. Chauncey had also led his children into the dragon wing of the villa where they could pick out spaces and create caves or actual rooms and rearrange piles of treasure and pillows and comforters for beds.

Elowen, Ariane and Dmitri had already created rooms on the south side of the villa, decorating them in a comfortable pastiche of what Kate immediately recognised as English Country House crossed with some of the more delicious aspects of faerie landscapes, all in spring colours. Perry had the end of that wing, abutting the eastern facing wing with its entrance opening on the Nile. Maggie and Kailen with Kate, Robin were in this wing opposite the dragon's main wing. This left the north wing that was partly dragon sized, for the comfort of Blue to stay close to Bastet, and part human sized and connected with the dragon wing for Bastet and Elvira and Feral. Here they immediately made sure the temperatures were more nearly like the Egyptian heat, but not so hot as to be uncomfortable for them, although it was rather warmer than the others would have been happy with. Still, it was their area, so they could configure it to suit themselves.

Maggie had asked rather tentatively if Bastet, being an ancient Egyptian Goddess, did magic, or was dependent upon her usual entourage to create her environment. "In which case," she said, "we would be more than happy to create your wishes as to shape, size and decoration of your rooms."

Bastet was uncertain about her own powers, as she had been waited upon hand and foot for much of her existence. "But I do remember that at a much earlier time, I did perform certain things that would in your language be called miracles or magic, so possibly I have powers I have not been aware of using lately. Except of course my transition from a large Imperial Cat to a woman with the head of a cat, that I can do with ease. Let me try, if it works, it would be a joyful thing to be able to create."

Elvira looked for support to Feral, who nodded. "My magic is small, but Feral helps me to create what I envision, so perhaps, if you find difficulties working alone, we could provide some of the support you have been used to."

Bastet nodded graciously. "Let us see what I might be able to do. This entire area is a magical place where even small powers are magnified it seems. I will ask you if I need help and I am grateful that you are willing."

Everyone stepped back to give her space to focus herself and not be distracted. Bastet felt within and found a universe tightly packed, full of potential. She was surprised and intrigued. So this was what it was to be a god and not just a figurehead. It had been so long since she had been in charge of her own life-force, she had virtually forgotten. Now she examined the web of her interior, its ebb and flow, and began to recognise the different threads of her power. It was from here, without conscious thought, she had reached out to Toby, the spirit-cat she had sent to help Kate and the Misfits disable Wyvern-Proteus on that island in the Venetian lagoon. She had passed power to him without even thinking about it. But now she contemplated the possibilities.

There was amazing destructive force waiting to be called upon, but also threads of glowing colour that pulsed with the potential to create beauty or heal or endow. She was pleased. *A house, something worthy of a god, but private,* she thought. *Just for me and my friends, with some rooms big enough for Blue also.*

As she stood deep in thought, the others saw that she was glowing softly and ribbons of many colours were unfurling from her hands, which were making gentle passes through the air. Wherever they touched, changes were made, walls came up, ceilings rose or descended, there were suddenly rooms, their walls decorated with frescos in the ancient Egyptian manner but of a surprisingly realistic nature. Bastet moved serenely, trancelike through each room, adjusting size, adding interior pools under what seemed to be large skylights. Beds appeared. And a very large central room where couches and chairs were scattered in comfortable groupings amongst the palm trees, gentle breezes blew, birds appeared in the trees and on the central pond. Finally, a gesture, and frescos grew on the walls depicting something ancient Egypt had never seen—Cat Goddess Bastet with her friend, the dragon Blue Moon. And then the Misfits, the other dragons and Elvira and Feral as well.

Bastet turned and smiled at her friends—who

were pleasingly astonished.

"I believe I have not forgotten after all!" she announced, clearly proud. "This is my main living area, where all of you are welcome at any time. And I hope Blue will find it spacious enough for her comfort."

As if speaking her name conjured her up, Blue appeared through an archway that led into the dragon area of the villa. She took time to look around, and then came over to Bastet, tiny flames of approval showing at her nostrils.

"This is a beautiful room you have made. I think only a goddess could do this. And I love the frescos, so very Egyptian, yet so modern, and celebrating your friendships. Thank you for thinking of me." And this time her beautiful bow was to Bastet.

"We are friends, as you said, we are equals, this is a tribute to that friendship," said Bastet. "So please do not bow before me, although it is a lovely thing to see. I would have us be as before, equals. And you know I understand that you will come and go as you please, that has been our compact, it hasn't changed."

It was then Elvira and Feral's turn to decorate their part of the villa, the area left after Bastet had made hers, that connected to the eastern front occupied by the Misfits. They moved through this area, easily creating an extremely colourful [like one of Elvira's caftans, Kate decided] suite of rooms, full of silken carpets, ottomans in coloured leather, comfortable chairs, cushions and throws in many fabrics, some embroidered, some woven, some printed, dripping with tassels and small bells, hung from the walls and draped over the furniture. The walls were also hung with vivid paintings showing scenes of Egyptian life, boats on the Nile, donkeys and egrets in fields and trees, Luxor as it was in the 19th Century, including the temple of Karnak and the Valley of the Kings.

Again there was one central room, also with a domed ceiling outlined in mosaic tiles and glassed in to let the sun stream down on a central pond where golden fishes flashed under lotus leaves and reeds and papyrus grew at the edge. This was the main sitting room, with couches and chairs and tables under the palm trees. Similar to what Bastet created, but somewhat smaller, and crowded with colour.

Finally there was the bathroom, a splendid room with copper tub and a huge separate shower, but the main delight was the tiled walls, again picturing scenes full of birds and lotus flowers and flowering trees, always with the Nile as background. It appealed to them all. It would have all looked rather Victorian, except Elvira's colour palette was bright and soft, making every room seem like a welcoming bower. Feral, black and piratical with emerald green eyes, still managed to look entirely at home here.

"This will be our 'home away from home'," Elvira announced. "*Heka* is our home, but I can see we will be wanting to move back and forth, and the dragons cannot do that easily, so if we are to help Bastet and prevent the rising again of the evil one then I think it will be necessary to gather here rather often."

Feral nodded his agreement as they realised what fun it was to create their own space and be able to alter it at will, and how well they seemed to get on with the others. Plus Elvira would be invaluable for her knowledge of the ancient Egyptian history of gods from the human perspective, whereas Bastet could give them the perspective of an actual goddess.

Chapter 17

Sitting down for a well-earned cup of tea or coffee or other drink, depending upon preference (Kate had introduced the Misfits to iced coffee with whipped cream some time back, and that was refreshing in the warmth of Egypt) they decided to have dinner in the main garden of the villa where Chauncey and his children could join them, and there finally discuss what Bastet had seen in the hieroglyphs of Rameses tomb that so distressed her. She declared herself to be quite recovered from her fright, due to Blue's care of her and her rediscovered magical abilities. But that did not mean she didn't feel there was a potential threat that might need to be dealt with.

"Who is making dinner, and where do we get supplies," asked Robin.

Lilac Moon laughed. "My father, Chen Shi, has a complete kitchen staff installed, capable of making dragon and human and. err…goddess food as well. He has been here for a few days, and he is known for how well he organises, especially food."

"Oh, splendid," said Kate. "I suppose we could have just asked some of the dragons in the Principality—it's just outside our front door really—but this is better, much better. Chauncey always produces amazing meals. Remember Robin?"

"Oh, definitely. But, Bastet, is there special goddess food?"

It was good to hear her laugh, even though her cat's head showed a lot of pointed teeth. "Not really, I have spent centuries eating what Egyptian followers left as offerings for me, which was identical to what they ate themselves. Of course when I was important to a pharaoh or his wives, the quality was better. Did you know there was even one pharaoh who named himself after me? The Pharaoh Pami, whose name meant "he who belongs to Bastet." But I am interested to see what dragons eat. And what they can make for humans and goddesses. Will it be edible?"

It was Kate laughing now. "Chauncey has developed quite a taste for human food, even gourmet food, and always keeps a human chef that he pays very well indeed. Of course dragons also need certain metals, coal, wood, and other minerals. Mostly it's for making fire, but also I think part of their necessary diet."

Blue, who was becoming quite out-going added, "We need a certain amount of limestone, and a fair amount of meat. Wild dragons cook their meat with their own fire, but we here in your world prefer it cooked by someone who doesn't just torch it."

So there was a gathering in the central garden of all who wanted to hear Bastet's story and find out if and how they might help. First, Chauncey's chef had prepared a multi-course dinner guaranteed to please dragons, humans, fae, a cat and a Cat Goddess. Apart from passing on the coal, limestone and metals set out for anyone who cared to partake, the humans, fae and goddess all dug in happily to the various other delicacies on offer. Finally, with the serving of coffee, brandy and wine plus small sweet morsels, the dinner finished and Bastet began her tale.

"I was showing Blue some of my world because she was so interested, and because of course we are both extremely long-lived. We had enjoyed parts of Luxor and the Temple of Karnak there, and she flew me to the Valley of the Kings after the tourists had gone. Here I was showing her illustrations and hieroglyphs in the tomb of Ramses the First when I saw a significant change to the ancient wall painting of Apep.

"The picture is of this huge serpent, the God of Chaos and Evil, showing many coils to emphasise his enormous size, facing the God Atum, some say another name for Ra, who prevents Apep from exerting his power to turn back the *Mesektet* boat carrying Ra. The hieroglyphs say, or are supposed to say '*The assembly of the gods, who repulses Apophis*'.

"Instead I was shocked to see that suddenly this inscription, so familiar to me, now said '*The assembly of the gods, unable to repulse Apophis'*. And the head of the creature, Apep, my deadly enemy, was no longer facing Atum but turned toward the viewer, me, and his mouth, shut before in capitulation to the power of the gods, was open with fangs dripping poison and his dreadful tongue flicking forward.

"You must understand these wall frescos are upward of two millennia old and have never changed. Some power was radiating from them now, and I became very frightened. Gods and goddesses of ancient Egypt do not suddenly become empowered to change the past or the present. And this God, the evil Apep or Apophis, dwells deep in the black night of the underworld, to all intents dead. But now he is not. Gods depend upon the power of belief to bestow life and power, and I swear to you Apep has never had a cult of worshippers or a sudden upsurge in belief. So what I saw was impossible within the old ways. And he has always wished to destroy cat goddesses." With this last utterance, Bastet shuddered and sank onto her seat.

"You say 'cat goddesses'?" asked Kate. "I wasn't aware of more, I thought you, Bastet, were *the* cat goddess. And surely you successfully cut off the head of Apep to protect the Tree of Life? I saw that illustration from an ancient wall painting on the internet."

"Ah, yes. But it wasn't me. It was Mau, a relative of mine, yes, but a different Goddess with much greater war-like powers. You saw it was a spotted cat? That's Mau, more like a lion or a cheetah. However over the millennia of course we became confused in human minds, and some inscriptions say that Mau killed Apep, some say it was Bastet. But I assure you we are different and I have never gone into singlehanded combat with Apep. Plus, of course, being dead already, nothing can really kill him. He may not have cults of worshippers or temples built to him or priesthoods, all affirmations of power to a god, but he existed before all that, and exists still. Only I thought he existed as he had long before Egypt existed, as a sleeping snake in the dark underworld."

"So in the modern world he is supposedly dead and buried?" asked Robin. "Exactly," responded Bastet. "Only now it appears he isn't. Ra the Sun God is sleeping, Mau also, even Sekhmet, the Lion God. And all the others. Various of the Gods used to ride Ra's Night Boat into the darkness every night where Apep was waiting to destroy the Sun. Now none of them is around or awake. And if that is the case, then it makes sense that he will be coming after me."

"But if the Sun God Ra is sleeping, yet the Sun still rises every morning surely Apep also has no power any longer." said Parry in an effort to soothe her.

"I think the answer to that is the same as in one of my favourite Terry Pratchett books, *Hogfather*," said Kate. "Let's see if I get this right... Okay.   After Susan saves the Hogfather, her grandfather asks her 'What would have happened if you hadn't saved him?' Susan answers 'The sun would have risen just the same, yes?' But he says, 'No. The sun would not have risen.' And she says, 'So what would have happened?'   And her grandfather replies, 'A mere ball of flaming gas would have illuminated the world.'   I've always loved that, it explains so much about the power, even need, for belief."

Bastet beamed at her, "Exactly so, this ball of flaming gas comes and goes, but it is no longer the Sun God Ra, and no longer does he fight Apep every night for the sun to rise again. But if Apep rises from the dead, without the other gods and goddesses there is just me.   And as you said a cat goddess was instrumental in killing him one time to save the Tree of Life.   That was Mau, but later writings say it was me. It was never me, but I think Apep doesn't know that.   It was written after all. And it now appears there are two ancient Egyptian Gods with new life and even power.   Myself and the God of Chaos. Without the others, I have felt more like a mouse before a cat than a powerful Cat Goddess with the power to subdue Apep. I am the Cat Goddess who guards the hearth and home, children and mothers, I am a gentle cat, a good mother, a house cat. Mau or Sekhmet are wild cats, Sekhmet is a lion god—*they* could battle Apep."

"How could this Chaos God awaken, then, if there is no cult of worship, no belief?" asked Chauncey.

"I can only think of one way. It is how he is different from the rest of us. It is written that Apophis could warp reality and control Chaos. That would give him the power, once his demons, or what you call minions, waken him."

"Minions? What minions?" Robin broke in. "From what I know — yeah, it's not a lot—the Egyptian Gods didn't have minions."

"We don't," said Bastet. "But Apep is unlike the rest, he has an army of small demons who exist to do his bidding. I am guessing that they had something to do with his waking up. Their existence could be one of the ways he can warp reality. If indeed that has happened. I have a feeling of *something* rising up, and it is tied in with the change in that ancient fresco."

"Maybe what we need is to wake up some of the other gods too," said Kailen. "That way you and they can face this Chaos God and beat him as you always did in the ancient times."

"I have no idea how to go about that," said Bastet. "My awakening—or rebirth if you choose—is the work of many Egyptians over some years gathering to worship me. Mainly that has meant to have a big party of course. It has seen me grow in substance and strength. It would take time, probably a lot of time, to encourage Egyptians to take an interest in the other gods. And that would result in revolution, because the country is now Muslim, and I think they would not agree. In any case, humanity as it is today here in Egypt and elsewhere would become distraught if the old gods came back. The gods are ego-maniacal and changeable, and not to be trusted. You could not just point them at Apep and tell them to get rid of him.

"I have had a rebirth because I am the house cat, and house cats have always been worshipped by humans. We are charming, affectionate, good mothers and have claws and teeth to dispatch rodents that spoil crops. We also maintain an air of mystery. A house cat Goddess is a deity humans can live with. I do not think they would want to live with many of the others. And as I said, it would certainly take years of renewed worship to resurrect the gods."

"Okay, we are without the help of other Egyptian gods," said Parry, "and it sounds as if that might be a good thing. But are you sure Apep is rising?"

Bastet again looked inward at her newly aroused magic and saw the definite signs of red and black tendrils of power circling a dark cloud. It pulsed with power, and it definitely was a warning. "I see within the warning signs of evil rising, and from the changes in the fresco of Apep, I must conclude that he is the source of this premonition. I don't think there is any doubt."

So Apep takes the form of a snake. Is that a cobra, a really large cobra?" asked Chauncey.

"No. Cobras are revered as powerful and appear on the pharaoh's crown of the two kingdoms, a symbol of his power," Bastet answered. "Apep is a huge serpent, said to be miles long, living in the night black waters of the underworld, the Duat. It's that underworld that the boat carrying Ra the Sun God enters every night, passing under the earth into the blackness of Apep's kingdom where Ra and other gods must fight him so the sun will rise again. Apep fights to devour the sun, so it is that he must be huge, and some say he is also golden."

"So definitely a mythical or god-like beast. There is no similar snake in Egypt or all of Africa," mused Chauncey. "Well, dragons are also magical beasts, we could not exist without magic, and the same with the fae, and probably gods. Witches are human, but are endowed with magic powers. We have here all these magical beings. I think that together we can defeat this Apep before he becomes a real threat.

Chapter 18

D K was simply simmering with ideas to get his ancient master back into the limelight. His best was to have an Apep Festival, similar to the one Bastet had had last year. Apep, growing more solid as he returned to 'life' was intrigued by the idea. "We can hold it at the same place?" he questioned D K. "It's a very inviting location I have been told."

"Ah…well, here's the thing Your Dreadfulness, it is, err, 'anointed' to Bastet. And more important, it's close to Saqqara, where the Egyptologists have recently discovered a huge cemetery, mummies galore, and artefacts. You can hardly move without tripping over something ancient and important to these humans. Or the humans themselves, they are there all the time. We, the ancient gods and their retainers, really mustn't be seen by the humans. Not for a long time, not until we are ready to dominate them and demand the worship that is your due. Not until we can restore the old ways. Your festival should take place in the south, near the Nubian border perhaps. There are some nice ruined temples there that would serve as a good backdrop for festivities and your introduction to the faithful."

"D K, you seem to know a lot about the world as it is now, were you not sleeping the sleep of the dead gods all these millennia?" rumbled his Lord.

"Not always, Lord," grovelled D K. "Your faithful demon army needed to keep watch over your sleeping form and be ready to defend you, or, as now, wake you to a possible new era of worship. Your faithful followers will rejoice when you are fully in possession of your power."

"Whoa, my demon, as I recall I was the fierce and loathsome God of Evil, never even morphing into more acceptable forms, as did Set and some others. I don't believe there were ever faithful followers."

D K squirmed slightly, knowing Apep was correct. "Well, it's a new era, as you say it's many millennia since the great gods of Egypt held sway over the populace. So with this festival, we will reintroduce you to your public. They may be fearful followers at first, but with a little image tweaking, they should become faithful. Once we entertain them sufficiently, they will be excited to follow you."

"Entertain? I never entertained, I brought fear and destruction!"

"Exactly, and I'm sure you will again. But to start you must garner belief or you will never grow in power. Hence the festival. I thought a rock concert to kick things off...

"A what—a gathering of rocks? You jest, D K, and I do not appreciate jests at my expense." The great head with its slitty eyes and venom-dripping fangs moved closer to the little demon.
"No, Your Horribleness, not like that at all. I would NEVER jest at your expense. Remember the music I played for you? You liked it, you *swayed*. Well, it makes huge crowds of humans sway and jump and lose their minds. It's called a Rock Concert. And D K and the Apepatones will give them a rock concert like they've never experienced. We will add refreshments with a few mind-bending ingredients, and introduce them to some smaller snakes, perhaps cobras such as decorated the crowns of the ancient pharaohs. Just to get them in the mood you know.

"And in addition there are a number of people in this world now who are ripe to become your followers. I would go so far as to say they follow Evil without having a suitable god to incorporate what they already both believe and practice."

"I am intrigued. Say on, D K, who are these people who practice evil?"

"Oligarchs, tyrants, plutocrats, psychopaths and plain ordinary villains, my Lord, very wealthy and powerful men who delight in the suffering of others, who make their fortunes from dealing in drugs and slavery and all manner of terrible things to do to ordinary people. They already worship you, even though they don't yet know it."

"Ah, yes, I am familiar with these people. Many of the Pharaohs were like this. Although they played the part of worshippers of the benevolent and protective gods, in private or in war they practiced all of these evils. Power, raw power of that sort fed me then. Can it feed me now, D K? Can we tap into this source and use it?" D K was astonished at how quickly his often-lethargic master had picked up on this idea. An idea in fact that had eluded D K himself until this moment. But, like any good vizier, he didn't acknowledge it wasn't his idea all along.

"Exactly what I had in mind, Your Odiousness! We will attract the ordinary folk with this festival, and also identify and tap into the power of the most powerful. They don't even have to know your name, but you will feed off them nonetheless. It will bring you to full strength in a very short time."

"Excellent, my small but potent little

henchman, then I can indeed pay back that pesky cat goddess for daring to challenge me. Ha!" If Apep had had hands he would have been rubbing them together with glee. Instead he used his tail to beat the ground and in the process flattened a number of his demon army that had taken up positions behind him, hoping that way to avoid his notice. They died with squeaks of horror pleasing to his ears.

Chapter 19

It was the next day on their dahabeeyah on the Nile. The Misfits had gone there where their computers and phones could work. Perry was chatting via FaceTime with Julien. He'd brought his partner up to date on the story so far and they were discussing how their magical group, now including the might of Chauncey, could possibly find Apep, the God of Chaos.

"According to Egyptian belief, Apep lives in the black void of chaos called the Duat that exists under the earth," said Perry. "Well that could be the black void of space, I suppose, since we know the earth is not flat and the sun does not go around it."

"But space or the universe isn't chaotic," responded Julien. "If anything it is amazingly well organised. Although I suppose the formation of the planets around our Sun seemed quite chaotic. But there are laws of physics that explain all of it. Mostly gravity. What about Black Holes?"

"Suitably awe-inspiring, but not as we once thought, the end of everything, and also I believe not chaotic," said Perry. "Look perhaps we are going about this all wrong. We are supposing that Apep is a creation of the world or the universe, but he is entirely a creature of tales told around firesides, and then of hieroglyphs and other writing—he is formed of belief and magic. Belief and magic that died out over two thousand years ago as the civilisation that created him and all the other gods changed. As Bastet says, she has been 'reborn' through belief that is mostly the result of a lot of booze and partying. And it's easy even for modern folk to believe that cats are somehow supernatural. Kate says she always thought they guard their house and people from evil spirits. She says it's the way they look into space as if staring at something only they can see."

"Then the answer is simple," said Julien. "Send the dragons to look for him, maybe with Bastet—she'd know the way if anyone would. And they are entirely magical you've told me."

"It's a thought, although I think Bastet might balk at having to go hunting for this huge snake thing in the—what's the word? The 'Stygian' darkness under the world. I will ask Chauncey, he'll know. Although they are the products of two different worlds, and different belief systems and different magic I would imagine."

"Then wait until this Apep reveals himself— if your Cat Goddess is right, he is 'rising again' and will no doubt be coming your way if she's the only ancient Egyptian God or Goddess also reborn, and he hates her. Perry, you're the magical one, and you are surrounded by magic people, fae and dragons and at least two magical cats. I'm just the scientific one, and this doesn't follow those rules. I love it that you want to ask for my opinion, but it really can't be too useful."

"Not true, talking it through has eliminated a load of possibles, that's always good. Plus I miss you and love talking to you,"

Kate interrupted their goodbyes, saying "Perry, don't sign off just yet. Hi Julien, I've had a thought. Are you in London?

"Yes, as it happens, is there something here you need?"

"I've found a picture on papyrus from a Book of the Dead, it's a copy called 'the papyrus of Hunefer' who was a scribe. It shows a picture of the brindled cat Mau, who is a form of Ra, the Sun God, 'killing' Apep to protect the Tree of Life. It's now in the British Museum.

"We've got into all this because the Cat Goddess Bastet saw a change in a wall fresco that should have showed and said that Apep was being stopped by gods as Ra's Night Boat sailed under the earth, but now showed that the gods couldn't stop Apep. I'm wondering if this papyrus picture is also changed to show Mau can't kill Apep. Could you find out?"

"If it's on display, very easily. If it's in

storage, it could be difficult. Egyptology isn't one of my fields, and offhand I don't know any of the curators to get in for a look. Find me the permission and I'll do it or get a curator to do it. Do you have someone there who can get permission from the Egyptian Museum or other important Egyptologists?"

Perry answered, "Yes, we have me, I might be able to, or Maggie through our contacts with the important auction houses in England, and I think one of the important dragons in the Principality probably knows how to get in touch and influence an Egyptian Museum curator.

"But Kate—that would blow this whole thing wide open I fear. And bring a lot of unwanted attention onto us because we started asking those questions and getting permissions in 'the real world'. If there is change the British Museum Egyptology Dept will go nuts, and also want to know why we were checking and what we know. And there's nothing we can tell them, is there?"

"Oh, hell's bells and buckets of blood!" cried Kate. "Of course, we can't afford to bring that attention to ourselves."   "Plus," said Maggie, "it won't add to our knowledge except for the very spooky idea that Apep can affect and change something in the British Museum. If we find out that he or his demons are making changes worldwide, because I'm sure pictures, frescos and hieroglyphs featuring him are scattered world-wide now, then we still have the same problem, how to defeat him, or otherwise 'undo' him back to the sleep or death that is the fate of all the ancient gods. But we don't want to call attention to ourselves—we could end up with court cases, even jail time! Or probably psychiatric 'care'. I vote no."

And, having a quick think about it, the others did too. It wasn't as if they were facing a worldwide apocalypse as in a superhero film.

Over coffee, Perry shared the rest of his conversation with Julien with the Misfits and Elvira and Feral.

They'd all been thinking about it, of course, but it was Kate who solved one bit. "We can't have magic that is very different from Bastet or the dragons or our and Bastet's magic wouldn't work so smoothly and with increased power in the Principality. If it were very different wouldn't it be like different electrical voltages—they were different in the USA and Europe, and you'd burn out the American product plugged into a European socket without a transformer."

"And here I still believed you thought electricity was 'the witch in the wall'," laughed Robin. "But you seem to have grasped the basic principles."

"I can't say I do understand it, but I did burn out my hair dryer when I first came to England because I didn't know about the change in voltages, so that is what came to mind." said Kate.

"Well it's a good analogy," said Perry. "You're right, if we all had very different magic, we couldn't interact with it as we have been doing. And Bastet's as well—so if her magic is compatible with ours and the dragons and the fae, then so must that of all the old god's, including Apep. They all had different powers, but they had to work within the same system. That solves that. We can fight him."

"But we can't *find* him," said Elvira. "It could drive me crazy knowing there's a threat but with no way to counter it unless and until he shows himself here, in our world."

"Frustrating," said Kailen. "But if Bastet is right, he is on the move in some fashion already. So it's just a matter of time. Meanwhile, we do our research, and figure out the best way to dispatch a huge snake."

"And make sure we protect our Cat Goddess in the meantime," Maggie was already thinking ahead. "If he is rising or coming back to life, it appears he will be coming after her, so she is both the focus of our area to expect him and to protect her."

"I suggest," remarked Robin, "that we go to

the Valley of the Kings and have a good look at this wall fresco in Ramses tomb. It should look like this" and he showed them a picture on his tablet. "But she says both the inscription and his head have changed. We need to get pictures of that. She got very spooked at that point and didn't spend a lot of time looking at it, she just got Blue to get her out of there. We need to see if there's anything more we can gather from it."

"And we need someone who can read hieroglyphs," said Kate. "I hate to ask Bastet, because she found it so upsetting."   "She's the only one we've got, though," said Elvira. "Feral and I can't, there's over 2000 years between this Egyptian and that language. But don't you think that knowing we're here to help, and only having to look at pictures, well, she'll be up for it. She's still a Goddess, and they are created with bravery built in. You don't have treat her with kid gloves, she has done her share of fighting and intriguing too no matter what she said."

"Is that the witch talking or the pragmatist?" asked Kailen.

"That's both. You ought to know, you're partnered with a witch—we're pragmatic as hell when it comes to it," laughed Elvira.

Maggie and Kate were both laughing too. "And Bastet, no ancient Egyptian Goddess would stand a chance of still existing without both power and pragmatism. I don't think we have to worry about her from that end. It was just the shock of it that sent her reeling. Since she's rediscovered her god-power, or magic, she is much more settled, I think, and knows she can cope. We just need to make sure we are all alert to come to her aid if Mr Slinky comes calling."

Everyone felt more settled after that, and 'Mr Slinky' became the code name for the fearsome God of Chaos.

Chapter 20

But Kate had been thinking, and now she shared her thoughts with Robin. "If these gods are being re-created, or reborn or whatever is happening, even if only two of them, then doesn't it make sense that somewhere some of ancient Egypt is still there, or maybe is being re-created as well? Inside some kind of space-time thingy, like the Dragon Principalities and Faerie?"

"I have absolutely no idea," said Robin. "But maybe it's possible, because otherwise where do they come from, or where have they been. Like the 'trousers of time' or innumerable universes stacked up next to each other like pages in a book. Doesn't make any kind of sense to me, but some say it might be scientifically accurate. Dragons make more sense."

"But there *are* other worlds, other Earths, apparently piled up against each other!" Kate was excited now. "Because that's where Chauncey and the other older dragons came from! And it's still there and accessible, because he said if Dawn was incorrigible, they could send her there to live with the other dragons with no moral compass."

"And he can't exist without magic, he says that too," added Robin. "So, yes, he might know about other magical worlds within worlds, or alongside, or asleep and waking up. We need to talk to Chauncey."

"Of course," said Kate, grinning. "Chauncey is the oracle here. If anyone would know if there's an ancient Egypt tucked away somewhere, he would. And if there is, we might be able to get there."

"And surprise the hell out of Mr Slinky!" laughed Robin. "Rise again, would you? Nope, sorry, that's a 'no' from us."

§ § §

Kate was sitting in Chauncey's cupped hand, and Robin was standing beside her leaning against one of the huge dragon king's fingers.

"So you see, since there are magical hidden countries and principalities and worlds, we are wondering if Bastet and Apep actually are from an existing ancient Egypt hidden in some kind of space-time bubble. Well, Bastet is from there and Apep is still there, so it would include that black domain under the earth where the sun goes every night. Do you know?" Kate looked up at her dragon father with trust and love, while Robin still had a look of awe and a bit of nerves about him when he was this close.

"That's very possible," mused Chauncey.

"No, my dears, I don't know. How clever of you to have put that together, though. Of course it would make sense. I would go in search of it, but again my size is a disadvantage."

Kate and Robin looked crestfallen. "Don't worry, we already have the perfect people for the job," Chen Shi assured them.

"Oh, not Bastet," said Kate. "I know she is feeling much better, but to send her out as bait…"

"No, not Bastet. Apparently when she found herself here in this Egypt she had no knowledge of where she was before, not geographically anyway, it's not as if she has the knowledge at this point to lead any of you there. We'll have to send out a search party to see if they can find it. And we can start with the internet and reading a lot of hieroglyphs. Tucked away there, particularly in the Book of the Dead, should be some clues."

"That's a lot of reading for Bastet," Robin remarked.

"Oh, I was here back then you know," remarked Chauncey. "And long before as well. I and several of the Dragons of the Egyptian Principality can read hieroglyphs — the vizier is particularly good with the old texts, but I'm not bad."

"Chauncey, you never said. Wow!" Kate was squeezing his finger happily.

"Yeah, wow, and why?" asked Robin.

"If you'd lived for over a million years, young man, you might not be asking that." Chauncey tried to look stern, but his eyes were laughing. "I can read the old texts of any of the civilisations I have found interesting. Reading is a wonderful way to pass the time, to learn how the different worlds work, and we dragons have huge brains and a lot of time. Especially once humans came to dominate, after that we weren't free any longer to roam about being visible. Dragons had to make Principalities and hide-outs or be invisible when out and about. But with humans came writing and with writing came the possibility to entertain ourselves with their books."

"But can it really be that a country as big as Egypt can be tucked away in a, well, a little magic bubble?" asked Robin.

"Yes, the Principalities aren't really that large, and Kailen says Faerie isn't either, not nearly as big as a country, either of them," said Kate. "Unless maybe Monaco," she added.

"Probably the only part that is tucked away would be the area around the Nile. Out in the desert on each side there was no ancient Egypt, just within the long fertile strip of the Nile valley and a bit into the surrounding hills and desert. So, we would go looking for Mr. Slinky's country in a magic bubble shaped like a long snake." This time Chauncey did laugh.

"And you said we have the people for the job—is that us?" Robin asked.

"Not to begin with. I think that could be a waste of resources, hunting out a magical ancient Egypt that may or may not exist. No, I was thinking more of a few of my more restless children, who would love the adventure of it, know how to sniff out and gain access to 'magic bubbles of space-time' and who could be trusted not to interfere with it if they found it, of course."

"So how long might it be before you can set this in motion?" asked Robin.

"A few days or a week, perhaps. You just brought me the idea. It's a good one, but I need to talk to two of the viziers of the Principalities — my brother Chen Da, the Prime Minister or Vizier of the Oriental Principality and the Vizier Imhotep here in Egypt. Because, yes, I know of our own world from which we emigrated so long ago, that's another Earth and not really in a spacetime 'bubble' but laid against this one, a fully-fledged world. And there is Faerie, definitely a space-time bubble with great mobility within this Earth. And our Dragon Principalities here, also space-time bubbles. But we haven't run into ancient civilisations still somehow existing alongside the modern civilisations that took their places. Of course, we haven't been actually looking either. But it wouldn't make good sense to form an exploratory party without first trying to ascertain if such a place, or places, are real. Although, on the other hand, it might be the only way to find out is to set them to looking. But if there is any knowledge of this or other ancient civilisations still accessible, these two viziers would almost certainly know it."

"Wouldn't they have said?" asked Robin. "Wouldn't they have spread the word?"

"Ah, Robin, yes, in an ordinary world of humans, yes of course. But we Dragons have lived so long, seen so much, if it was just a rumour or a mention in an old manuscript, well, the knowledge could have been known and then forgotten. I don't think it would have been forgotten if we had actually had dealings with such a place, but second-hand stories…"

Chapter 21

"So will you be flying off to the Oriental Principality?" asked Kate.

"Yes, I think I will do that," responded Chauncey. "I haven't seen Chen Da in quite a long time, and we have always been friends as well as brothers. So it will be a treat for us, and if he doesn't know, we can have a little look in their archives. But before that I will spend a little time with Imhotep, looking through their archives where there is the greatest chance that if we knew anything back when, it would be written down here. I love libraries!"

§ § §

"Sniffing out a space-time bubble?" queried Perry. "Sounds like you need a specialist sort of blood hound."

Everyone was gathered for dinner in the spacious central garden of their magnificent villa. But Chauncey was missing. Kate and Robin felt it was safe to share their idea and Chauncey's endorsement of it, and that he was off talking it over with the very knowledgeable viziers of the dragon principalities that were modelled after two of the most ancient kingdoms on Earth.

"We think he will send some of his children searching. They are magical, they are used to finding the special and rare, and they know already that a number of these anomalies exist."

"There are?" said Elvira, "Where are they?"

"Right here, the Egyptian Principality is one and all the Dragon Principalities are space-time bubbles, places that exist alongside or within or somehow magically overlap with our ordinary world. Yet remain invisible and undetected in the ordinary world, except by creatures like ourselves, magical, or magic-using. And Faerie is another, more flexible than the Principalities in that you can find doors into it or make such doors from virtually anywhere on Earth. We were thinking that if two ancient Egyptian gods are among us, then possibly they came from somewhere, and that somewhere would be a space-time bubble which contains a version of Ancient Egypt. Unless of course they are entirely a creation of an upsurge in belief." answered Kate.

"Or, they could be both," said Robin. "Being, like, dormant in this Ancient Egypt bubble, and awakened by a renewal of belief."

The Cat Goddess laughed, "Well that could explain it, as in my personal experience I was indeed sleeping or just 'not being' and awakened when I became aware of the festivities at Bubastis in my name. I wasn't aware for a while that I was not still in Ancient Egypt, but somehow transported to this future time. That happened when I began to notice differences in clothing and language. And a general improvement in the food and drink!" She turned to Elowen. "You are the Queen of this place called Faerie. Is that a new magical 'bubble'?"

"No, my dear Bastet," said Elowen. "In fact I think it must be much older than Egypt of the Pharaohs, which I learned lasted for more than 30 centuries—from its unification around 3100 B.C. to its conquest by Alexander the Great in 332 B.C. Ancient Egypt was the preeminent civilisation in the Mediterranean world, but Faerie, my home, is older. The Celtic people believed in faeries for at least twice that long, so the land of the fae grew up from that belief.

"However, the Dragon Principalities are far older than that, the dragons created them when human beings began to develop as a species similar to what we know today, and that they say was around a million to three hundred thousand years ago—Chen Shi might know more exactly. Dragons understood that either they would have to fight these new beings or go into hiding. The dragons of this Earth were essentially peaceful and wished to avoid wiping out this new species, which they realised would fight them, having seen them bring down mastodons and other huge creatures. But dragons would have won any fight, being magical and of a different earth and possessing fire long before humans did. I believe later on they remained hidden because humans had developed weapons that could kill even a dragon rather easily. But that was many thousands of years later. However they co-existed beside humans long enough to create stories and legends and in the Orient they even cooperated. Hence dragons appear in many forms in many cultures. But almost never any longer in the flesh."

"I'd have thought that it would be an awful thing to be driven into hiding to avoid terrible wars," remarked Perry, "except that Chauncey told me that when humans started creating writing and art, dragons here—after all these are the intellectual, peaceful branch of dragon-kind—were so delighted by both that they mostly felt it was a worthwhile trade, since dragons with all their advantages are clumsy creatures without the kinds of hands that can create beautiful delicate things or even printing, except on a very basic level. They fell in love with both art and history and legends and even all kinds of fiction."

"Bastet, do you think or know that you came into today's world from some kind of 'space-time bubble' where Ancient Egypt still existed or exists, or was it more that you ceased to exist and were called into being by increased belief?" Maggie, who was particularly close to Bastet, tried to phrase her question carefully so as not to distress or antagonise the Goddess.

"   "I…I am not sure.   I haven't particularly probed my consciousness to look for anything before I awakened to the festival at Bubastis. I was pleased, you see, and felt renewed. And I was busy, so I was simply accepting that I existed and was enjoying it. Do humans often probe for what or where they were 'before'?"

"Quite right, no, most humans don't, and I would guess those that do either are philosophers or malcontents, those who aren't particularly happy where they are," laughed Maggie. "So we can't tell from your experience if there is a sort of space-time bubble of Egypt under the Pharaohs. Well, it was worth asking."

"Of course it was," said Bastet.   "I don't mind. But more to the point, perhaps, is Apep still 'asleep' and if so since he is also making some changes here, then that would argue for his existence in another place or space or page of the book of worlds as I've heard some of you call it. So quite possibly in a 'bubble' of Ancient Egypt."

"And you don't think that the change in the

fresco means he is already here?" queried Perry.

"No, definitely not. Apep would announce his presence a lot more loudly, even violently, if he were here in his full form. We would be in no doubts. There would be storms, earthquakes, the Nile might run red. Rains of frogs perhaps. Certainly the Sun would be obscured. As you know Egypt is not a country given to cloudy skies. No, Apep in his strength would be much more than a change in a fresco."

"So would renewed belief bring him here?" asked Kailen.

"Probably, but Apep didn't have followers or worshippers. Quite the opposite, the people hated and feared him. They prayed that Ra, the Sun God, with the protection of other gods, would fight off Apep nightly so the sun would rise again. When earthquakes or dust storms or other weather phenomena kept the sun in hiding, back then the people believed that Apep was gaining strength, and they prayed and sacrificed more to Ra, and a few other gods, but not to Apep."

"So worship isn't necessary to bring Apep back," mused Robin.

"Apep was not worshipped, but he was very strong back then, so I don't believe he relies on worship. Fear is also a very strong motivator to believe in what you fear." Bastet was searching her memory.

"I realise I am being old and silly, but this reminds me of a Broadway musical I knew in my youth," said Elvira. It was called Brigadoon, which was a Scottish village of some hundreds of years ago, where the village pastor, fearing the changes that he believed were evil in the world, cast a spell that put the village to sleep only to waken for one day every hundred years. The villagers didn't feel like they'd slept for more than one night each time, and they stayed in this magic bubble so long as none of them left the village. It protected their way of life and their innocence I suppose. What I most remember was it had a number of wonderful songs. I used to sing them to myself as a girl."

"So that was it? They just lived this bucolic life away from the industrial revolution and the—what was it? The Highland Clearances?" asked Robin, not impressed.

"Oh, no," laughed Elvira. "No—first some Americans sort of crashed into the place on the one day it appeared. And one of them fell in love, of course. Then a young village man, a teenager, tried to make a break for it, and was dragged back before he broke the spell. I forget if they killed him or not. I never saw it you see. I only heard the recordings and fell in love with it."

"Actually, it has some aspects of Faerie

there," said Elowen, who of course would know. "Legends and folk tales have the fae appearing and disappearing, and luring unsuspecting humans inside where they sleep what they think is a normal time, but when they get back home find out their loved ones are dead and their grandchildren are all grown up. At least those are the legends in Ireland and Scotland (where we're called pixies or pictsies). Mostly total codswallop of course, but some of *the folk* do maze human minds and lead them far astray. However, if anyone attempted to abduct a child or keep a human as a sort of pet—well that used to happen, yes—but believe me I'd put a stop to it very quickly."

"So lots of legends, folktales and even modern fantasy novels and musical plays deal with hidden lands, or possibly spacetime bubbles." remarked Perry. "But I'm only aware of one that deals with ancient Egypt."

"There is?" cried Kate. "I didn't know that."

"Glad I could surprise you," said Perry, grinning. "I'm not always reading reports and articles from learned journals, you know. Look it up, it's a three or four book series about a modern man visiting Egypt and he goes through this door and finds himself in ancient Egypt, really ancient, because he meets the Pharaoh Djoser and ends up being the Imhotep who builds the step pyramid, the first big pyramid, for Djoser."

"Doors, there have to be doors, either those we can create, or those that are just sitting there," remarked Robin. "I would guess that if there is an ancient Egypt within a space-time bubble it would have at least one door, and our search party would have to find it. Generally, except for Faerie, those doors would be in the area where the ancient place actually existed."

"And right there we have narrowed down our search area to exactly where we are!" exclaimed Kate. "Robin sometimes you are so clever it scares me."

He grinned at her and swept a low bow, "Anything to please my lady.

Chapter 22

Chauncey arrived back the next day, full of legends and strange happenings in the Oriental Principality, none of which had any bearing upon what they were looking for. Neither Chen Da nor any of the oriental dragons knew of an ancient oriental spacetime bubble other than their own. The Egyptian Vizier Imhotep also said they knew virtually all the history of Egypt under the Pharaohs, including the gods and the demonic presences, but weren't aware of any other space-time bubble that might contain them.

"So that could indicate that there isn't one, but doesn't rule it out entirely," he finished as he and all the other inhabitants of their villa within the Egyptian Principality sat around with cool drinks and snacks.

Kate was eager to share that they had come up with a probable location for such a magical place or space. "Doors, everywhere we travelled with the Rain youngsters, we went to the actual country or area on our Earth, and then found the door that led into the Principality. In every case of a Principality space-time bubble, like the one we are in now, the door to it was within the actual country or area. Except, of course, Faerie, which is somehow movable, and doors can be found or made almost anywhere. But probably or hopefully this narrows it down—if there's an ancient Egypt space-time bubble it will be here, somewhere along the Nile, or as you said a while ago, a long skinny bubble like the Nile. And there will be a door, or we or the ancient gods can make doors."

Chauncey was impressed. "So I can send my little band of searchers off sniffing out focuses of magic and possibly even doors up and down the Nile."

"Yes, especially where we know there were once great palaces, towns or temples, where power would have been strong."

Just then there came a sort of low rumbling, a sound that seemed to travel toward them in a wave, but was then as suddenly stopped, as if a large wave that looked to be about to crash violently upon the beach, just subsided into a ripple and retreated.

"What the hell was that?" said Kailen looking at Chauncey for clarification.

"Possibly an earthquake," the Dragon King replied.

"It's an earthquake, or a tremor," said Perry. "They aren't very common in Egypt, but they do happen. Nothing to worry about, it was very mild."

Chen Shi disagreed. "As it happens, it could be something to worry about. We aren't in Egypt. We are in the Egyptian Principality, and as such are not often encroached upon by nature's effects. We created the Principalities to be immune to the fluctuations of Mother Earth. And indeed, that is why it simply met our boundary and subsided. But that we heard or felt it at all means that it was possibly very strong or happened just beside us."

Bastet stood up and came to stand beside Chauncey. "My friends, you were going to look for where there might be a remnant of Ancient Egypt where there are really the old gods and the old ways. It appears that it, or the God of Chaos, might have found us. Somehow, rather than us searching him out, he might have been attracted here. I don't know if by me or by this locus of magical power or both. And it was supposed back then that Apep's movements were responsible for the upheavals of the earth."

"Well, then we may have a starting place to find this creature, or even the spacetime bubble of ancient Egypt," said Perry. "That can save a lot of time. Chauncey, I suggest we gather your specialist children and brief them on what we need to find out."

"For this job we need just a small group, and to lead them my best spy, my stealth dragon child— Silver Moon. He guarded the island in the Venice lagoon while you planned how to retrieve Kate's mother Amanda. In any night sky with a few clouds he would be invisible with his colours, wouldn't have to waste energy on invisibility. Then there are some of the Rivers whom you haven't met—Tigris, Thames, Ganges, Volga and Amazon. They are very intelligent, but always on the move, can't settle to anything for long. And as they have an affinity for water, searching along the Nile would suit them. Plus, I am genuinely thinking this might be good for Dawn."

"Dawn? But, can we trust her?" Robin was astonished.

"And she's not old enough surely," said Kate. "She couldn't keep up with those others flying. And she might be dangerous."

"Dawn is extremely intelligent. With better teachers, she's progressed far beyond her nest-mates. I think much of her seeming perversity was due to that—she was brighter and she was bored and, yes, she wanted to be treated with respect. She's got all that now, and she has been thriving. She also showed she could care about people when she made that bond with Elvira and Feral. So I think she will want to be part of this, since they are part of it.

"They love Bastet, so she wouldn't want to see Bastet hurt. Plus she's an adventurer at heart. It all went badly wrong when she was a bit younger and being treated essentially like a badly behaved small child with no say in her future, as it seemed to her. If we give her this chance, with Silver to monitor her, we will find out at least. And I am quite hopeful. Sometimes you just need to find the right place to find yourself as well."

Kate and Robin were both nodding, as something similar had happened to both of them. They remembered the sick anger of being in the wrong place with the wrong people, and feeling helpless, and then the incredible relief and joy of finding out who and what they were and being respected and loved for it. Chauncey of course knew this. "But the flying part?" ventured Kate.

"She's coming along very well, can fly for at least an hour without a rest. Plus a lot of this doesn't require actual long journeys. Sometimes you find a secret magical space by just being in an area and sniffing it out. Silver is good at that, sniffing out magic and what kind of magic, and he could teach Dawn. I think she'd love to know how to do that and might be very good at it.

"But you're right, of course, she'll need to be carried or ride sometimes, so the others will have to do that. And I need to make sure they agree to have her along before I say anything to Dawn. Please make sure you keep this a secret, no one else must know until I can first get the agreement of my search team and then ask her myself."

On hearing this about Dawn, Elvira joined them, "Feral and I have a good relationship with her, and Feral is both very magical and as knowledgeable as any person can be about the Nile, the old places, the magical places, and I can give Dawn the mothering she still needs, she's not a grownup after all, however intelligent and advanced for her age. Why not let us use the dahabeeyah to transport us, Bastet and Dawn as your young dragons search. Then they won't have to be carrying Dawn, and we can look after her when she's tired."

"And we should come too, the Misfits, and Ariane and Dmitri and Elowen," said Kate. "If our scouting party runs into Apep, they could need help if he's as powerful as he is supposed to be."

"So much for keeping you all in reserve until you are needed," laughed Chauncey. "I can see you are wanting adventure and to keep your friends safe. But please think carefully before you pile all your resources into one boat. Err…that is a figure of speech, but I see that it is also the reality, and reminds me that a boat is an easy thing to sink. I also honestly think it is not wise for all of you to go together. We need some here in the safety of our own space-time bubble in case of trouble. A good general never sends all his troops into unknown territory to meet a force he does not yet understand."

"So, what is your plan, then?" asked Kailen.

"I would send Elvira and Feral to help take care of Dawn, plus Kate and Robin and Perry and Ariane and Dmitri. And your special dragon friends as extra protection and should you need to fly—or abandon ship. But I would keep Bastet here because if we lose her we have lost our entire reason for being here at all. And Maggie, Kailen and Elowen to give her company and provide protection. So that means having your dragon friends Blue and Peony and Dance here. Plus myself. I will, along with Lilac Moon, provide daily contact with the scouts, and protection for Bastet. Even Apep can't foresee the might of a fully grown Dragon King or that of the dragons of the Egyptian Principality. We aren't a part of his world, so he wouldn't be expecting us."

"But he is a monster himself, as long as you are, Chen Shi," said Bastet. "And he is a constrictor—if he got your neck in his coils, he could very probably crush your windpipe. I am not as certain as you as to your ability to withstand or overpower him."

"So how did the gods of old successfully fight him off every night as the sun barge sailed under the earth?" asked Perry.

Bastet laughed. "Not like you might suppose. Various of the gods came with Ra on the night boat to protect him from Apep. And they did it by chanting special spells that repelled the serpent. In the temples of Ra, the priests also stayed up at night in a rota and chanted the same spells. These overpowered Apep's strength, and somehow repelled him. I would guess that this was the age-old method because a pitched battle pitting physical strength and weapons against him every night simply didn't make sense."

"No, it wouldn't," said Perry. "There would have been wounded and dead to deal with, and to have to manage the rebirth or even healing of a number of gods on a nightly basis only to have them sacrificed again…even the fertile Egyptian imagination couldn't really deal with that."

"Exactly," said Bastet. "Daily life in Egypt would have had to grind to a halt to cope with the carnage. Everyone would have been enlisted to literally fight Chaos every night to get the sun to rise again, and as we know, war has a devastating effect upon all the necessary things of ordinary life— farming and building and making and selling goods. Ordinary Egyptian life, and Royal life, depended upon the population going about its ordinary business. The nightly battle was left to the gods, and they depended upon magic, not upon actual battles. Actual physical battles between the gods only happened occasionally, not every night. Too tiring and destructive altogether."

"But many of those chants involved not just cutting Apep with swords or spears or knives, but using fire," said Kate. "So if we do meet him, and we aren't the old gods, then dragon fire would be a very good method of fighting him off perhaps in this world."

"And my neck is armour-plated," remarked Chauncey, smiling at Bastet. "I can also dive to the depths of the ocean where pressures are so great as to crush even a battleship, so a huge snake wouldn't crush me or suffocate me, as you fear, my dear Bastet."

"I think," offered Robin, "that if the dragons couldn't be killed by WP even though they had over a century to attempt it, then they won't be severely threatened by Apep, and as for us, we have magic at least as strong as the Egyptians of old. This God of Chaos may be a threat, but he won't be able to beat us." Which neatly summed up the matter and left them free to plan their own attack.

Chapter 23

The earth tremor that had been strong enough to be felt within the Egyptian Principality was in fact the God of Chaos himself in a furious state. It had been caused by the appearance of D K with a leaflet such as could be found plastered to the walls of derelict buildings and telephone poles worldwide.

The leaflet was not shocking or hellish, rather it depicted a group of 4 of his minions, all in dark glasses, two with guitars, one with a drum kit and one holding a microphone. All wore bright yellow tee shirts with Apepatones in red with lightning bolts printed on them. In the background was a rather dreary brown mound—true, there was coil upon coil, and his head was on top, but it was all quite small and lifeless. He was not the centre of the stage at all. And the words—nowhere was there fitting homage and fear of the most evil god in all of the Egyptian pantheon. He was hardly mentioned. In small type across the top it said 'In honour of the God of Chaos, Apep,.. then in large red type PRESENTING A CONCERT BY THE APEPATONES, THE GREATEST ROCK BAND TO COME OUT OF ANCIENT EGYPT. 2 DAYS OF MUSIC, FOOD, SPECIAL DRINKS, DANCING. COME GO CRAZY WITH US! FROM (dates to be decided).

Apep's fangs were dripping venom, and where it landed, the rock fizzed and dissolved. "Thisss travesty," he hissed, "will not go unpunished. Where is the depiction of my power, my venom, my very appearance should have all mortals trembling and groveling, not dancing and drinking strange concoctions *and* not listening to you, D K, you vile excrescence. This thing there, this brown worm could be just a pile of dung."

D K, who'd had eons of placating his master, was not particularly scared by this display. In terms of what Apep could produce when riled, this was very minor indeed.

"Oh, Master of Chaos, First of all the Gods, Evil Incarnate," he spoke while grovelling. "We wish to see you gain in power, to have the Egyptian masses once more fearing your wrath. But first we must gain this power, first we must make them aware of your existence as a force. But not scare them into retreating from you, that will not allow you to suck from their gathered masses the power you must have before you can once more, err, scare the living daylights out of them. They must believe in you and feed you thus. But to terrify them prior to regaining your legendary strength, well, that will not work.

"First comes belief, and to get belief they must no longer believe that earthquakes, floods, famines, volcanic eruptions are natural parts of earthly workings. They must be led carefully toward you, toward belief, and wishing to believe. Then, when properly educated, they will once more not just believe, but know that you are the first of the gods, the never-changing God of Chaos, always there, always to be placated.

"One step at a time. This will bring them flocking, a free party always does. Then will come the time when they believe in you and your powers are restored, and all Chaos will be yours once more."

Apep listened. D K had not survived the eons by being stupid and Apep had come to rely upon this demon. D K was his chief advisor, his loyalty unquestionable (although Apep questioned it constantly). D K was the ancient serpent's vizier, and even Apep knew you didn't come upon one of those who could be trusted to have your best interests right up there with their own. D K was valuable, loyal and usually right. The rumblings of the earth around Luxor died down and stopped.

"Well, if we must, we must," grumbled Apep. D K exhaled a deep sigh of relief.

Chapter 24

However confident the rest felt, Feral was not about to leave it at that. He and Elvira had been followers of Bastet for ages, and he felt, as another cat, albeit not a cat god, but with magic powers and a great deal of experience at stealing, that he had to provide Bastet another layer of protection. And he knew exactly what that was and had a good idea where to find it. He asked Elvira if they could retire to their quarters on the dahabeeyah for a talk. So they excused themselves and made for the door from the Principality to Luxor dock and their Nile boat *Heka*.

Settling with cups of strong Egyptian coffee for Elvira and water and some sardines for Feral, she asked him what he was planning, for she knew of old that when Feral needed a private meeting it meant he had a plan.

"Every time, least ways every picture I've seen, where Mau or Set or Bastet is protecting the Tree of Life or Ra from Apep, the cat is stabbing or cutting off the head of Apep with a knife," said Feral.

"Yes, that's true," replied Elvira. "Even when they are on the Sun Barge on the nightly journey under the earth, Apep is often being cut with a knife, either welded by a Cat God or Goddess or where strokes of a pen indicate he has been sliced."

"Exactly," said Feral. "The priests of Ra practiced nightly rituals which included what the Pharaoh and the gods on the Sun Barge say to drive off Apep and protect Ra and the Sun. But sometimes that isn't considered enough. So I thought, we need to impress upon Apep that Bastet, the only other ancient god who has been revitalised, is off limits to him by attacking him with a knife. But not just any knife, an important knife, a knife of his own time, that will have the magical power to really hurt him. I need to get the only knife that could kill Apep."

Elvira smiled, but there was sadness and concern in her expression as well. "And you my brave magical cat have just the knife in mind, don't you? But Feral, it is guarded so much more safely than anything the tomb robbers ever found."

"Yes," said Feral almost on a hiss. "And I have …"

Elvira interrupted him. "And you my dear thief have just the plan of how to steal it. Feral, I love you, you are Egypt's best thief, but you will be caught, and you will be killed, and I cannot bear that. Why must you do this?"

"Because if prayers and playing at being gods don't work, then it is a cat god who must stop Apep, and with a knife. *The* knife."

Feral jumped from the hassock on which he was stretched into Elvira's lap. He raised a soft paw to wipe away the one tear that had escaped her eye. He rubbed himself against her. Then he sat up quite tall.

"I can confidently promise you that I will not be caught or killed, and my plan has taken into account various aspects of this little caper. You and some of the Misfits and their magic as well as ours will play a big part. We will have the knife to protect Bastet, and when this adventure is over, we can also return the knife secretly and safely to its special place."

§ § §

Three days later, Elvira, Maggie and Kate were all robed in full black *abaya* dresses and Muslim *hijabs* with face veils showing only their eyes, but even these were concealed by a small spell that made Kate's green and Maggie's blue eyes seem dark. Elvira was carrying a bag that contained Feral, Maggie was carrying a small briefcase and Kate was carrying a handbag. For entry to the museum and when it came to entering the storage areas of the sprawling new Egyptian Museum, Chen Shi, the Magical Misfits, even the Fae including Queen Elowen had worked on spells that would produce innocent images on the electrical scanning equipment that would check their ID, what they carried and anything that might be concealed on their bodies.

Maggie and Kate had perfected a spell that had the guards believing that the blank pieces of paper Maggie took from the briefcase also showed official permissions to enter the areas they wanted. It also identified them as experts in the objects they wanted to examine.

"Whenever I do this," whispered Maggie, "I always feel like I'm doing those little hand motions and saying, 'These are not the droids you are looking for'."

"Well we are doing those little hand motions," said Kate, stifling a giggle. Indeed, the spells, which they didn't have to say aloud, were accompanied by small gestures that gave the guards a complete picture of their visitors as specialists in the field of ancient Egyptian weaponry, and especially that of Tutankhamun. It didn't surprise the guards that these experts were also vailed Muslim women, since in Egypt now there were many devout Muslim females who were educated and had important jobs in many fields. That they preferred to wear the complete black *abayas* instead of fashionable suits or dresses and colourful *hijabs* was a matter of their own choice. That it helped immensely in making them nearly invisible just in case something went wrong, and they had to run for it never entered the guards' minds.

They had all memorised the location of the rooms containing all of Tutankhamun's treasure, especially the weapons. Because with them was a knife of such amazing power that it was among the articles of special potency enfolded in the Pharaoh's linen mummy wrappings, meant to keep his body especially protected. It was a dagger forged from meteorite iron, years before smelting of iron tools had been in use in Egypt. Experts had decided it was a dagger made in the Mitanni empire and given by its king to Tut's grandfather as a wedding gift. Along with the blade, definitely from 'another world', the gold hilt was intricately decorated with gold grains and lapis lazuli, carnelian and malachite, and a crystal pommel. It was of the right time period, it was royal, and it was stronger and more deadly than daggers made of bronze.

Maggie used her most feminine appearance and her softest voice asking for guidance to the special dagger. There was magic woven into her request, and she laughed softly as if sharing a special joke asking that the guard take them directly to it.

"Although I have the directions here," she gestured toward the briefcase, "it would save so much time if you would take us to it. That would be so kind." Kate nearly giggled again as Maggie fluttered her eyelashes at the entranced guard.

They all put on those blue plastic gloves as the guard carried the drawer containing several knives to an examining table with good lighting and magnifiers. Elvira put her bag with Feral inside on the table near the display of knives. Maggie picked up the knife next to the gold sheath and held it near Feral. His voice was shielded from the guard, but they could hear him, and he wasn't happy.

"It doesn't   smell right. Yeah, definitely, it's a fake," was his message. "This is not the original. Push me closer to the drawer with the other knives."

Elvira, looking like she was searching for something within her bag, managed to move it slowly close to the drawer with other daggers and ceremonial knives.

"Ah," breathed Feral.   "It is here, it is disguised."

"Thanks be," murmured Maggie.   "I was truly scared we'd stumbled upon a theft we'd have to report. But which one of these others is it? None of them look like it. Could they have used magic? Or maybe it's not here at all."

"Which one, and is it enchanted?" asked Kate.

"Not   under   a spell," answered
Feral. "It is the one with a full sheath enclosing both
blade and hilt, which can be opened by pressing a
small gem in the sheath. Inside you will find the
dagger in its original gold sheath."

"Like the three coffins that the Pharaohs were
buried in," murmured Elvira. "I will ask that that one
be put out for us to investigate." Which she did in
perfect Egyptian.

The guard looked startled and anxious.
Maggie and Kate both carefully gave him calming
and the magic message that it was smart to conceal
the real one so cleverly and have a facsimile in the
same drawer, but they required the real one.

The guard, again calmed and reassured that
these women were indeed the experts who knew
what they'd come to see, replaced the forgery in its
carefully shaped space and gave them the rather
larger fully sheathed knife. Elvira pressed the jewel
that Feral indicated to her, and there was an almost
inaudible click as the two parts of the sheath parted.
Carefully she pulled the handle with its crystal hilt
out of the dummy sheath.

Although identical except in age to the fake
(which was almost certainly not meteorite iron), the
original somehow did give off a feeling of age,
authenticity and even magic. All three women sighed
with relief and pleasure.

Then came the tricky bit—it would have been impossible except that all the women and the cat were in possession of serious magic powers. Feral had suggested leaping out of Elvira's bag, taking the priceless object in his mouth and running like hell. And given his talent to conceal himself as he escaped, this might have worked. But it would leave the guards and all of Egypt suddenly with the knowledge that there had been the theft of one of King Tut's most wonderful objects. Elvira was more used to dealing with Feral the magical thief, and not quite so anti this possibility, but Kate and Maggie convinced them both that such a dangerous and publicity-laden theft was not what was needed when they had serious magic that could leave the guards believing that they hadn't been burgled at all.

Kate did her 'party trick' of reproducing the dagger, this time with meteorite iron blade and its beautifully inscribed gold sheath and handed them back to the guard to be carefully replaced in the false sheath while Elvira used her powers to distract him from the sleight of hand that had put the real dagger into a specially lined compartment in the scruffy bag that held Feral. And the three experts in ancient Egyptian artefacts left the special room and were escorted to the exit, where once more they put their bags onto the X-ray conveyer belt and submitted to being searched in a most respectful manner. Again, magic kept the machine from seeing either Feral or the dagger in Elvira's bag, and the three ladies were clean as a whistle.

Back in the car driving from Cairo to Luxor however, they were treated to an awkward half hour where Feral complained about virtually everything.

"I should never have told you what I was planning, I could have pulled it off by myself. All this preparation and keeping everyone hypnotised and unknowing. All gussied up like old Muslim biddies…and me in a shabby bag! Never in my life… And it'd have been all for naught if I hadn't pointed out that the dagger they were keeping so closely guarded was itself a fake, wouldn't it? But would you trust me to do what I'm best at? Nooo… Too much chance of being caught, certain to set off alarms, sure to be discovered. Bah! You all make me…"

"Aye, and you'd have left me to live out my last days trying to mother a dragon as wicked as you are, and we'd both have probably died of grief, you self-centred, misbegotten son of a street cat and a demon!" cried Elvira, smacking Feral on the head. His verbal outpourings skittered to a stop. For long minutes they simply sat and looked at each other. Kate and Maggie sat stunned and quiet. Then Elvira and Feral both started to laugh.

"Oh, come here you untamed streak of

Sheitan himself!" said Elvira, scooping up the big black cat, who clasped his front feet around her neck and nuzzled her ear.

"I'm sorry you didn't get to show off all your tricks to impress everyone," she said. "But this time the results were just too important, and we have all had to learn to work as a team. We know you're the real star of the show, it was your idea after all. And you can present it to Bastet that way and none of us will say a word."

§ § §

Bastet was indeed mightily impressed and gave Feral all the praise he could possibly want. But she would not accept the knife. "I am more than impressed that you thought of bringing me a weapon with which a Cat God could indeed fight off Apep. But I still do not want to have to do this. I am hoping there is another way. Meanwhile, you must keep it because you may not be a cat god, but you are brave and magical and with talents I swear even the gods would envy. So, *mon brave,* I hereby pronounce you my Paladin, my chivalrous hero, and bearer of the sacred dagger."

"We will have to get a special harness made for him," whispered Kate to Robin. "He can't just carry it about in his teeth, and if he needs to use it, a cover for the pommel that allows him to hold it in his claws."

Robin said, "You do know that you're talking about sending one of the most precious artefacts in Egypt out to possibly do battle. Couldn't we just make a replica?" "After all the trouble we went to obtain the original? Bastet and Apep, even the demon army, are precious, indeed gods, of ancient Egypt. By making him her Paladin, Bastet has invested Feral also with more ancient magic that we can imagine. I think we can guarantee that whatever happens this beautiful, magical dagger will not be in danger."

Feral was suitably honoured, and also felt that goddess or not, he was more capable of protecting her than she would be herself. He tried to accept all the ceremony and his new title and being bearer of the magic dagger as no more than his due, but deep inside was the kitten who'd have died horribly without Elvira and who'd dreamed brave dreams he never expected could come true. But here he was, looking almost regal, and standing proudly but with a face for once showing humility and gratitude. Inside however, he was leaping about manically, and his face was split with an exultant grin.

Chapter 25

Chauncey was doing something he hadn't done in a very long time. On the terrace that stretched the entire length of the long side of their villa, he was lying on his back, legs and wings spread, his spinal spikes folded carefully, tail and neck extended, and his entire front exposed to the sun and the breeze. His eyes were closed. It seemed like centuries since he had felt safe enough to be this exposed. And relaxed. He was drifting in and out of a doze, something he usually allowed himself only when he was curled into his usual resting position resembling something like a tightly curled cat.

Ah, he thought. *It is a most agreeable sensation to feel the sun on my belly. I must try this more often now that I am finally free of enemies who could possibly do me harm.* Still, it also left him with a small niggling feeling of unease to be thus exposed and potentially helpless. The sudden slight weight landing upon his chest brought his head upright to stare down the length of his neck to see Feral standing there, all four feet planted and a look of something like triumph on his face.

"Blue bet me you would jump like a— what was it she said? Oh, like a scalded cat, if I jumped on you. I bet her you were much too cool to jump. And see, I won." And Feral strolled up the length of the mighty Dragon King and rubbed his head against Chauncey's neck just where it joined his head.

Chauncey tried to roll his eyes sufficiently to see the black cat but could only feel his rubbing at that point where his jaw met his neck. A pleasant sensation. "You are indeed fortunate, offensive black furry thing, that I was and am feeling particularly relaxed and benevolent. Blue might have told you that if I'd been startled enough to jump I would also have very probably used the power of my reptilian neck to strike you with these extremely sharp teeth," rumbled Chauncey.

"And I've have leapt as quickly as a cat pouncing on a bird and avoided them," remarked Feral complacently. He continued to rub himself gently against Chauncey. It was soothing, and shortly both cat and giant dragon were snoozing, Feral having also adopted the position of a completely relaxed animal, belly exposed to the sun.

And there they stayed until Kate inadvertently woke them returning from one of her shopping trips to equip the dahabeeyah for their journey up the Nile in search of the elusive evil Apep. *Well, I never...* she thought, seeing the two, Chauncey still basking in the sun, Feral now almost invisible in the shade of the Dragon King's head since the sun had shifted away from midday. Both were awake but chose to feign sleep.

Hating the thought of waking these two whose lives were mostly spent on alert, Kate started to back slowly away, when without moving, Chauncey's voice appeared in her head. "Don't go, Daughter, we are resting, but are awake, or at least I'm awake. What a pleasure it is to be able to completely relax in the warmth of the sun."

"Something I haven't ever enjoyed with my redhead's sensitivity," remarked Kate without rancour. "Still haven't found the spell that will take the place of factor 50 sunscreen. Or the need to wear a sunhat."

"You haven't?" queried Feral, proving that he too wasn't really asleep. "I will ask Elvira. That should be something even basic witchcraft could deal with."

"So far, no," said Kate. "Plus the sun striking my skin doesn't feel warm and comforting, but more like being too close to a fire."

"Oh," remarked Feral in what for him was a sympathetic tone. "What a drag. How about this?"

His tail flicked a couple of times and suddenly Kate was no longer feeling the heat of the sun, but merely pleasant warmth. She looked up, yep, there was the sun, no cloud had come to cover it. Then she looked down and yelped...or rather yowled. She was a large ginger cat.

"Not funny!" she hissed — yes, hissed — at Feral. "Change me back this instant!" Chauncey reached out a claw and pinned Feral gently to the ground. "Never do magic on a friend unless there's a damn good reason."

Kate was instantly herself again, and instantly the sun was again too hot. "Let him go, Chauncey, he didn't hurt me. Feral, could you teach me how to be a cat and how to change back?"

"Of course," said Feral, shaking his fur back in place and resuming his indolent pose.

What a fabulous way to avoid being a redhead in the super-heated sun of Egypt! thought Kate. *And I could travel unnoticed, I could spy, I could slide into places like Feral does without anyone bothering.* It was extremely attractive and gave rise to fantasies of all sorts of fun and adventures.

Chauncey, who could so easily sense what she was feeling even without permission to be in her mind, held up a claw. Certainly a claw of caution it seemed to Kate. And Feral oozed gently into the deeper shadows of the foliage in the flower borders.

"Kate, that is both high level magic and also here, where we are in search of an ancient evil god who hates cats, I would suggest that this is not the time nor the place to be practicing changing your form just to avoid a sunburn, or for fun." He could see her disappointment. "I'm sorry my daughter, but changing shape can be dangerous, many practiced witches who have done it find themselves stuck in a shape they do not wish to keep. Why do you think it is so rarely seen?"

"But Bastet does it, and often," Kate flashed back.

"Bastet is a goddess and many thousands of years old, and it is part of the myth and magic that created her in the first place. None of these ancient Egyptian gods could ever have existed without belief, and that belief created and empowered and also changed them over the millennia—Bastet is not like us, magical beings who exist with or without belief, and as ourselves, not as some construct of myth and faith."

"Then why can Feral do this magic, he isn't a god, or a creature created out of belief?" Kate was truly perplexed.

"I confess I don't know. All I can say is that he is a cat, and like the spirit cat Toby, and I must suppose all cats, is in some kind of connection to Bastet, or another cat god, making at least part of their magic part of his. Remember, Toby totally subdued the Chimaera Proteus or possibly it was Bastet's power working through him."

Feral spoke from the shade where he blended in, "I was born with magic. Every cat is, all are somewhat magical, just as dragons are in the world where you originate. But I am an Egyptian cat, and that has added power to my abilities, as has being in close contact with Bastet. Of course, being with Elvira who is a witch has also increased both our magics. Just as you, Kate, have grown magically in the close connection with your Magical Misfits."

He strolled back out. "But I confess the Dragon King is correct, it is not the time or the place for you to play with being a cat. It was my sense of humour getting the better of me, and I ask your pardon."

"Oh," said Kate. "Of course, no harm done. But I must admit it's a little hard to let that possibility go."

"We all learn over our lifetimes, short or long, to let go of tempting possibilities when we see they carry the possibility of harm as well as fun or power or whatever else we found attractive." sighed Chauncey. "It's part of the whole responsible adult thing, and I will admit it is sometimes hard to be faced with those choices. What are you mourning for that might be possible, Daughter?"

Caught off guard, Kate answered honestly, "I hate it that I can do a warming or cooling spell, but I cannot prevent the sun burning my skin. Even my best cooling spell is weak when I'm in direct summer sunlight, and it doesn't prevent sunburn."

Chauncey pondered, then he entered the outer layers of her mind and spoke there. "As you know dragons are always changing their colours within their own colour palette to communicate, to express changes of feelings, even to make themselves blend into the scenery or go entirely invisible. I could impress a very small bit of that into a part of your mind that takes care of things that aren't conscious, and some melanin into your skin, perhaps it would give your mind the ability to shield your skin from sunburn. If you don't like how it works, I will have kept careful note, and could undo it."

Kate was very interested indeed. Then she laughed, "I'd love that, but don't slip in any stripes or sparkles like you and all the dragons have, okay?"

"That's communication, either to another, or of feelings—no none of that," he promised. "I've got it, I think. Step out of the shade into the full sun, please."

Kate did that, almost flinching with the expectation of the heat beating down. But there was no feeling of heat, she still felt comfortable. "That worked! You did it! My skin feels comfortable." She spread her arms to the sun, and then noticed they were just a shade darker, not a deep tan, but slightly, slightly darker. She used her spell that allowed her to see herself as in a mirror, and saw her face also was just slightly tanned. It looked great but not like she was actually sun-tanned.   Robin and the other Misfits would notice of course, and they'd be happy for her.

"You've given me a make-over!" she laughed. "A slight 'sunglow' and a protection as well. It's perfect, it works. Thank you, you have no idea how happy this makes me." She hugged one of his large fingers.

"So you won't miss being a ginger cat?" he asked mock-seriously.

"Not at all, this is what I've been after all my life," she was ecstatic. "And I must thank Feral too, if he hadn't played with me, we wouldn't have worked this out. So my profound gratitude, Feral, you were the catalyst that finally solved one of my most aggravating problems."

Feral preened and strutted, with no false modesty.

Chapter 26

Chauncey invited Silver for a private chat, asking if he would head up the scouting party of several dragons from the River clutch to go looking for evidence of Apep in this world, or where Apep himself 'lived'. Silver Moon, Chauncey's 'stealth dragon', his spy, used to working alone, took time to think it over, then announced it seemed a workable idea, and he would do it, but he wanted to pick the Rivers he felt he could work with. These turned out to be Amazon and Tigris.

Amazon was a sleek dragon, her main colour a deep red- brown, so that she bore some resemblance to the giant otters that live in the river from which she took her name. But unlike the otters, she was all dragon, her wings shaped something like a swallow's, and her scales had a sheen like well-polished mahogany. Her spikes and the edges of her wings were jade green and iridescent blues, while her body displayed streaks of deep gold.

Tigris, named for the river that flowed through Mesopotamia, was mainly dark green, with scalloped wings and spikes showing many lighter shades of green, blue-green and silver. His body had streaks of silver that changed to black when he was agitated.

Silver Moon himself had modified his colours, as he sometimes did for weeks or months at a time. Now he was indeed Chauncey's 'stealth dragon' his silver body colouring had been toned down to a more steel-like tone, and there was a cloudy effect overlying the silver, that made it look very like the moon being reflected on clouds. His black scalloped wings were streaked with muted silver and blue and edged in grey and his spikes were deep black with muted silver edges that looked like weapons from some ancient oriental hoard. His eyes were black with silver rings around the pupils. He looked both beautiful and dangerous but could also blend into any dark area of sky or background with his colours subdued when, as now, he was in 'stealth' mode.

So another meeting was set up with Chen Shi, the scouting party of Silver, Amazon and Tigris, plus Kate and Robin on their tablets.

Perry and Kate had made a list of ancient Egyptian sites along the Nile that should be focus points of magic and power from the time of the Pharaohs and might therefore be places of access to Apep. Copies of information on these, plus maps were provided to everyone.

Finally, Chauncey asked the three dragons how they would feel if their spying mission were to include a younger dragon with a mixed history of adolescent rebellion. This included bullying and fighting and finally resulted in her running away and nearly getting herself killed, but revealed a hitherto unknown compassion and a keen intelligence coupled with a yearning to test herself. To his surprise all three, Silver, Amazon and Tigris, exchanged looks and then turned to him and grinned.

Silver, as leader, spoke for them all. "You are telling us about ourselves, you know. All three of us as young dragons were misfits, were rebels, made trouble. If we'd been human, we'd have been 'juvenile delinquents'.

"It was fortunate we all found outlets for being misfits and adventurers that weren't so socially unacceptable. But we'd need to meet this youngster and assess her ourselves. Is she much younger than we are?"

Chauncey was smiling with secret delight. His unlikely plan might be coming together. "She's one of the Rain Clutch, so yes, she's about three hundred years younger. Younger than I would usually promote for such a job, but she's hungry to learn and to, well, to 'matter', to test herself and to do meaningful things. She also is very adventurous and intelligent. A lot of her trouble, I think, has been that she was very precocious and the Fae who cared for the Rain clutch didn't know what to do with that. So she rebelled."

Tigris said, "Oh, the Rain Clutch, the ones the Fae found when we were all, err, absent. That group must have had difficulties being raised without their mother and no other dragon society for over a hundred years. Is she very damaged?"

"Not so much anymore, I've made sure she has dragon teachers and carers here in the Egyptian Principality who are encouraging her gifts. She's been doing well, but I feel she may be at a tipping point, and needs a challenge such as this, or she may be inclined to find her own challenge."

"Then, if you think she can do it and if she's interested, let us meet her," said Silver.

§ § §

Sending them off to start making their plans, Chauncey then requested that Dawn be sent to visit him. She came promptly escorted by her companion and favourite teacher, a young Egyptian dragon named Nefertari.

Kate and Robin were watching on Kate's tablet from their own rooms in the villa.

"She's grown a lot!" said Kate in surprise. "Look at those spikes and tendrils, and she must be two feet or more longer."

"She certainly doesn't look like a baby

anymore," said Robin. "But then she was small for her age before, as if somehow she'd been stunted."

Indeed, although still predominately green with gold wings and spikes, Dawn's body colour had darkened from light to more leaf green with some streaks of darker green and blue green. Spikes were growing down her tail and the arrow-head shaped end was a deep, dark gold. Her eyes no longer showed red but were a beautiful green with golden flecks.

And Dawn also no longer looked either demure or sly. She looked self-confident and even contented. Kate was impressed. This was not the practiced deceiver she had known; this was a young dragon becoming aware of her worth, and no longer feeling the need to plot against her own kind. Kate could feel it, and she reported all of this to Robin.

Chapter 27

Chauncey had made the overall plan, three young dragons led by Silver, Chen Shi's best spy, would follow the course of the Nile to the south looking or sensing anything that might be evidence of recent activity by Apep or his demons. Chauncey also believed this could be a good placement for Dawn, so he decided to interview her alone.

Dawn bowed to her father, as did Nefertari. Chauncey replied to that with an inclination of his head, and then invited them to sit beside him. He asked Dawn various questions about her schooling and about how she felt in this new environment. A bit shy at first, Dawn thawed in the warmth of Chauncey's obvious interest. He then asked Nefertari for her opinion of Dawn's progress.

The lovely dragon (her name meant 'beautiful companion') smiled. "Dawn is so intelligent, and since she's been with us she has grown in so many ways. I've never met a youngster so eager to learn, and so quick too. She came to us emotionally traumatised, both afraid and arrogant to cover her confusion and fear. She knew she was special, but she was afraid of what she'd done in trying to assert herself."

Dawn raised her hand to interrupt. Both

older dragons indicated she could. "I grew up so uncomfortable in a group of nest mates who all seemed to fit and I didn't. I thought it was my fault, but that made me angry because I didn't know why I should be singled out to be unhappy. I found myself wanting to get back at the world. I've been told that was adolescence and hormones kicking in, and is pretty normal. It didn't feel normal, it felt even worse. I did lash out, I did bully, I did make my mates do things they didn't want to do because they were afraid of me. It made me feel big, but it didn't make me feel better. I felt like I was harbouring a nest of snakes inside, all struggling.

"Then I escaped and the world gave me some horrible lessons—I was no longer the smartest and the one the others were afraid of. I was small in a world I knew nothing about, and I was scared stiff. Feral found me." Dawn smiled at the memory. "I thought he was the rudest most horrible thing I'd ever met. And he wasn't at all afraid of me even though I was so much bigger. He saved my life. He took me to Elvira, and they tried to help. Even though they couldn't do much, they made me feel safe and, well, accepted. I was a mess and they made me feel it was okay. And later here in this Principality they've made me feel okay too. They know who I am, what I've done, and they understood, and made me understand. And now they are showing me how to become what I always wanted to be."

"And what is that?" asked Chauncey gently.

"Someone who matters for who they are. Someone who is respected and encouraged. Someone who has been forgiven for making mistakes, even bad mistakes. And they've let me forge ahead to learn and to try things without being criticised. Nefertari always says, 'If you don't make mistakes, you won't make anything at all.' And she says it is wonderful to be different, even unique. That learning who we are and celebrating it is important. That's what I am learning to be. What I want to do is learn more and have adventures. We watch human television— these tiny people without wings or protective scales or fire, out there climbing things, white-water rafting, diving, exploring, and working so hard to try to save the planet their ancestors messed up. And I think, I've got scales and wings and fire, and I could help somehow. I could do things that matter. We haven't got yet to where we know exactly what that might be…"

Kate, Robin and Chauncey all noted that Dawn said 'we' not 'I'. That was important—that, remembering the Dawn of old—might even be crucial.

"Dawn," said Chauncey. "Would you like to join a small group of dragons doing intelligence gathering about a possible enemy force? In fact, would you like to be a spy? Would that interest you? Would you be afraid?"

Dawn looked up with sparkling eyes. Her colours darkened, and gold flashed over her sides. "Yes, oh, yes…" she breathed. Then she stopped. "I *would* be afraid. I still get afraid of criticism, of doing the wrong thing, of being stupid, and I'd be afraid of getting hurt or endangering the others. Would that mean I couldn't be part of an intelligence gathering group?"

"Not at all," said Chauncey. "It means you have common sense. No one wants to be hurt or make a mistake that endangers their group. I hope it means you would be careful. And you would be a cadet, the youngest, the one who is learning. Not at all a leader. Could you be a good follower?"

Dawn looked at Nefertari for support. "Maybe. I can follow if I think the leader is good at their job. I'd follow Nefertari, I respect her and trust her. And a few of the others who are teaching and caring for me. But not all of them." Dawn wrinkled her nose, an expression that spoke to Kate of grownups who didn't earn her respect—she knew exactly what Dawn meant.

Dawn continued. "I'd follow Feral. I'd follow Elvira. In different ways they are both very wise." She stopped and took a breath, gathering her courage to say what she wants to find out. "Is this a test? Are you kind of finding out how I might have changed? Or is there really such a group and you are thinking I might join?"

Chauncey grinned with pleasure. Robin still drew back slightly when the dragon king flashed all those teeth, even on a tablet, but Dawn didn't. His colours flashed his pleasure with her, and she could read that, as could Kate.

"There really is such a group, you've met the leader, Silver Moon. They tell me they will take you on, that your history of rebellion sounds a lot like their own, that all they needed was to put their energy and intelligence into something they could believe in. And they believe in this mission, and that younger dragons who don't quite fit the mould should be given chances to find their place. Don't be afraid to ask questions, they will be teaching you a lot you don't yet know, and don't feel you've failed if you don't do something as well as they can. Remember you're learning and they will protect you if you make mistakes. Don't try to be a hero."

Dawn had been nodding like one of those dogs that used to be so common on the dashboards of cars. "A lot of what I've been learning is how much I don't know!" she said with a grin. "I can take orders even."

Chapter 28

Ready at last for their journey up the Nile helping the dragon scouts to find any focuses of magic and hopefully the centre of Apep's power or even his lair, the Misfits and Fae stepped through the door from their villa in the principality directly onto the waterfront where their new dahabeeyah, *Heka*, ancient Egyptian for Magic, was docked. Though it was not the first time she'd seen it, Kate looked it over with an eye for both its beauty and its history. She had read a lot about this type of vessel and could now compare *Heka* to dahabeeyahs both ancient and modern.

A gift from Chen Shi, *Heka* was built along the lines of the big shallow-bottomed barges that used to travel the Nile thousands of years ago.

These boats had an illustrious history. Dahabeeyahs hadcarried Pharaohs and their families and important courtiers and wealthy merchants up and down the Nile. Royal barges were often painted gold. In fact, the name derived from the Arabic word for gold because similar gilded state barges were used by the Muslim rulers of Egypt in the Middle Ages. With the suffix 'a' or 'ah' it could translate as 'the golden one'.

In ancient times when the winds weren't

favourable oarsmen provided power. In modern times when once more the wealthy sometimes travelled by dahabeeyah, these barges still had no motors, but were pushed or pulled by tugboats when there was no wind to fill the sails. So even now in the early 21st century, a dahabeeyah could be hired by those who didn't want to travel in one of the big tourist boats but have the privacy and cachet of renting one of these replicas of the vessels that carried the Pharaohs. *Heka*, though, would not have to depend upon a tugboat—when the winds failed, she would be pulled along by dragons. The thought made Kate smile.

Heka was half again as long as their old rented dahabeeyah, *King Arthur*, and there were eight double cabins each with ensuite bathroom and windows with views of the Nile. The bow of the boat was pointed with a long bowsprit.

The stern was rounded and held the big salon. The height of two 'floors', it was high enough to allow the Moon and River dragons to stand upright and was entered by a door that led to a ramp into the water for them, and by another door at the end of the corridor between the cabins. Chen Shi had indulged his passion for opulence, with rich oriental rugs in deep hues on the floor and sofas, easy chairs and great poofs for the dragons, all done in shades of red, maroon, orange, and flame, with highlights of sea blue and gold. There were end tables of elaborately carved wood, some holding excellent replicas of Tiffany table lamps. There was a long table against one wall that could be wheeled out to become a dining table in inclement weather. From the high vaulted ceiling hung Moroccan lanterns and Venetian globes.

The rest of the upper floor was a large open-air terrace topped with a canvas awning and set with tables for dining and easy chairs and lounges for relaxing. Kitchens and storage and cabins for crew (a human couple who cooked and cleaned and two young Egyptian Principality dragons who were adept at handling the two huge sails) were on the lower deck just above the water line. There was one mast at the very stern of the boat and the other about a quarter of the way back from the bow. They were rigged with huge sails, similar to those on a felucca, still a common sight on the Nile.

Heka's sails were a beige-gold colour and the hieroglyphs for *Heka* were emblazoned on them in a sunset red orange. The boat itself was also painted this sunset red orange, the paint colours blending and changing slightly as the eye moved along the hull, because a bit of magic was incorporated into the work. The name *Heka* with the hieroglyphs for Magic was on the stern and along the side, carved within a cartouche and painted the soft sandy gold of the sails.   *Heka* would carry Kate, Robin, Elvira and Feral and their Fae friends Ariane and Dmitri and follow along up the Nile from Luxor behind the scouting party of Silver Moon, Tigris and Amazon River and Dawn Rain. Lilac, Peony and Dark Moon would come too, either swimming, flying invisibly or resting on the large upper deck. Most of the dragons could be accommodated for sleeping there as well or could find places in the surrounding countryside. And Dawn would have her special friends Elvira and Feral to offer comfort and support, plus she would sleep on board. Too young to fly long distances invisible, having the dahabeeyah following with her friends on board would provide both emotional security and physical resting place.

§ § §

The other scouts would also join the boating party for some meals and exchange of information and news, plus rest. Silver, in spite of his loner tendencies, had joined the Misfits a number of times as scout and as guard and fighter. He also, rather to his surprise, had helped at times with raising the Rain Clutch, finding a certain talent for interacting with the young ones.

      The two River dragons were less used to this mixed gang, and quickly made it known they would prefer to be going it more on their own.

"I thought it would be just us with the young one," said Amazon with an edge of complaint in her voice.

Tigris backed this up. "How can we operate with sufficient stealth with this 'party boat' following us?" he queried with a note of ill-concealed contempt.

Silver laughed. "I know how you feel. Our sire called me to be scout and watch over the island in the Venetian Lagoon while some of these human witches and some fae were attempting to rescue Kate's mother from the clutches of WP. Even though I was mostly alone, I was not happy to be involved with what I assumed were bumbling humans. Plus doing something so feeble as playing watchdog over another really unpleasant little group of humans and two nasty fae. And at the time I hadn't much faith in the capabilities of Kate and Robin or even my sisters Lilac and Peony when it came to battles, as it was sure to.

"All I can tell you is—they totally changed my mind. They will stay well back on the barge, not interfering at all or alerting our prey, while we do our scouting. But if it comes to any sort of confrontation, I assure you I'd rather have Kate and Robin at my side than almost any dragon. Although it turns out Lilac and Peony are very good fighters as well. And if they vouch for the others, that's good enough for me. We need Feral and Elvira and the boat for Dawn's sake, they are her chosen family, and she hasn't the strength yet to keep going long days with little food and less rest. Plus you may find you like these folks. I did. So remember what we've all learned over time — no judgement prior to investigation."

It was a well-worn phrase in their training as intelligence agents, and the two Rivers laughed and relaxed a bit. They were among the trees and reeds, watching from across the Nile as those going on board *Heka* were making ready to sail.

"I suggest we take this opportunity to meet with Dawn and explain what we're going to be doing and what we expect of her," said Silver. "It'll be hours yet before they sail." He took wing over to the dahabeeyah to fetch Dawn. She was watching the preparations with interest but sprang up all attention when Silver came in for a quiet landing and hurried to meet him.

Chapter 29

Dawn made a small bow to Silver, who responded with a slight inclination of his head.

"Come with me," he said. "They'll be hours here getting ready to leave, so Amazon and Tigris and I thought this would be a good time to brief you on what we will be doing." Dawn's colours rippled over her sides, indicating interest and enthusiasm. Silver smiled briefly and then turned and took off. He didn't look behind, but Dawn was learning fast what was expected of her, and she took wing and flew behind and slightly to the left of him, where she could pick up the slip stream of his wings and get extra lift and speed, plus being in a properly subservient position. They landed quickly near the stand of palms where Tigris and Amazon were lounging.

"Hi, Dawn," said Amazon. Tigris merely raised a seemingly negligent hand. Dawn made a good landing and bowed her head to them. Then they all sat down, digging themselves into the moist mud of the riverbank for the coolness and to help to make themselves less visible. Each of them altered their colours a bit, adding stripes and zigzags and more earthy tones as camouflage. Dawn watched in wonder. They all smiled at her.

"Go on," urged Tigris. "Try for a bit of blending in." Dawn's sides flashed her confusion rather brightly. The others laughed. She looked slightly annoyed, but then downcast, and that feeling of being downcast made her golden spikes and wings turn dull as if tarnished. She was astonished when they all nodded approval until she saw her own tail and how dull it had gone. But it took a while to get the hang of it because her feeling of getting it right made her glow gold again.

Silver explained patiently. "Yes, our colours are important to communicate both feelings and even language. But we don't want to have to feel depressed or wrong for our colours to go dull and less obvious. So we need to teach our bodies to respond to actual orders. Therefore, if I tell myself to become camouflaged my body is attuned to that word, and doesn't just respond with going dull, but will actually adjust itself to whatever environment, colours or patterns it perceives. And with training we can override our automatic emotional responses that would change our colours and keep the camouflage even if we are suddenly happy or sad or frightened.

"We have our ordinary brains that think, process information and talk, but we also have parts of our brains that control our usually unthinking reactions, like fight or flight or raising our temperature when it's cold or lowering it when hot, or our hearts beating faster when aroused. Or our colours changing with our emotions. So we must practice being camouflaged just like we trained to learn to fly."

Dawn nodded understanding. She looked around at where she was crouched and thought about what colours she manifested with different feelings. "So if I want to be green brown with some grey and some stripes of green I need to get in touch with what makes me that way, but then link it to a command I give myself? And the same command will turn me bright green and red if that's my surroundings?"

"Exactly," responded Amazon allowing a shifting gold pattern to dapple her side in approval. "But it's easy to say and not very easy to do. So don't be discouraged if you can't do this quickly. Some dragons can't do it at all, and they'd never make it as spies. But I heard that you managed invisibility months and months ago at an age where so far as we know no other dragon has ever done so."

This was news to Dawn. *No other dragon? Wow.* But she simply nodded her head.

"Well, that would indicate that you could have some kind of natural talent for colour changes at will as well. Invisibility usually takes years of training to master, and you had no one to train you. Take heart, young Dawn, you may have the makings of a spy!"

Dawn blushed and a small riot of colours ran across her sides. But she somehow, she wasn't sure just how, muted these into green and brown and sandy stripes and her golden wings into sandy beige. She couldn't hold it long, but she could see the astonishment on their faces. She grinned. Not the sly, calculating smile of the Dawn of old, but a grin of pure happiness. Then feeling suddenly as if she'd been holding her breath too long she let out a wuff and collapsed slightly. "Takes energy," she gasped.

"It does," remarked Tigris. "You've done well."

"I'm not sure how I did it," said Dawn looking abashed. "I just wanted to, and it happened."

Silver laughed. "Exactly, that is how it works, but not many dragons can do it even so. Remember that other big part of learning— patience."

"And not being afraid to make mistakes," murmured Dawn.

"Yeah? They taught you that?" Amazon turned to the others. "That's important for sure, someone in that principality has the right ideas."

"But, young Dawn, there will be times on

this expedition when it's possible we can't afford any mistakes. So at times like those, you take a back seat, yeah? Do nothing unless you know you can do it perfectly and it is what's needed. Take orders."

"I can do that," she stated confidently. "But can I ask you a favour? Could you just call me Dawn? We know I'm young, but I don't like being called that."

The others exchanged grins, but also nodded. "Okay," said Silver. "From now on it's Dawn, possibly Dawn Rain, but we will try to keep from embarrassing you, it's not a nice feeling."

"Thank you," she said, heartfelt. It might have been an easy request, well, more a command from the Dawn of old, hiding her fear behind a facade of bullying, but from Dawn now it had not been an easy thing to ask, and she was properly grateful to be taken seriously and with kindness.

She dared to ask the question she'd been wanting to know from the first. "Where are we going and who or what are we supposed to be looking for? Can you tell me that or is it like a state secret?"

Amazon smiled, "Shall I fill her in or is that your job, Silver?"

"Go ahead," he said. "If you miss out anything we can fill it in."

"But, just to begin, we don't really know that much," offered Tigris. "We'll tell you what we know though."

"There's this ancient Egyptian Cat Goddess, so far the only ancient Egyptian god that has shown any signs of, err, 'life' for thousands of years," Amazon began. "Her name is Bastet, and she's become friendly with your father, Chen Shi and the Magical Misfits and some of our group of younger dragons because she was instrumental in helping them all to disable Wyvern-Proteus and getting him into a granite sarcophagus and burying that really deep in an area of Egypt no one goes to. He's been disposed of entirely now, so he's gone, and therefore all threat to the dragons, you and us included, is gone.

"But Bastet got this real thing for dragons and the Moon bunch introduced her to Blue Moon, who is even more of a loner than Silver here. They hit it off, and Bastet was showing Blue her own history as an ancient deity when she spotted a change in an illustration and some of the hieroglyphs about another really ancient god—maybe the very first one. Anyway, Bastet freaked, because this other god—his name is Apep or Apophis—is a huge snake and hates cat goddesses. Especially Bastet because he thinks she killed him once eons ago.

"Bastet swears it wasn't her, it was a brindle

cat named Mau who attacked Apep. Bastet is not a warrior cat, she's the goddess of women and children and the home, the cat by the hearth sort of thing. She's afraid Apep is awakening and will come after her. Our job is to find him first and then Chen Shi and the Misfits can defeat him before he can hurt her."

"Yes, Elvira and Feral have told me some of this. But why is it our job exactly?" asked Dawn.

"Because she was instrumental in saving all the dragons from WP, and we owe her. Why us, exactly? Well I volunteered, sort of," said Silver. "And it's what we do, we are the sort of elite corps, we are the James Bonds of dragons, we go out and hunt down the bad guys and if necessary, call in the heavy artillery to help us finish them off. It's dangerous, but it's exciting, and it uses up all the energy and brain power that would otherwise probably get us in trouble."

"We're troublemakers on the side of Good?" queried Dawn.

"Yep. Got it in one," laughed Tigris.

"Like the Three Musketeers? I haven't heard of this James Bond." said Dawn.

Silver laughed. "So you read human stories too? Yes like the Musketeers. James Bond is also a fictional character, a spy who always wins."

Amazon took up the tale, "We're going to

hunt along the Nile for places that have all the energies associated with eons of god-worship or 'spooky stuff' and try to pin down where this old god is looking to make his comeback. The dahabeeyah will follow at a safe distance so as not to disturb Apep, but will be there to help if we find him."

"Our reasoning is," said Silver, "having seen how Bastet re-awakened and then gained in strength and power due to her big festival at Bubastis, Apep, or his demon lieutenants, will have decided to try something similar. A big festival with lots of entertainment, free food and drink may also give him the power he needs to attack Bastet."

"And then we kill him?" asked Dawn.

"Not exactly," said Silver. "We pinpoint him, we watch him without him seeing us to find out if possible what he has planned. Once we know, we call in the cavalry, so to speak. He is a god and he has demons, all are magical. We have magic too, but so do all of those aboard *Heka,* and we don't try to be heroes, we try to scare him and convince him to leave Bastet alone.

"But it might be that Bastet, since she's the only cat goddess available, will have to take part in this. The only portrayals of Apep being 'killed'—for a given value of dead, as he is immortal—are when a cat goddess attacks him with a magic knife.

"There's another part of the plan, the one most likely to be used because it is illustrated in Ramses the First's tomb. *Heka* will be enchanted to become Ra's Night Barge and the Misfits take the places of some of the gods who accompanied the Pharaoh and the Sun God, Ra. For the ancient Egyptians, the sunset was a dangerous time, they were never sure that it would rise again, and they depended on it for life itself. So Pharaoh as Ra sailed Ra's Night Barge under the earth with other gods, where they did battle with Apep, who was there trying to kill Ra, but Pharaoh and the gods always beat him, so the Sun would rise again in the morning."

Amazon joined in, "This doesn't require actual fighting with weapons, even tooth and claw, it is done by saying or reading texts from the Book of the Dead which overpower Apep and allow the Sun, and the Night Barge, that's *Heka*, to rise out of the darkness under the earth. It will all be magic."

"Although," said Tigris, "most pictures of this 'battle' show evidence of either Apep in pieces, or lines depicting knives, so cutting him up seems to be part of many of the stories of the nightly defeat of Apep."

Dawn looked thoroughly perplexed.

"Yes, I know, confusing," said Silver. "Look,

these ancient gods aren't like humans or witches, fae or dragons, we are difficult to kill but we can — humans certainly—be killed and stay dead. The gods of ancient Egypt were invented by men way back, and they changed to suit new beliefs. They live because of belief topped up with worship or, as with Apep, fear. Very powerful, fear."

"And if they die," continued Amazon, "they were reborn, sometimes every day, sometimes after eons if belief starts up again. They changed their jobs and their characteristics too—except Apep, he never changed, he has always been evil and always done the same job—try to destroy Egypt by keeping the sun from rising. When we deal with them we are in a world like the spacetime bubbles that contain the Dragon Principalities, or Faerie, existing alongside or within Earth, but somehow not *of* it."

"So if we conquer this Apep, this big snake under the earth, he dies then, but he is there again the next night, and every night? How does that help Bastet then?" colours of confusion were running down Dawn's sides.

Amazon and Tigris both looked at Silver with questions in their eyes and colours too.

Silver said, "I can't say I understand it really, but if we do it once, we don't keep him from his job, trying to keep the sun from rising, but apparently we can drive him away from being any threat to Bastet. She was not involved much with the ritual of Apep trying every night to stop the stop the sun from rising, and Ra and the pharaoh and other gods fighting him off. So if the Misfits as gods beat Apep badly, worse than usual, at the same time warning him to stay away from Bastet, Chen Shi believes that will work. They'll do that in the form of an incantation as similar as possible to those incantations they use every night. The form of words and the warning that they will be able to 'kill' him if he forgets should be enough to get him to forget any grudge he has against Bastet. Either he goes back to the sleep of the other ancient gods, or even if he manages to keep doing his nightly duty, he will forget Bastet. It's most likely he will disappear back to the underworld of ancient 'dead' gods and just sleep.

"And the sailing a Night Barge under the earth part?"

Dawn's questions, it seemed to Silver, were making his headache. "I think our father, Chen Shi, and the Misfits plus Bastet and that Egyptian witch and her cat are all working on that. That is an important part of what we are going to trying sniff out—the space-time bubble that contains the ancient Egypt where the gods are or were worshipped, and Ra's boat did navigate the dead waters under the earth where those on the boat did battle nightly with

Apep, using ancient texts that would...I suspect 'disable' might be the term here...stop Apep so Bastet is free to enjoy her own rebirth as a benevolent goddess for as long as that lasts."

Dawn thought for a while. "That Egyptian witch Elvira and Feral, her cat, saved me. And with Bastet and all our heroes and us...I can see that it could work. I can see that it *will* work. Thank you for explaining."

The other three dragons looked at each other in perplexity. Something that seemed to be clear now to Dawn wasn't at all clear to them, but then she knew all these people better than they did. It was ancient magic and modern magic and reality and something like spirituality of a kind, and apparently it clicked with her. They'd have to hope it would eventually make sense to them too.

Chapter 30

The three spy dragons and Dawn drowsed during the heat of the day in the mud near the Nile, but Dawn had 'borrowed' a James Bond book from Silver's mind-store of books and had discovered MI5. Like the Dragon King, many of the dragons had the ability to read something once and keep a copy in their mind for later re-reading. As human books were so small for a dragon to manipulate, many who loved reading had developed this talent. It wasn't quite so necessary now that they could easily project type onto big screens, but it had become quite a usual thing to have a mind that stored vast quantities of information they could easily access. It was much less usual to borrow information without asking first.

She knew about the Magical Misfits and the Fae Free Spirits and how they had eventually taken to calling Wyvern-Proteus WP. This group she might join was certainly designed to be spies, and could profit by an easy acronym (it was Feral who'd told her what an acronym was), and she'd thought of one. RMR for River Moon Rain. It depended of course upon her being made a member. But she was beginning to feel she had a very good chance of that, they'd admitted she had the talents, which were rare, and they'd confided in her about at least some of the plans.

As the day cooled a bit, the others woke and stretched, and they all had a large snack followed by a nice swim. "No more crocodiles in the Nile," Amazon assured her. "When humans built the Aswan Dam they moved them all upriver past the dam, and now we can swim without any fear. Not true above the Dam though. So if and when we get there, you need to be careful, Yo…, err, Dawn. You'd make a good meal for a big croc."

"I'll remember that," promised Dawn. "What exactly are we trying to find as to evidence of this Chaos God?"

"We're going to concentrate on the major sites along the Nile from here in Luxor up to Abu Simbel and also keep alert for any sites of interest that humans may not know about but that have concentrations of power, even if there's nothing to see."

"How do you sense those, then?" asked Dawn. "I mean, if there's nothing that shows they were or are places of power or worship."

"We stay alert for any signs of concentrations or accumulations of power. Just as we can find the Egyptian Principality by sensing the assemblage of dragons and their power. I'm sure you were aware of that when they brought you here." said Tigris naively.

Dawn displayed a certain amount of agitation in the colours that shifted down her sides. But only the truth would do. "No, I wasn't at all aware of the location of the Principality when they brought us here from the Creche. That's way I jumped ship and got in so much trouble. I had no sense at all of where the Principality was, got completely lost. Oh, I know now, of course, I can sense it now, but I'm over a year older, and I've been there most of the time, so of course I can sense it."

"Ah, of course, sorry, I'd forgotten that bit of your history. Never mind, as with all our other talents, they manifest themselves at different times and different intensities, and some never appear at all."

"The point is," said Silver, "that we will not just see evidence of activity over the millennia, we will also sense where there have been areas of activity, and even the sort of activity — worship, or sacrifice, or just living, working, the kind of work in many cases, but mainly when there is a large concentration of worship or fear or both combined, and the types of beings that have been involved. These leave indelible traces, and for those of us with our senses honed to sift them, we can also usually tell the timeline, whether this was an ancient site not used for ages, or an ancient site still used or recently used, or possibly a new site where ancient beings have recently been active. Although there is no blame attached to being 'blind' to most of this, as many dragons are, it is very helpful for a spy to have senses finally attuned to all this sort of thing."

"And if I do not?" asked Dawn with some trepidation.

"You have some real ability," said Amazon. "There are dragons who, if they are out of their principalities must always be accompanied by a dragon with a good sense for locating it, because some simply have no ability in that direction. You do, it may be rather ordinary, or it could, with training be very good. As we travel, we will be both training and testing you, so we will find out. You already show precocious abilities in various areas so we can't be certain, but we can be quite hopeful that this precocity will extend to this area as well, since it is quite important." Amazon gave her a friendly pat with her wing. "Don't worry, we won't throw you to the crocodiles just because you aren't super good in this area."

"Although it would be very helpful," remarked Tigris, leaving Dawn with a shiver of discomfort.

"It's why there is more than one of us," said Silver. "We all have these skills, but at different levels. Tigris is very good at picking up the sense that an area has been used for evil practices, or just major sacrifices. She's not as sharp as Amazon, however, at sensing the times when these things happened. I'm very adept at sensing what is going on at the moment, and the identity of who or what is doing it even when there is nothing to see. I'm rubbish at sensing the exact nature of what went on in the past, there I get only general ideas of what went on or when. Amazon is immensely gifted at the timeline of things, good things as well as bad, it's amazing how accurately she can pinpoint things.

"So whatever aptitude you show, and there are other areas as well, such as invisibility, you were flying invisible long before any other dragonet we'd ever heard of. Yes, I know you 'flickered' and it nearly got you killed, but you did it. This would almost certainly mean that as you grow you will be expert at staying invisible while doing anything and everything else. That is rare. Should you show special talents, we will encourage them.

And of course we know all kinds of fighting, much of it not encouraged as a general rule, but although you were out of control and behaving badly, you showed you weren't afraid to do whatever you thought necessary to get the freedom you craved."

Dawn stared at him as if mesmerised. She hadn't realised how much they knew, although to include her in such a venture of course it made sense.

But to find that even her worst behaviour (she had drugged several of her creche mates, knocked another cold and badly clawed the one who'd been her 'best friend') could apparently be seen as being potentially valuable. Well, spy, clandestine operator…suddenly she felt as if a number of puzzle pieces were coming together. She was meant for this. And Chauncey, her father, had seen it. From being the one who didn't fit, she had found her place.

But Amazon was moving away from the particular and onto the itinerary they expected to cover. "We'll start with Luxor and Karnak Temples right here plus the Valley of the Kings and Hatshepsut's mortuary temple. Then we move up the Nile—that means going south—and stop at Edfu and Kom Ombo, Elephantine Island.
From there it's on to the Aswan Dam and Lake Nasser, where we will see two important temples moved from their original locations when the dam flooded their locations, and they were saved by being moved to higher ground, these are Philae and Abu Simbel. Quite honestly, we don't expect to find evidence of Apep in these areas at the moment, because they are very popular with tourists, and although he might have hung out around there in times past he wouldn't now."

"But we must look, especially at the

carvings and frescos," said Silver. "Plus the entire area is full of ancient buildings and even cities long ago destroyed and covered in sand. These also could lead us to some information. Amazon and I will be acting as 'eyes' for both Chen Shi and Imhotep, both of whom read hieroglyphics extremely well, and they will be looking for carvings that might tell us more about Apep."

Dawn wondered if Silver was aware that she'd mind-linked with Silver when he was sleeping and 'borrowed' the James Bond book. She felt his mind-link, which made her jump slightly. "Yes, of course I did, and you're welcome, but it's usual to announce yourself first" said Silver in her mind.

"I'm sorry, I thought you were sleeping," murmured Dawn.

"So you thought you'd just make off with something while I slept? You do realise that's stealing?" But Dawn could hear the smile in Silver's mock-serious tone.

"I only borrowed a copy, you've still got yours, I made sure of that," said Dawn. A sense of confusion came down their channel from Silver, who came back with, "So you did, my copy is here." They'd been whispering, but suddenly he was speaking aloud. "Dawn here has done something else rather rare. And very good for spying if she can repeat it without being caught." Tigris and Amazon were surprised and looking around to see what evidence they might have missed.

"She 'borrowed' a book from my mind," explained Silver.

"Oh, that is precocious, but not all that rare," said Tigris.

"It is when she left the original in place and made off with a copy she made herself," grinned Silver.

"Oh, my fire, that is, err, that might be unique?" gulped Amazon.

"But you noticed it? So not so unique," said Tigris.

"I was aware she came in and borrowed the book, I was not aware that she left my original safely behind," said Silver. They were all looking at Dawn now with expressions that made her feel quite peculiar.

"Wow!" was all Tigris could say. "But Silver, you were aware of her presence, so that might not be so useful for listening in unnoticed to beings we want to find out things from."

Amazon added, "A mind-link with a different species, as some of the Misfits now have with some of us has to be set up as a cooperative effort."

"Well, let's file it for now under possible useful things for the future." Silver grinned at Dawn and put a companionable wing around her. "I have a feeling you might continue to surprise us."

"I have a feeling I wish I were actually a little more ordinary just now," muttered Dawn. They all laughed, and after a moment, she joined in.

"Shall we get back to the business of the day?" queried Silver.

Tigris grinned, "Yes, this whole thing started when Bastet saw a change in an ancient tomb fresco, which she interpreted as evidence that Apep is rising, and will be coming for her. So we will be looking long and hard at that one. And for any other such evidence as we go.

"What we are especially looking for is evidence in some abandoned temple complex along the way that there is, was or will be a gathering. Something like the celebrations at Bubastis that brought life back to Bastet. Lots of booze and drugs involved we heard, and a lot of adoration, and next thing you know, there she is. She wasn't even aware she was a few thousand years into the future at first. We think Apep, although not expecting worship, could be planning something similar—a big party with lots of free food and drink and entertainment. Just like a huge rock festival, most people won't care who's behind it, but it will feed his power. So we'll be checking the well-known well-preserved temple complexes for the hieroglyphs, but spending at least as much time sensing out any possible really big noisy festivals.

"And if nothing comes of all that?" queried Dawn. "After all, if he's after Bastet, she's being kept safe in the Egyptian Principality guarded by half the Misfits, a lot of dragons and our father himself. Wouldn't Apep try to infiltrate that?"

"He would if he thought he could, but he may not even know it exists, it's a space-time bubble totally outside his own experience, and it's never been penetrated by any of the ancient Egyptians, or their gods, although they had their own main capital and pharaonic seat for many many centuries at Thebes, cheek by jowl you could say to the Egyptian Principality. And never the twain did meet in all those years. We are betting he will make himself manifest in this time with some kind of big splash that will increase his power, and then lure her out."

"Why would she fall for that?" asked Dawn, amazed. "She's safe where she is."

"Because she knows only a cat can 'kill' him (for a given value of killed), and because for her the Egyptian Dragon Principality is not her home, she's in exile there. And she will begin to fade in power. She's a very important goddess, she won't want that, plus as frightened as she may be of him, she is also quite aware of her duty as the only presently existing Cat Goddess. She is the daughter of Ra and Isis.

Some say her father created her specifically to kill Apep! Others say that was Mau, others Sekhmet. But they aren't here, and she is."

Chapter 31

Silver stretched and shook like a dog to get all the sand off him. "I'm going over to talk to Kate and by mind-link to Chen Shi. The others have already studied the hieroglyphs in the Tomb of Ramses the First for what they say, and if they could have been altered recently by human hands. They know what they used to say and they've agreed now they say exactly what Bastet said she and Blue saw.

"And the experts who examined them in situ and using special instrumentation are all agreed these changes weren't made by new carving or any other method they can figure out. The block of stone hasn't been replaced with another, and the painting and carving are definitely from the time of Ramses, yet are also and at the same time newly changed. Only they haven't a clue how. Even magic has been suggested by scientists who don't believe in it.

"So I think we should go there after closing time tonight and study them with these other senses we've been talking about. Between us we may be able to tell who was there, and when and what they did. It's worth a try anyway. We're all meeting for dinner anyway, and Dawn you'll be staying overnight on the dahabeeyah."

"But can I come too?" asked Dawn.

"Oh, definitely, you are displaying all sorts of latent and precocious talents, and who knows what you might pick up."

Dawn felt as if she'd been declared a winner in some way. It was a really good feeling.

When Silver returned he was carrying Feral, who was looking quite pleased with himself.

"What is that, and what's it doing here?" demanded Tigris.

He's my good friend, my very good friend, Feral, and he's a cat, a magician and a mage!" Dawn almost spat the words, she was so upset that Tigris was being so disrespectful with no reason.

"That may be so, but we depend upon stealth and few people knowing our business," replied Tigris.

Amazon intervened, "Isn't the very fact that Silver has brought him proof enough that he is needed now. Tigris, you are too much alone. We must get used to working as a group to accomplish our purposes. We have heard of Feral."

"Of course," murmured Tigris, backing down. "Silver, why does our business this evening require Feral?"

"Because when Bastet and Blue explored Ramses Tomb Bastet's magic was sufficient to allow them entry through the usual entrance without anyone questioning them," explained Silver.

"Either they were entirely invisible, or Bastet enchanted the guards into allowing them access without anyone else. Whatever it was, we do not have that magic or other power to gain entry. Feral can either find us a back way into the tomb or possibly he can gain entry to the guards' hut and come away with a key."

"I think," offered Feral, "it wouldn't be possible to find a back way into the tomb that would accommodate the size you are, not even Dawn anymore."

There was agitation amongst the dragons. "But!" Feral raised a paw imperiously. It was astonishing just how he managed to project power and leadership when he was not much larger than one of their feet. "I can either find a way into the guards' hut that is big enough for me or, failing that, I am practiced at mind magics that will have them opening the door for me and offering food. I can do this with virtually any human, and the night guards here are usually alone and happy to have a bit of company. It is then easy to perform a sleep spell and bring you the key."

"And this sleep spell is deep enough to keep the guard from waking and discovering the missing key for as long as we may need?" asked Amazon.

"I will have replaced the key with what

appears to be a duplicate. And even if he wakes, the guard will feel drowsy, too drowsy to start doing rounds. Budget cuts mean that there is only one, and he is usually quite happy to remain in his comfortable chair rather than go out poking around in the late hours. In fact doing rounds hardly ever happens anymore, they depend upon the locks and the fact that there is no longer anything that can be stolen, with the possible exception of the art on the walls, and that is such a laborious process that no one would attempt it who couldn't import equipment and take special care—much more time consuming than one night. And much too noisy." Feral sat looking smug.

"Oh," said Dawn, "Feral also knows the location of Ramses the First's tomb, so we won't be wasting any time."

"KV16," said Feral complacently.
"If you're going to start speaking in code, you must excuse our ignorance," said Tigris.

"It's the numbering system people have given to all the tombs discovered in the valley of the kings—KV for King's Valley and they are numbered in the order in which they were discovered," said Silver. "We brought maps and some information."

Feral grinned, "Ramses was one of the later pharaohs, he ascended the throne when Pharaoh Horemheb died, but of the sixty-something tombs discovered, his was the sixteenth.

"Horemheb came after Tutankhamun who was the last of the great 18th Dynasty, when Egypt was strong and powerful. Tutankhamun died at only 18 or 19 of wounds, whether in battle or in military exercises, or possibly murder, with no living children. So Horemheb, as general of the army, was well placed, powerful, to take over, and he named Ramses, also not of royal blood, to succeed him. Ramses was old though and was only Pharaoh for two years before he died. His tomb is small, probably because there wasn't time to make a big one, but it is very beautifully decorated. And the particular wall paintings are in the room with his sarcophagus—easy to find once you are there. However, because of the size of the sarcophagus, you may only get one or two of you at most around it to examine the art. I have to warn you about even brushing the walls, your scales could damage the paintings. I've brought measurements and pictures so we can find out if you can get past the sarcophagus to be close to the paintings. However, Blue could, and you are of about the same size, yes?"

"Yes," affirmed Silver, "at our age males and females are virtually the same size, and Blue and I are of the same clutch— the Moon Clutch—so if she can go there, so can I. But it would be helpful if

Amazon and Tigris and Dawn can also examine them. What about light? We can see in the dark, but it is better if we have good light sources so as not to damage anything."

"Ah," said Feral. "Lighting, of course. Sorry, we may have to go back to *Heka* and get some good torches. Silver, can you carry those?"

"In some sort of carryall, of course," Silver replied.

Shortly they were airborne again, and landing on the roof deck of *Heka*.

"Back so soon?" Robin asked from where he was arranging lounge chairs and tables and rugs under the large sail being used as a shelter against the sun.

"We're going to the tomb of Ramses the First tonight and will need good torches with full batteries to explore without danger of damaging anything and also to examine the wall painting in the main room that so upset Bastet." explained Silver.

"Oh, the one where Apep isn't bowed down before that god I can't remember, but is looking out at us with his fangs showing? And the writing is different? We've got lots of pictures, but...well, could I come along? And Kate. We've both been really thinking we want to see the real one. And Perry, I know he'll be gutted if he can't help or see what you guys are doing."

Silver took a few minutes to think about this He knew Amazon and Tigris wouldn't be happy, but really there was nothing to be unhappy about, except they enjoyed their loner status, and they already were four dragons and a cat. But he was the leader, what he said, went. And he felt a sneaking feeling of comradeship with Robin and that getting Tigris to start accepting major changes of plan wasn't a bad thing at all.

"Yes, you can come, but I don't have saddles for you human folk so Lilac and Dark Moon will have to join us then," said Silver, a tone of resignation in his voice. "But you all must be prepared to do exactly as I say, and it is imperative we don't damage anything."

"Hey, Kate would cut off my hand if I brushed it against a frescoed wall!" said Robin with a grin. "Don't worry, we're well trained, and Perry is an art and antiquities expert, he'd be the most careful of us all. What about getting in?"

"Feral assures us he can mesmerise the guard and borrow the key. The guard will sleep soundly for hours. Feral says they usually do anyway. Other than occasional thrill-seekers, there's not much to guard really, the locks on the gates are good, and nothing is left inside but the wall paintings, and it would take a lot of time and equipment to remove any part of one. We will go at 11pm to make sure all is quiet, and no

one is still around. We'll fly invisibly. But once
we're at the tomb we'll use torches and maybe a
good bigger light to see the entire painting."

"I can hardly wait to tell Kate!"

Chapter 32

Kate was as enthused as Robin had expected, but
also quite in agreement with Silver's cautionary
attitude.

"But what exactly is it you hope to find?"
she asked Silver. "Chauncey, Imhotep, and Bastet
plus the rest of us have examined all the pictures
Blue went back to take and a special instrument was
used to check the age and type of paint used to alter
the originals—it seems to be original too. It's a
magical change so far as we can tell, with no other
clues as to when or how it was done, or by whom."

"That's why our father has me, Amazon,
Tigris, and Dawn doing the searching for any
evidence of recent activity that is or could be Apep-
related. We have instincts, or senses we've
developed and trained, that can tell more than your
instrumentation or visual inspection. Call it
something like a hyper-developed sense of smell for
things if you want."

"And Dawn has this too?" Kate was
fascinated.

"She is showing signs of it, yes, and she has a lot of other talents that could make her a good spy. So we've taken her on board and this is on-the-job-training."

"Wow! I'm so pleased for her. It did look for a while there as if she could be a no-hoper and would have to be controlled somehow. This is great."

Feral said, "She was just ahead of herself, or ahead of her clutch mates, and it frustrated her. She was a right mess when I found her, but she's something else now, she's kind of growing into herself. I know how it is. If Elvira hadn't found me, I'd have been—well, dead for a start—but if I'd survived, I'd have been a nasty piece of work. She saw what I could be. Now I've been helping Dawn. Well, and Elvira of course, and the carers in the Principality."

Kate was laughing silently at Feral's usual way of telling a story, plunking himself front and centre as the main action hero, then recalling his raising by Elvira and, with only a slight diminution of enthusiasm, giving credit where it was due to others as well. Feral was in so many ways his own unique creation from the shattered bits and pieces of his dreadful beginnings, but also with a deep kindness he tried often to conceal, and the way he had of sounding like he was ungrateful for the help he'd been given whereas he was in fact very grateful indeed. In any other creature, this almost schizoid character would have been disconcerting and not very appealing. But somehow in Feral it was endearing—but then Feral was a cat. And a mage.

Kate longed to hug him, but she refrained, knowing that Feral would at best be embarrassed. At worst he might give her one of his looks, or even a smack, and stalk away. Only Elvira had his complete adoration and could do anything with him.

But Dawn it appeared was spreading her wings in more ways than one, expanding her circle of friends and finding her way. If Elvira and Feral had been her nursery, the caring dragons of the Egyptian Principality had been her therapists as well as educators, and now Silver's spy 'school', with help from her father Chen Shi, was to be her next step in becoming what might be someone quite extraordinary. Kate, who had had the unpleasant job of alerting Chauncey to Dawn's anti-social activities and potentially sociopathic tendencies, was more than pleased, she was delighted.

Robin had already alerted Dark and Lilac Moon and Perry's special dragon, Jade Moon, and had himself gone to fetch their saddles in anticipation of their trip across the Nile to the Valley of the Kings. But the sun was still above the horizon and there was a good five hours before it would be safe to enter the Valley. Silver and Robin were discussing lighting and Robin was asking Perry where on *Heka* the necessary stuff was stored.

It turned out Perry, with the help of Julien, had anticipated the possible need for good light of various kinds, and the storage area had lights, ranging from battery powered torches to powerful lights for illuminating a larger area to lights in various spectrums to check for layers under the most recent layers of paint or for providing light for humans not visible to some other species and vice versa. There were also some magical equivalents, provided by the fae, and by Kate, whose ability to conjure fire from her hands under stress she had trained to provide light without heat.

So the dragon spy group plus Feral and led by Silver, and the Misfits Kate, Robin and Perry and their own dragon friends, settled in with an early dinner, to wait for sunset when it would become safe to fly to the Valley of the Kings and do a little prospecting of their own. The Misfits were fascinated by the idea that the dragons could sense things that might prove helpful.

"Like dogs trained to sniff out drugs, or bodies or other things," mused Robin.

"Is it mainly smell, or do other senses come into play?" asked Perry.

"Smell certainly" said Silver, "but other

things too. Our eyes can see in different light spectra, as well as that which humans use, our skins are capable of all sorts of things, not just flashing colours to project feelings or as more complex communication. We can pick up sensory signals when we are close to an object."

Seeing Perry's worried look that they might brush up against the walls, Silver hurried to reassure him. "We don't have to touch the walls, Perry, being close is sufficient if there are messages we might get and be able to interpret. It is similar to you feeling another's body warmth if you get quite close, you don't have to touch. Whether what we pick up will be meaningful is another thing. It is good we have several different kinds of people to hopefully help interpret what we experience."

Kate ventured, "Magic might be useful. Only Bastet and Blue have been there, it might have been Bastet's magic that interpreted what the changes in the wall paintings mean, or just her fear of Apep. Blue is a magical animal, but she didn't sense anything but the actual pictures and how upset Bastet was. Blue can't read hieroglyphs. Maybe if we use some simple spells. There's one that can sometimes tell me who did something if I see something like a theft but no thief, or a crashed car but no driver. I can try that."

Robin said, "And I can often tell how long

ago something was changed by being close to it. So can Perry, he taught me, very useful in authenticating antiques he said, didn't you?" He grinned at Perry.

"And there's a spell that can heighten my sense of the emotion behind what was done," added Perry. "If it was a joke or prank, if it was mischief or malice behind it. Not fool proof, often what I get is a mixture, but then people who mess with stuff often have a mix of emotions."

"Mainly, it's important that we share what we experience so that if we don't know the meaning of it, maybe another one of us will," said Amazon.

Chatting and eating, exchanging information, they were ready when the sun went down.

Chapter 33

The Egyptian night following quickly upon the sunset, twilight did not linger this far south. By the time the riders had saddled their dragons, and the bits of electronic equipment were packaged up on Amazon, full dark had descended. There was a lot of light pollution from Luxor, where *Heka* was moored, so the stars weren't visible.

So the dragons chose invisibility to fly over the river and into the hills around the Valley of the Kings, including Dawn, who was carrying Feral. As they'd discovered a few years back, anything a dragon was carrying also became invisible when they did, so a complete 'invisibility cloak' was cast over all the dragons and their cargo. Except that, handily enough, the dragons could still see each other and what or who they were carrying. The non-dragons, however, could not, and invisibility meant they could not see either their dragons or even themselves, a drawback they had had to get used to.

As Feral was their guide, he and Dawn took the lead. He guided her easily to the entrance to the valley, well out of sight of the guard's hut near the entrance. Except for a light coming from the single window, there were no lights in the Valley. The other dragons all landed gently in this area, out of sight of the door and window of the guards hut.

Feral jumped down off Dawn and strolled with complete cat confidence to the guard's hut. Here he jumped up on the window ledge, where the window was open to allow the cool evening air inside, but a screen still covered the entrance. Feral gave a soft meow that caused the guard to raise his head from where he was sitting with his feet up a magazine open on his lap. He was a large man of late middle age, his guards' tunic strained over his belly, and his feet in sandals showing puffy ankles, rather than the boots that stood in the corner. "Ah, my friend, the cat of the night," said the guard. "How are you, my friend, hungry as always?"

The *merow* sound from Feral was clearly meant to signal that, yes, he was hungry. The guard laughed softly and rose with some difficulty from his well-padded and somewhat sunken chair. He went to a covered plate on the table and uncovering it, displayed the remains of his own dinner. Then he came over and unlocked the door, where Feral had already jumped down and was waiting. He did the expected cat thing of winding around the man's feet as his sandals flip-flopped back over to the table where he put the plate down on the floor. Feral made a to-do of lapping up some bits and pieces of fish and turning up his nose at the spiced vegetables. Then he stalked over to where the man was once more sitting and leapt into his lap.

This was apparently a well-known visitation, and the man settled back absently scratching Feral under the chin and around his head and ears. Feral purred. Then he rested a paw on the man's hand and became quiet. The guard looked down and met the green eyes staring into his. Feral broke into a sort of singsong that was just barely cat-like, and the man's eyes began to glaze over. As the chant continued the man fell into a deep sleep, soon followed with soft snores. Feral tested the depth of the sleep by gently biting the man's thumb. When there was no reaction at all, he jumped down and over to the table, above which was a rack of keys in a wall case. This should have been locked also, but the key was there in the lock, and not turned and locked, so that Feral could hook it easily with a claw and pull the cupboard door open. Inside were keys on hooks numbered from 1 through 63, the last of the tombs so far discovered.

Feral carefully unhooked the key for tomb KV16 from its hanger, and with a few soft mews and a wave of a paw, he produced a shadowy facsimile of it on the hook, one which seemed to grow more solid as it hung there. Then he closed the door and turned the key. Bouncing soundlessly off the table he came out of the hut, where Dawn carefully closed the door behind him.

"He'll sleep soundly for at least 8 hours," announced Feral. "Nothing but an earthquake or an explosion under his hut will wake him now. Plenty of time to get to KV16 and have all of us do whatever we do to find out how and who. Shall we go?"

He handed over the key to Kate and led them quietly and confidently up the main 'avenue' where off to both sides were various tomb doors labelled by number.

"Why are the numbers so out of sequence?" asked Robin.

Perry answered, "Because they were numbered in the order they were discovered by archaeologists, not according to the reigns of the pharaohs.

"Ramses the First is tomb KV16, and yet he is one of the 19th Dynasty, not long after Tutankhamun, who was the last but one of the famous and most successful 18th Dynasty. Ramses wasn't even of royal blood—he was an army general, like Horemheb before him, and Horemheb nominated him as his successor. Ramses however only lived for two years.

"But although the might of the Dynasties was declining, their tomb decoration was getting more elaborate. Seti the First, who succeeded Ramses, has the most highly decorated tomb here. It was his son who is called Ramses the Great.

"However, enough history. We're going to

see KV16. It's small compared to some others but highly decorated."

They had walked about halfway through the Valley before reaching the door of the tomb.

Feral explained, "It's an easy tomb to get through, just you bigger dragons be a bit careful—tuck in your wings, okay? It's basically a straight line from entry to burial chamber at the bottom. The entryway has steps going down. About twelve of them, curving to the right, there are handrails, and rails all along to keep people from brushing up against the walls. After the first steps there is a straight bit, then many steps going down, then another walkway without stairs, but it slants downward. Finally we come to the last set of stairs, and these open directly into the burial chamber."

Kate took up the narrative, "And we find the wall painting we want on the corner of the wall to our right as we face the sarcophagus. It shows the night barge with the Sun God Ra in it, and under that is the dark of the underworld with Apep in many, many coils facing the God Atum who is there to keep him from devouring the sun. Except of course it has changed now."

Suddenly she stopped and turning, took Robin's hand. When she looked up into his eyes, he saw hers shiny with unshed tears. "What, darling, what?" he whispered.

She gripped his hand tighter, "It's just hit me, I've never, never been here before. Never at the door of an ancient tomb in the Valley of the Kings about to go in and down and see, really SEE it."

"Of course," he said. "I can see how that is, that is your dream, the dream that kept you going when everything was almost unbearable, somehow you escaped to ancient Egypt. And as much of it as you've experienced of Egypt already, this, this is the bit you always dreamed of. Well, we'll go now, together. I cherish you, I will keep you safe and I will embrace this new special adventure with you, if you will have me."

"Of course I will have you, of course. You are the person I was meant to do this with. Your heart knows how special it is."

Chapter 34

All the rest followed in single file, except Lilac, Peony and Dark Moon, who waited close to the entrance since they had no talents to bring to solving the mystery, and they could stand guard invisibly in the unlikely case that someone should come their way. The spy dragons kept their wings tight against their bodies and tails tucked under to avoid any possibility of brushing against the walls. It was quite a long way down, and even though the night outside was very cool, deep inside the tomb it was very warm.

Kate and Robin stopped immediately they stepped off the last stair onto the floor of the tomb with the side of the massive stone sarcophagus facing them, but they hardly looked at it, turning to the right where facing them from the wall was the painting that had so distressed Bastet.

But Kate was also in thrall to the fact that she was seeing the beautifully decorated inside of a Royal tomb, the actual room with the painted sarcophagus and all the walls completely covered in beautiful images. She stood and drank it in like a magic elixir, even while holding onto their purpose for being there.

The background of the walls was painted

blue, except around the figure in the sun barge, where he stood facing forward in a white box, perhaps to indicate his sun god persona. Or, since there was yet another depiction of Apep completely surrounding the box, more likely it was to protect the image with the disc of Ra on his head from the Serpent of Chaos in its unending nightly attempt to destroy the sun and bring chaos and destruction to the Egyptian world. There were only two other people in the long barge with him, one before and one behind.

Lighting the special torches that gave them clear vision of the walls without, Julien promised, any harm to the frescos, Kate, Robin and Perry went closer to the one they were there to examine.

"Who is that in the barge?" asked Robin. "It should be Ra? Or not—his head could be a ram but it's *green.*

Perry had some research papers on his phone. "I think in this case this is supposed to be Ra as a ram with ram's horns and a sort of standard sun disc such as many of the gods and the pharaohs wear, but there is also the interpretation that the white box that surrounds him is also the sun disc Ra, and it is protecting the God Ra from Apep, who is surrounding the white box. Ah, here there is information—even more confusing—Ra was pictured as a beetle, phoenix, heron, serpent, bull, or lion among others. *But* it says when Ra was in the Underworld, he usually had a ram's head. I think therefore we can take it that this is Ra because the sun barge is definitely in the underworld here."

"But *green*?" asked Kate.

"I have no idea," confessed Perry. "Artist's license perhaps. Also, it is confusing that the snake appears surrounding the white box and again below. I think we must accept that the tomb painters were given a lot of room for self-expression.

"For instance, the hieroglyphs talk about the assembly of the gods, yet there are only two other figures in the sun barge, and as they have ordinary human heads it is doubtful they are gods. So, again to the Egyptian way of seeing things, possibly saying in hieroglyphs that there is an assembly of gods means it isn't necessary to picture them as well. Atum, the first and most powerful god, is below, and should be able to repel Apep, which he was doing quite efficiently, until the picture changed."

Underneath the sun barge there was a huge snake, its many coils meant to indicate just how large he was. This was also Apep, God of Chaos. In the pictures they had on their cameras it showed this Apep as docilely facing the creator God Atum, whose staff was keeping Apep at bay. But, just as Bastet had described, now on the wall the serpent's head was turned toward the viewer, its jaws open showing the forked tongue and the fangs and a look of menace. In the fresco, Atum appeared not to have changed at all, just standing there as if he wasn't aware of anything different. Robin had to mentally shake himself, he had somehow expected Atum to be either attempting to repel or perhaps beating the no longer docile serpent.

"Where are the altered hieroglyphs?" asked Kate.

Perry was scanning the wall as well as the picture he had on his camera. "I honestly can't tell. I don't read them well, you know, and there are so many of them around the pictures. Plus it's possibly only one hieroglyph, the one that indicates 'unable to repulse'. But I'm sure we can take Bastet's word for it that they have changed."

"Do you suppose," asked Silver, "that the somewhat unfinished aspect of this whole wall fresco could account for it being chosen as a possible place to start Apep's entry back as a living God? I mean, the hieroglyphs saying one thing and the picture showing another. Maybe those other gods should have been pictured to make certain of Ra's safety?"

"That's definitely another possibility," allowed Perry. "We'll ask Bastet and Chauncey and Imhotep, who know a lot more about Egyptian iconography that we do. I have read that in ancient

Egyptian, the word is the thing—to say something is the same as doing or having it. It may work that way here, the hieroglyphs saying the Gods cannot repel Apep serves the same purpose as a picture showing that happening. We will ask Imhotep and Chauncey. But we should get out of your way now and let the four of you see if you have other senses that can pick up what we aren't getting—if there's anything."

Each of the dragons starting with Silver and ending with Dawn came carefully close to the wall fresco and allowed themselves to be open to any 'vibrations' they might experience. They did not share these out loud so as not to influence any of the others, but afterward they retreated to the back of Ramses' tomb, and each spoke of what they had experienced. Perry made sure this was getting recorded on more than one phone, so no data would be lost.

The combined information they gathered was both informative and confusing. Some sort of a magical being or ancient Egyptian minor deity had been there at the wall with the fresco. It had happened within the past year. The thing was described as smelling like a rodent, but with undertones of rotting flesh. *So not a god then* thought Perry. There was also another objectionable smell that Dawn identified as being like a Shield or Stink Bug. *Two different animals or one?* Perry

made a mental note.   And
they agreed that the changes to the fresco had to be
magical because there was definitely no change to
the painted image made by using paint or any other
substance, it was as if the change had used exactly
the same materials and just moved them around
without touching them. They hadn't sensed any
spells, but spells by small ugly magical beings
weren't something they could sense, so it didn't
mean it hadn't happened.

        Now each of the Misfits came forward and,
clearing their minds and saying a small spell to
increase sensitivity to what had happened to the
fresco, they stood in silence, concentrating. Again
they gathered at the back of the tomb and exchanged
information.

        Kate said, "The dragons sensed some really
unpleasant small magical being, and I have a clear
mind picture of it—it's a rat-like thing that seems to
be in a state of decaying, as if it had been dead for
some time, yet it is alive and, yes, it is wearing as if
it were some sort of armour, wings like shields, and
they appear to be rusty, in keeping with the general
look of something old and falling apart. But rather
than moving like a decrepit thing that is dead or
dying, it is quite quick. I think it was doing spells on
the fresco, since it—the fresco that is—was changing
slowly while the rat-bug was making gestures and

saying things I couldn't hear. So were these hieroglyphs here." And she showed her phone to them.

Perry took close-up photos of the wall where Kate could point out that a few hieroglyphs had been altered.

Robin added, "This happened less than a month ago, only about a week or so before Bastet saw it. And whatever the thing was, and I will make a guess that it is one of Apep's little army of demons, that are written about, since he is the only god to have any sort of army. Anyway, he was absolutely enjoying what he was doing and thought it a good joke, but also had the serious purpose of adding some power to his 'boss' (well, that seems to be how he thinks of Apep)."

Feral also, although wrinkling his nose in disgust, and later cleaning his paws where he had stepped where the little demon had walked, confirmed the rodent look of the demon, and added that it was about twice the size of a rat.

They then had about a half an hour where they simply enjoyed the beauty of the tomb frescos and the immensity of the sarcophagus. They didn't sense any other changes in the rest of the walls, and Perry was more inclined to agree with Silver that the disjunction between what the hieroglyphs said about the gods and the lack of pictured gods had made it easier to make the change.

Chapter 35

The group made their way back up the long tunnel and out into the Valley of the Kings. Kate carefully locked the door and wiped the key before putting it in her pocket.

Robin hugged her and whispered, "I'm sorry this is the only tomb you've gotten to see so far, but we will come back before we set sail."

Perry added, "Oh, yes, it only makes good sense to explore all the tombs we can both for the pleasure of it, and to sense any disturbances. But I doubt that there will be important things to find, unless small clues. We are thinking that if a festival of belief is the key to re-animating an old god, then that will be what Apep is planning. And he won't be able to do that here in the Valley or in or around the temple complexes of Luxor or Karnak."

"But what about the big flat area around the Colossi of Memnon? That seems just perfect for a large gathering, and they could put up a stage between those two huge statues of Amenhotep the Third." said Robin.

"That would work for a God like Bastet—a God associated with protection and kindness. Tourists and Egyptians would gather and the enjoy a festival to honour one of those," replied Perry. "But when the God of Chaos, a huge python- or anaconda-like snake appears with his demon army it would cause a general panic, and troops would be called in. No, I'm betting that if Apep is holding a festival to add to his power it will be well away from tourist areas, and intended to demonstrate his power, which is usually by earthquakes or floods or violent storms that hide the sun or show that he is able to shake the underworld and therefore the earth itself."

"But who will go to it then, who will see it?" queried Kate.

"To be honest, I don't know," replied Perry.

Silver said, "Talking to our father, Chen Shi—he has said Imhotep, who has made a study of all the ages of Egyptian civilisation —after all he was here for most of them—has plans for thwarting Apep to the extent of keeping Bastet safe for eons to come. I don't know what these are, but our research is important to choosing how and what plans to put in place. So we do the ground work and our esteemed father and the Lord Imhotep will use our information to make this happen. We can trust them, they have powers the old gods do not.

"I do know that our first and longest job will be to search along the Nile for places of power and see if any of them bear hallmarks of Apep or this demon army, especially recent ones. There are no temples or places dedicated to Apep, so we must check out all the temples and places that radiate ancient power from here to Aswan and Lake Nasser."

Robin had been musing on the differences between a Chaos God of Evil who wasn't worshipped and the other Egyptian Gods, who, although changeable and even wicked occasionally, were worshipped, had temples, priests, and offerings. What would Apep do to declare himself in this world?

Robin had an idea. "I think it could be that Apep will have a festival of sorts. A kind of Kiss, Black Sabbath or Alice Cooper type—all heavy metal—I bet his demons might be able to conjure up some of that. Everyone dancing after a lot of drink and drugs—and then Apep appears, just on stage and makes a storm happen. That's what I'd do if I wanted to get attention and start up belief. Not worship, because he's never been worshipped, but attention and a display of power."

"Do you think he could do that in a tourist area?" asked Kate. "I mean, they would come, they would party, but mostly they wouldn't be Egyptians. And even if he doesn't need worship, doesn't he need belief? Tourists wouldn't believe that a staged event with a python and a storm was a real thing, they'd just think it was special effects."

"And it would have to be like a Rave, those things that were so popular in the 80s, where they happened almost spontaneously," said Perry. "Otherwise, a proper rock concert or festival involves all sorts of licenses and permissions. I'm betting Apep doesn't have either the staff or the patience to deal with bureaucracy—if his, err, personality is what we've been led to believe, unadulterated evil, he would just explode with wrath. Might get noticed, but by all the wrong people."

"So we're back to thinking he or his demons will probably schedule such a thing in an area without tourists, and where the government wouldn't know about it," said Silver. "My personal bets are on areas around some of the ancient temples and/or the quarries down by Aswan. There are only a few popular tourist destinations, and the area is without the kind of policing that would discover it ahead of time.

"But there are lots and lots of Egyptians who still live all around there, and work for archaeologists during the season and farm or do other jobs when the digging season isn't on. They would go, they would definitely be impressed, a lot of them would believe it is Apep, so it would increase his power."

"Of course we don't know that this is what is actually being planned, but it makes sense, and he's got the example of how successful it has been for Bastet," said Perry. "The changing of the fresco by his demons—ok, yes, Robin, 'minions' if you must—is like an advertisement that something is going to happen. Maybe we will find more of them."

"So in essence we are still going to check out every temple, quarry and area where we can sense ancient power between here and Aswan," said Silver.

Robin was looking at his phone, "Ah, guys, it appears there already are some bands call Apep, with album covers showing the solar boat, and song titles like 'The Innovation of the Deathless One'. Will that mean that Apep can't use the concert idea?"

Perry checked the listings, "No, there have been several called Apep, that one seems to have got the farthest, but the others just flickered and died. There's nothing to stop Apep from doing his thing, if that is his thing. After all, he is the *real* Apep. But these guys seem to have done their homework all right—the titles of the songs are great, all about the nightly journey of the solar boat and the gates and how to get through the night. We should get a copy."

This discussion about the myriad possibilities of finding Apep and doing something definitive about him had taken them back along the path between the tombs almost to the guard's hut.

Now Kate intervened. "What? And give it to him for inspiration? We're getting off track here. Ancient Egypt and all its stories and gods and legends and treasure—everybody loves it. No surprise that some bands have called themselves Apep. Maybe Apep has hired one, even," said Kate. "If there's a rock concert, maybe Alice Cooper will show up to carry Apep. Come on, guys, it's not the point. The point is to find out where he is and if and how he is gaining power to challenge Bastet. Then we help Chauncey and Imhotep develop a plan to neutralise him again. That's our job, and Silver's right, we are going hunting." Turning to Silver she asked, "What's the itinerary?"

"The dragons of the Egyptian Principality who read hieroglyphs will examine the temples of Karnak and Luxor for any other changes that indicate Apep is rising. You humans with copies of all the decorations on the walls and ceilings of the tombs here in the Valley of the Kings will spend the next few days doing the same inside all the tombs. Chen Shi has arranged for you to have special access to any tombs with decorations that are presently closed to tourists. We are counting on Perry particularly to spot any changes in the hieroglyphs but you all should be able to spot any changes in the frescos that might pertain to the afterlife, the sun barge or Apep."

Oh, my stars! I get to see all the tombs in the next few days, even the ones that aren't usually open! Kate's grin caught Robin's attention and he grinned back. He knew exactly what she was thinking.

Having reached the guards' hut, they became quiet. But the guard was still soundly asleep. Kate unlocked the door, and Feral took the key back to the box on the wall and hung it on the hook numbered KV16. Then they left the guard to sleep it off and walked to where Lilac and Dark Moon and Jade River were waiting behind some rocks that concealed them from both the hut and anyone walking in the area.

Silver finished imparting his information. "Back at the dahabeeyah are maps of the Nile in detail from here to Aswan, showing all the tourist sites, all the temples and other workings of man, like quarries or villages that aren't for tourists and other maps showing buried evidence of any of these things. My spy dragons and I will take off each morning and fly some two hours or so ahead of you to examine every one of these. I will have my mind-to-mind connection with Imhotep and Chen Shi who can read and interpret any hieroglyphs we find. Dawn will return most nights to the dahabeeyah to spend time with Elvira and Feral and the rest of you and to get a good night's sleep. She will join us each time we return to share what we have found, probably every other day. If we have found anything we think she might help with, we will take her there. But we'll proceed slowly and carefully over each possibility. Meanwhile you on the dahabeeyah will behave like normal tourists, taking a leisurely Nile cruise and stopping at every point of interest. Apep shouldn't notice you at all."

Chapter 36

Everyone returned to the dahabeeyah, where there was a buffet ready of all sorts of foods from snacks to filling stews and extra dragon food as well. Elvira was so pleased to see Dawn and Feral and they both rushed to her. Dawn had watched how Feral would rub his head against Elvira's and she now did the same thing, very, very gently, and settled beside her like a big dog, with Feral in Elvira's lap and Elvira's arm around Dawn's neck.

It made Kate, Robin and Perry very happy. Their potentially dangerous, totally misfit dragonet had become the kind of misfit they all were and appreciated. They were family, human witches, dragons, cats, Egyptian goddess, and fae, all together, working at what they were best at, and bonding more closely with every adventure.

Now Kate told them that for the next few days they would explore the temples at Karnak and Luxor looking for anything that might indicate that Apep was using or planning to use the temple areas to increase his power through increased belief. She showed them the changed hieroglyphs in Ramses' tomb and explained how they'd each used their magical strengths to make a sort of picture of the creature who had, magically, altered the story.

"Using all the knowledge we each could gather we figured out that this was a rat or rodent-like creature with some insect features, mainly shield like wing casings over its back, that also left a smell similar to what we commonly call a 'stink bug' or 'shield bug'. This thing was also sort of 'rotten' in parts, as if it had been dead for more than a few days, and that stench plus the look of it made it quite repulsive. We think this is one of App's demon army. We don't know if all the others look similar or are the same size, for all we know they could all be different. But this one was definitely Apep's minion, and also left behind feelings of a sort of excitement and even thought what it was doing was fun, as well as increasing Apep's power. However, if they have a lack of any kind of morality it would fit with their master's reputation as being unalloyed evil. So his demon army are perhaps like juvenile-delinquent followers, totally without empathy, enjoying destruction. Unless some are larger, we'd have to be careful if we ran into a lot of them at once. Otherwise, I'd say more of a nuisance than a big threat. Apep is still the big threat."

Putting his arm around Kate, Robin told them, "Then while Silver's spy group continue up the Nile, we on *Heka* get unlimited and special access to all the tombs in the Valley of the Kings, looking as before for any evidence of Apep, any changes. It's a once in a lifetime treat as well as a detective job—very few people get to see all the tombs." Kate's smile was glowing.

Perry picked up the story as Silver had laid it out. "After that, ladies and gentlemen, we will be sailing *Heka* on a leisurely cruise up the Nile, stopping at each of the tourist attractions, ancient temples, archaeological digs, quarries and any other place that the stealth dragons, Silver's spies, have identified as having been a locus of power in the past. In this way we hope not only to gain more knowledge, but also to discover where Apep is planning to throw his own version of a rave, probably a rock concert. If, indeed, that is part of his plan. We think that it is quite likely, because he has and will never attract worshippers, or have temples, prayers and offerings from priests. But it will increase belief so he will want to attract as many actual Egyptians as possible, because it is their belief that will increase his power. And as it will be in the nature of a rave, to avoid local or national government license or permissions, it will have to be in a place removed from usual tourist spots, but also in a place of ancient power."

"If that's the case," offered Elvira, "there are only a few places along the Nile from here to Aswan that answer all those requirements. My guess would be the quarries at Gebel-el-Silsila. They are the source of much of the stone used to build the temples and tombs of the Middle and Late Kingdoms. And because generations of ordinary Egyptians spent their lives working there, there are also villages and very substantial temples amongst the quarries, so there was a priestly class and governmental class as well as a large working class. The area is still busy with archaeologists and local workers, but there is almost no tourist trade there. They could hold a rave amongst the valleys of the quarries and be gone before any police showed up, plus attract a large contingent of local Egyptians and those working the digs. We could save a lot of meticulous searching perhaps."

"Only if that is indeed what Apep and his minions are actually planning. We still need to carefully work with all the other sites to find any evidence of Apep and any possible alterations. These might tell us that he is planning something quite different, or in a very different location, or might give us insight into other ways he is accumulating power to rise again," Robin said. "Sorry, and all that, but we are going to be going over every place as carefully as possible. We can take some consolation from the fact that Silver's spies will have to be going over all of them even more intensively than we are and will be directing us where to spend our energies."

He turned to Kate. "It does seem, however, that your wish to see all the sights is being granted, even if it is in conjunction with searching for evidence. There is no reason why you, in fact all of us, shouldn't also enjoy the wonder and beauty of these unique places while we also scan them for evidence of the Chaos God."

"Absolutely!" said Kate. "And isn't it totally typical of us that a wonderful sightseeing expedition should be in conjunction with the hunt for an evil entity?"

"I wouldn't expect anything else," remarked Perry without a hint of sarcasm. "It appears to be what we do."

Their laughter rang out over the water, causing a flock of Sacred Nile Ibis to take off.

§ § §

Late the next afternoon, after the heat of the day and the majority of tourists were gone, the group arrived at the Karnak temple complex, having given the search of the temple complex over to Silver's spies the night before.

Karnak was significantly older than Luxor Temple complex and held the work of many pharaohs. As writing and acknowledgement of Apep was more often found in the ruins of later dynasties, they didn't expect to find much relating to that, but were excited to be seeing this ancient holy place.

Kate, as always, had been reading up on it and now gave them a potted history. "It's the largest temple complex ever created," she told them as they walked up the long avenue toward the huge pylons that marked the entrance, "and is nearly four thousand years old now, being started around 2055BCE as a cult temple dedicated to the major gods Amun, Mut and Khonsu. Ah, I haven't heard of that last one. Anyway, it stayed in use until about 100 AD.

"Being the largest building for religious purposes ever constructed, the Karnak Temple was known as 'most select of places' by ancient Egyptians. With continuous additions, it became eventually a village of many smaller buildings as well as the main temple complex. In addition to its religious significance, it also served as a treasury, administrative centre, and palace for the New Kingdom pharaohs. Even now it's thought to be the largest temple complex ever constructed anywhere in the world.

"During the New Kingdom, the Karnak Temple Complex was the centre of the ancient faith while power was concentrated at Thebes (modern-day Luxor) and its significance is reflected in its enormous size. Because of Karnak, Thebes became the centre of power in Egypt during all that time. Just imagine it—for over fifteen hundred years, each pharaoh added temples, sanctuaries, pylons and halls and obelisks to memorialise themselves and their power."

Perry added, "They were certainly trying to outdo each other in the size and importance and sheer 'muscle' of decoration and expense. And they weren't above trying to obliterate previous pharaohs when they had a grudge. In fact, one of the best-known pharaohs with the exception of King Tut, Hatshepsut, was nearly totally wiped out of history by her stepson Thutmose the Third. He claimed all her fabulous work, as one of the few female pharaohs, as his own and tried to erase her entirely. He nearly succeeded, but painstaking archaeology has reclaimed so much that is hers, from the journey to the land of Punt to her memorial temple set into the cliffs of Deir el-Bahari and a lot more, including the enormous obelisk now sited in the middle of a temple to Thutmose—mainly because he couldn't get it moved! Careful research has found evidence for her cartouche and hieroglyphs telling of her achievements, nearly destroyed by Thutmose and replaced with his own name."

"We'll never, not even with weeks, be able to check this enormous place carefully enough to find evidence of Apep," said Robin.

"Not to worry," remarked Feral, strolling along ahead of them his tail erect and waving like a tour guide's flag. "The spy dragons said they will leave little markers that I will be able to smell if they find any evidence of Apep or his minions. Our job is to scan over the whole place in a general sort of way because we might pick up other evidence of magic or just the sense of something out of place."

"What, with all the tourists and all the years all piled up together?" asked Perry.

"We all have different areas of special abilities to sense things," said Kate. "So, yes, that may well be true. Anyway, it's a starting place, because of its age and location no one really expects to find anything important, but we can't afford to just leave it either."

They separated at this point, each going off to see things that held special interest for them. Kate and Robin, arms around each other, walked slowly into the Great Hypostyle Hall. Kate, who although she knew much of its story, was reading bits off her phone to Robin.

"Apparently until recently it was believed that this magnificent hall was created by Horemheb or Amenhotep the Third. But now they say it was entirely created by Seti the First who is also responsible for the engravings of the northern wing. The decoration of the southern wing was completed by Ramses the Second.

"Oh, now this *is* interesting—the pillars represent the prehistoric papyrus in a lake or swamp from which Atum—the first god, self-created apparently—rose up at the beginning of creation. Oh! Wonderful, my favourite Pharaoh, Queen Hatshepsut's mortuary temple at Deir el-Bahari is the prototype for the design. This style of pillar representing papyrus was initially used in the chapel to Amun there. I'm looking forward so much to seeing that."

"So those huge pillars are the papyrus growing out of the primordial swamp? Okay, I can just about see that," said Robin. "But please tell me what 'hypostyle' means. Does it have anything to do with hippopotamuses? I could see that it would be a lovely place for a hippo if you included the swamp part. And really, those enormous round pillars look a lot more like a hippo's legs than a papyrus."

"Yeah, I see what you mean, Robin. But no, it's an architectural term, and has to do with having pillars to support the roof— the roof that is no longer here. So 'hypostyle' is a roof resting on pillars or columns rather than on arches. The word literally means 'under pillars.

"There's a lot more about different pharaohs adding inscriptions and decoration, and sometimes erasing, or trying to erase, some previous pharaoh's work. Ramses the Second also went over the decorations of the main processional ways, so most people think it was all his work. Sounds just like him, doesn't it? Self-important, grandiose."

"Honestly, I wouldn't know," replied Robin. "Although his stuff does crop up a lot, and usually it's very big."

"Well, that's how to ensure your immortality, lots of monuments, statues, and your name all over everything," laughed Kate. "Although they were awfully cavalier about abolishing their ancestors. Plus the tomb robbers, they didn't seem to have much interest in keeping their pharaohs alive in an afterlife."

"Still, it's in these later dynasties that Apep gets so much attention and appears so often as this much feared God of Chaos, total destruction," remarked Robin. "I wonder if that came about because the pharaohs of these times were so incredibly self-aggrandizing. Maybe something in the psyche of the people and the rulers felt there needed to be a big bad god who could potentially wipe them out."

"That's a really intriguing hypothesis," said Perry. who had caught up with them. "And, if you think about it, if Amun was self-created as the first god, and rose out of a primordial swamp, then the idea of the one great Chaos God that cannot be destroyed or changed living in a primordial swamp under the world is a very good one too."

Chapter 37

They spent two days in Karnak and another in the temple of Luxor, going over every inch of the temples, tombs, palaces, and halls. No signs of Apep except the occasional hieroglyph or illustration. There was nothing that indicated that he was on the rise. It was frustrating at times even for Kate, whose enthusiasm for these sites and learning more about them was almost endless. Almost but not quite.

As they walked along another avenue between the partially destroyed statues and those that had been reconstructed, she told Robin, "I never thought I'd say this, but even I am getting quite full up with so many statues and painted walls and hieroglyphs that I can't read. I'm having some trouble remembering who built what and when."

Robin laughed, "No I never thought I'd hear you say that either, but now you know how the rest of us feel. I can see being astonished, overwhelmed, and excited to spend a few hours, but this is getting to be 'much of a muchness', particularly when there are no clues to find. I suppose if we could read the walls or remember, as you say, who did what when it wouldn't all begin to look a bit same old same old. But I'm afraid it does."

They were now walking along the Nile back

toward *Heka* when he suddenly noticed that she wasn't wearing a hat. "Hey, no hat, you could be very sorry later if you have sunburn. Did you forget it? I should have noticed and got it for you."

Kate laughed and did a bit of a twirl, "Yeah, no hat. I don't need it. Chauncey found out that I have always had to protect myself artificially from the sun, and he gave me this great present."

"Present? He has the world's best sun block?"

"In a manner of speaking. You know how all the dragons change colours for lots of reasons? Well, one of them is to provide varying degrees of sun protection, it's built-in and happens automatically. And somehow, I'd never said to him how I wished there was a spell I could do to keep me from getting sunburn and even allow me to tan a bit. Well, I did tell hm the other day when I was chatting with him and Feral and Feral turned me into a ginger cat! Can you imagine? I looked down and there I was, a very large ginger cat!"

Robin was indeed looking astonished. "So being a ginger cat kept you from sunburn?"

"Yes, yes it would have. But Chauncey made him change me back. He said it was not a good idea to change someone so entirely, and not to a cat when cats could be in danger from Apep. I was quite sad about losing the ability to withstand the sun though, so Chauncey questioned me about it and then he gave me the little part of colour changing that the dragons use to provide complete sun protection, which includes being a shade or two darker than I was. I was waiting for you to notice."

Robin looked embarrassed. "I've been concentrating too much on our job. I think I did register you looked particularly relaxed and were looking just, well, good in the kind of heat you usually suffer in a bit, but our minds were on other things." He hugged her, "But I'm totally delighted for you, I know you've been frustrated by not being able to find a spell that would do this. Will this last, is it a spell Chauncey did? You aren't going to get scaly, are you?" His gold eyes were twinkling in a way that made her know he was teasing about the last bit.

"Would you stop loving me if I went all scaly? Would it be too much? What about if I could then change colours like the dragons? Think of the savings on buying clothes!" By this time they were both laughing, hugging each other to keep from stumbling.

"Seriously, Chauncey would never do anything to or with me that wasn't totally safe and for my good," said Kate. "He wouldn't let the ginger cat thing last; it might have had a lot of problems besides any sun protection. Feral was showing off, like Feral does. I think he also meant it as a joke, not something to be stuck with. But I'm glad he did, because it got me to tell Chauncey about this annoying problem I had, and he had the cure for it. I got just the tiniest bit of what you might call epidermal dragon, and it has solved the one problem without any side effects.

Robin nodded, "Yes, we can trust Chauncey totally. Not just that he cares for us, but he's had so many centuries to learn things and to study humans." They'd reached their dahabeeyah by then.

"What's next on the agenda, by the way?"

"We have some maps of the Nile with all the old temples, the villages, any ancient site all marked out. Plus Silver and the others have marked some you can't see—just mounds or even just dessert that resonates with power. They are going first a couple days ahead and will tell us which ones we should also spend time with. The first of course is another two or three days in the Valley of the Kings—I finally get to really see that properly! And at least part of a day at Hatshepsut's Mortuary Temple at Deir elBahari, which looks almost like modern architecture of the best sort in the pictures I've seen. After that it's on up the Nile stopping at all the tourist places, and a lot of places tourists don't go, like the digs and the quarries and anywhere the spy dragons call our attention to."

The next few days were indeed the days Kate had dreamed of. In a loose adaptation of ancient Egyptian dress, she wore white with turquoise and lapis necklace and bracelets set in gold and comfortable sandals that were also decorated with turquoise and lapis. She felt like this was only appropriate for going the places she'd spent her life dreaming about. Although her childhood books depicted Egyptians as having black hair (or wigs, they were mostly wigs), there were also redheads among those ancient people, including some pharaohs and their women. So she was proud to wear her hair loose and flowing, or in a long braid. or piled up on her head.

Arrangements had been made that they would not be among large crowds of tourists or hassled by the vendors trying hard to make a living selling postcards and other souvenirs. Robin had dressed as usual in lightweight beige trousers and white shirt, but with his tan and his gold eyes and black hair he was as striking as Kate. Elvira was also as usual in a multi-coloured kaftan, and Feral either strolled alongside her or draped around her shoulders. When she needed a bit of a rest, it seemed a chair would appear out of nowhere. No one amongst the guards and guides questioned this, and they began to realise that some bribes or magic had been done to keep them from being bothered. Dawn was two days ahead of them with Silver, Tigris, and Amazon. When they got to their first stop after Deir el-Bahari, she'd rejoin them for a day of rest and some family time with Elvira and Feral.

Meanwhile, they strolled the wooden walkways and the stone floors of the tombs, enchanted by the wall paintings and the carvings. All the mummies and any movable sculptures or objects had long ago been taken, first by looters, then by 'collectors' to go to museums across the world, and finally by the Egyptians who were also working to preserve the walls and frescoed ceilings, even the floors and the occasional giant sarcophagus still in place. Feral could smell or otherwise sense any trace of Apep's demon army, and so far, there had been none.

Chapter 38

D K was mustering his band, D K & The Apepatones. They were proving less than amenable to learning to play actual instruments, most of which were larger than they were. So he was improvising with a variety of child-sized instruments ordered off the internet and a selection of the demons who could carry a tune but in voices with something in common with the Heavy Metal and Death Metal bands of the 70s and 80s. He also got hold of a drum machine and an electronic keyboard (much smaller than a real piano and much more rock 'n roll too). Determined to be up front, he appointed himself lead singer and keyboard player.

"But you can't play that, I've heard you, it's awful," said his best mate, Slime. Somewhat to Slime's surprise, D K didn't lash out at him, but smiled smugly and replied, "No I can't, I found that out. I'm not *stupid* ya know. See, it has a whole repertoire of tunes already installed."

"A whole rep-what?" questioned Slime.

"*Repertoire! Repertoire!* you stupid scumbag. It means selection, or bunch of songs and all you have to do is press one of the keys and it plays a tune. Meanwhile, I can be making playing motions and singing.   "I ain't stupid neither," whined Slime. "And Scumbag is me brover. I know we looks similar, but you know better than that.

"Yeah, yeah. Sorry. So do you have an instrument you can play?"

When Slime shook his head, D K said, "You look like a real rocker, so I want you up front, it'll have to be a guitar."

Slime 'auditioned' on various of the guitars D K had acquired. He couldn't play them, but he did get some amazing screeches from the electric tenor guitar that D K thought should work with Heavy Metal. He announced that Slime would be their lead guitarist. Slime was overcome, but then proposed that as part of the band he wanted to change his name to Slyme, which did look better.

Other potential guitarists were discarded one after another until Doom, who sported six appendages, two legs and four arms, brought forth amazing sounds from the bass guitar and was given the job. Another of his physical type got the job of drummer. The noise was, well, hellish. "Good!" pronounced D K.

All these instruments were electric, but there was no electricity and even they couldn't 'magic' a large generator hundreds of miles into the desert, but D K and several of the others could use magic to take the place of electricity. They included plenty of sparks to add excitement.

And D K presented all the band, including the backing singers, with earphones and old iPods loaded with Heavy and Death Metal music until they were totally caught up with the beat and the screaming or basso singing. D K also acquired a huge marquee with the back side a large screen on which he projected soundless videos of human Heavy Metal bands, plus Alice Cooper and his snake and Iggy Pop crowd surfing.

When they were practiced to his satisfaction, he presented the results to Apep and explained that they would be chanting his name in the chorus of all the songs, and at the end of the concert proper, Apep could make a brief appearance if he wanted. Or they could film him, again briefly, saying something friendly.

"I don't do 'friendly' you misbegotten whelp of a Tasmanian Devil and a cockroach!" snarled Apep.

"No, no, of course not, Your Dreadfulness," D K hurried to agree. "But this is about your first festival appearance, and it is all about attracting *favourable* attention. So a *very* brief appearance and a friendly word or two will go a long way."

"I have a better idea," said Apep, proving he hadn't been quite as ignorant of his minions' efforts as they'd thought. "These human Metal guys, they don't go all friendly at the end, they sign off with some kind of mix of scary and 'keep coming back'. I could do that, be very scary and drip a little poison and say something like "I'm back, risen from the dark depths, and you will all belong to me.' Then a big thunderclap and everything goes dark. Then lights come up and you feed them and give them more drugs and drinks."

"And you promise not to eat any of them, or squeeze them, or us?" Slyme asked carefully.

"I do so promise," said Apep. "I can see this is part of the plan to return me to full strength, and I will play along. But if I am to appear in person, I suggest you have a good feast for me arranged when I disappear in the dark and thunder. Or, perhaps, since it seems you can do this, I will appear looking smaller on the film screen, and I won't have to attend this spectacle at all."

D K thought this latter idea would be by far the best and was only relieved that his master had thought of it himself.

Grovelling appropriately, he said "As my master wishes, always the most brilliant ideas. You will be spared the noise and the crowds and not terrify them with your actual enormous appearance. We do not want to scare them to begin with. Thank you, oh Gracious Ghastliness.

Meanwhile the dragon spies started to discover recent evidence of Apep's demons in various places along the Nile Valley. Most surprisingly on small stone stelae on the outskirts of villages where small hieroglyphs of the God of Chaos and his picture plus a strange amalgam of hieroglyphs and paintings of the heavy metal band either incised on the stelae or painted on mud brink walls.

Chapter 39

The search party settled into a routine, where the four spy dragons went ahead to every tourist spot, every ruin, every place where Egyptologists had dug, past or present, and every place that they 'sniffed out' any buried ancient architecture.

Following a day or two behind came the dahabeeyah with the Kate and Robin, Perry, Ariane and Dmitri and Elvira and Feral on board, plus their dragon friends Lilac, Dark and Dandy Moon, taking in the sights like the tourists they were—but always aware that there might be more to it than that. Hatshepsut's Mortuary Temple had delighted Kate, and she'd showed Robin the ancient graffiti of two figures making love that could be identified as the Pharaoh Queen and her architect, Senenmut.

"Even then it was okay for a man to have multiple wives, and a harem, but not for women. However, I hope Hatshepsut and Senenmut were lovers," said Kate. "Because I've always felt sorry for Queen Elizabeth the First. Royal women could get in so much trouble if they strayed."

The morning before they were to reach the Temple of Esna, Kate woke up feeling a pleasant tickling on her back. "What are you doing, Robin?"

"Trying to write "Daughter of Dragons' in

hieroglyphs on your back," he said softly.

"But ancient Egyptian didn't have a word for Dragon," murmured Kate.

"I've been finding that out," he laughed softly, so I made one up, because the only thing close is either 'snake' or 'crocodile' and I'm not going to do that."

"You're not using ink, are you?" she said, waking up properly.

"No darling heart, just magic, and it will fade quickly. Anyway, I really just wanted to wake you up gently."

"It was gentle until you started about the snake or the croc," she said. But nevertheless she rolled over into his arms.

They spent the morning enjoying the Temple of Esna, its red sandstone and the beautifully carved lotus-leaf columns, the wall carvings. It was a very late temple in Egyptian history, made during the Ptolemaic period when Greece and then Rome ruled Egypt, but the Romans had gladly taken up Egyptian customs and lifestyles and built temples to Romano-Egyptian gods. Esna Temple was dedicated to Heka, the Egyptian god of magic and medicine, which made it even more special to them. For this reason the voyagers from *Heka* brought offerings of fruit and flowers and some ointments useful for skin diseases.

They disembarked at the temple of Kom Ombo, literally 'the hill of gold'. There were temples here from the time of Hatshepsut and Thutmose III, but the main building now was a beautifully preserved and restored temple built by the Ptolemies during the Greco-Roman era. It was unique in being exactly symmetrical and dedicated to the worship of two gods—Sobek, the crocodile god and Horus, the falcon god, over the the ruins of a much older temple to Sobek. Kate found it beautiful and Robin was amazed at the condition of much of it. The carvings were exceptional, and paint could still be seen at the tops of some pillars.

Then they went off to see the museum of mummified crocodiles. Here there was an armed guard, something they'd seen very rarely during their journey. But this was a large, efficient and mean looking weapon. Kate left Robin admiring how carefully a particular croc had been wrapped and went to ask the guard what kind of weapon it was.

"A Kalashnikov,' he said proudly.

"But why here?" she asked.

"There is still a, what you say, black market for mummies. I guard them." said the guard simply.

"Even for crocodiles?" asked Robin who had come over.

"Even these," the guard, whose name was Fawaz, replied. He and Robin discussed the gun a bit and then Fawaz asked if they wanted to see something interesting. He pulled a water bottle out of his jacket pocket and held it up. Inside was about an inch of water and a small snake.

"She is a cobra, I find her, only a baby, here in the temple this morning. When I get off duty, I will take her down to the reeds by the Nile. Maybe there is something for her to eat there. Maybe she will live, Inshallah." Kate asked what such a small cobra would eat.

"Big insects, small mice, who knows,?"

"Can I hold her?" Kate asked.

"No, missus, no, they are born with poison. She might not kill you, but if she bit you would be very sick. No, I let her go away from people."

"You don't kill them? asked Robin.

"No, many do, but I don't. Once they were revered, once they were royal. I am Muslim, but I think maybe the word of the Prophet could have sort of removed the old gods, they may have been here then, they are not now."

"So you think that they were once here but that the Prophet displaced them with his own faith?" Kate was fascinated.

"I don't know. I just feel that perhaps such a beautiful civilisation, such buildings, such stories—

well they say it was all lies or stories, but I sometimes think they might have been real for them then. But please do not repeat this, it is only that you like my snake. I would not like my friends here to think I am a, how you say, heretic."

Silver's group only reported very slight evidence of Apep or his demons, and those were either ancient or just like a quick stop, as if they too might be looking for something. The magic of the group on board *Heka* added little or nothing to this. Those with an interest in ancient Egypt, Kate especially, but Robin and Perry and Elvira too, were very happy to be seeing the places they stopped at, but the lack of evidence was also a bit of a nagging feeling.

"It's not a worry," said Kate. "After all we don't really want to encounter him or them planning something vicious, but I guess it's that we'd rather know than keep coming up empty. Because we do believe he's planning something, and we want to catch him at it and stop it."

But then the spy group returned full of excitement.

"We were right!" announced Dawn, skidding to a landing in the water near the dahabeeyah. "Well, Elvira was right all along!"

It was Silver who explained. "We've found evidence of what we thought they might decide to do to increase Apep's power. They're holding a big party this coming weekend in an area of that huge dig site at Gebel El Silsila."

"You see," said Feral, 'it's the one Elvira told us about, where most of the sandstone used during the Middle Kingdom was quarried. My mother knows things, she always knows things."

There was a short pause while everyone commented and congratulated Elvira on her wisdom, and then it was back to business.

Silver continued, "It seems that Apep's minions have been putting up signs attached to stelae and there have even been a few carved into new stelae, announcing a party with music, food and drink. It doesn't mention Apep by name but there are snake-like wavy lines and music is to be provided by the, ahem, 'famous' Heavy Metal Band 'DK and the Apepatones'.

"The archaeologists who have the digging permit for that area are away, so it will be aimed at the Egyptians who live around there and perhaps the occasional tourist, like us.

"So it's for sure they are trying to add to his power by holding a Rave in his name—although that name isn't exactly out there, and I'm sure they will have various tricks to show Apep as the one who has provided the entertainment, food and drink without scaring the population. Probably not bring up his identity until after everyone has been suitably mind-altered by music, dancing, drugs and drink. Then they'll be ready to yell approval at the devil himself."

Dawn approached Kate on the upper deck, where she showed Kate one of the posters that Silver was talking about. It was in red and black with writing in white. The writing however was not in Egyptian hieroglyphs, but modern Muslim characters and Kate had to admit she couldn't read it.

"Can I read it to you?" asked Dawn.

"You can read this!" exclaimed Kate, surprised.

Dawn seemed to blush slightly, but she spoke up quite confidently. "Learning to read and write and speak modern Egyptian has been part of my schoolwork. I'm not really fluent, at least not talking, but I can read it really well."

Kate felt something like a wave of pride and affection for this misfit dragon she had once feared might be a psychopath. "Oh, that's wonderful! I don't know any language but English, and I really think it's splendid that now you already know three. Yes, please read it."

"Okay, I'll translate as I go so it may be a little, em, patchy." And Dawn read. " 'In honour of the old gods of Egypt and a new age of belief, we will gather in the…err, it's a phrase I don't know, but I think it means 'place where they used to hold great festivals for the honoured dead'—Silver told me it's a big open, flat area surrounded by limestone hills where they both quarried stone for important buildings or sometimes buried important people who lived or worked here."

"Like an amphitheatre?" asked Kate.

"Yes, sort of like that, not like Roman ones— no seats." said Dawn. "Anyway 'to celebrate and listen to the great new Heavy Metal Band: D K and the Apepatones. This Heavy Metal Band will have you mesmerised. It will blow your mind! Free admission and free food and drink."

She'd been running one talon down the page as she read, and Kate saw that mentions of old gods and belief were in quite small print, while the band name and free food and drink were in large type. It was certainly attention getting, with red and red-gold flames against the black background.

Toward the bottom was the date and a list of the band members of D K and the Apepatones: D K - keyboards and vocals; Slyme - lead guitar; Doom - bass guitar; Sludge - drums.

Robin was leaning over Kate's shoulder, "I'll bet you my MX5 that with names like that those are some of Apep's demons and that D K is really 'decay'.

Chapter 40

No dragons could appear at the rave, so it was only Lilac and Dark Moon with Kate and Robin and Peony carrying Elvira and Feral who flew invisibly close to the big open area amidst the hills and valleys of Gebel el Silsila. The dragons let their passengers off some distance away and hid themselves inside a large opening in the rock face.

Silver, Dawn, Amazon and Tigris also few in invisibly, but settled themselves closer to the action on a cliff top to the side of what would be the stage, using their ability to adjust their colours to blend into the surroundings.

Kate, Robin and Elvira had all dressed themselves in what they hoped would be appropriate for a day of festival in Egypt. Robin had wanted to wear something similar to pictures and films he'd seen of 'the summer of love' in NYC in the 70s, and more recent club garb. But Kate and Elvira had argued that most of the participants would be local Egyptians and probably just where gallabiyahs or, possibly jeans and shirts. If women did attend, they would be wearing the usual galabia and a headscarf.

For a festival jewellery might be added. So Kate and Elvira wore gallabiyahs with colourful headscarves and necklaces in complimentary colours, in Kate's case, green and blue to set off her eyes and for Elvira gold and red. Although they wouldn't be taken for local Egyptians, except from a distance, dressing like the locals helped to blend in and could also be taken as complimentary. Feral disappeared. He would be close by, but even midnight black, he could take advantage of all the rocks and pillars and clefts in the stone. He wanted to be close to the actual minions, those mostly rodent-like little demons, to overhear anything of interest and if it worked out that way, maybe do a little hunting.

They'd arrived while recorded music by rock bands was playing, before the advertised D K and the Apepatones came on stage. The crowd was already dancing, swaying, jumping, and drinking and eating. There were a number that the Misfit's magic could tell were already well under the influence of drugs. They had brought their own snacks and water to drink. Who knew what would be available at the refreshment stands?

Music Kate knew well from NYC came over her in a wave from the speakers. She began to dance, swaying, stamping her feet, raising her arms above her head, closing her eyes until she tripped against a stone and nearly fell, but arms caught her, and she opened her eyes to see Robin's gold eyes near hers.

"I…I never saw you dance like that," he was saying.

"It's music my mother played, a band she got, err, 'involved' with I think in the 70s. I love this song though. Dance with me!"

She pulled him closer, and they swayed together. The song that followed was Jefferson Airplane, and Grace Slick's amazing voice. Even though they hadn't taken any substances, her embrace of this music and his closeness to her took them out of themselves. Fleetwood Mac followed and they just kept dancing.

Finally, hot, breathless and thirsty, they came to a stop. Moving away from the centre of things, they drank from their water bottles and Robin laughed.

"What? Why are you laughing?" but Kate was smiling too.

"You, you and me, we just went back in time sort of. And I loved how we were together. That must have been a magic time," said Robin. "We weren't even alive then, but it felt like we were there. Did you think so too?"

"Oh, yes, oh most definitely yes," said Kate, her green eyes sparkling. "But I think I need to sit down now for a bit."

They found a reasonably comfortable rock. "Funny I did enjoy that music when my mother played it, but was never swept away, and I was always thinking of how she knew how to spoil things for me, which I guess sort of spoilt it for me. But just now, here in the middle of Egypt, I was suddenly transported and swept up and forgot all the bad memories and just felt it all. It was good. Like, really good."

The recorded music had changed to some of the old heavy metal bands. Neither of them recognised most of it, but it came down hard and they saw Elvira dancing in a way they didn't really know old ladies could dance.

Some while later, as the sun was going down, after multi videos of Iron Maiden, Cradle of Filth, Black Sabbath and Motorhead, then finally a video of Alice Cooper plus boa constrictor started, lights came up on the stage at the front of the video.

And there, with a large but obviously phoney snake wrapped in and out of the live band, DK and the Apepatones appeared. They picked up on the music playing on the video, and the speakers, possibly with added magic got louder. And more discordant as the Apepatones became more front and centre. Kate and Robin moved in a vaguely dancing way through the crowd and closer to the stage, where they saw for the first time Apep's demons, or at least four of them.

"Look, Robin," whispered Kate, hanging herself against him in a very rock'n roll way, "D K there on keyboards, he's just like what I envisioned in Ramses tomb, the rodent body, the insect wings, sort of mouldy, even that sort of grin."

"Hard to grin with mandibles," muttered Robin, "but yeah, he is, isn't he. Still they are big rodenty things, more the size of small cats maybe. Gods, I wish there was a spell to make this cacophony more bearable."

Kate did know a spell and she muted the noise down considerably for them. They also moved out of the front and found a space off to the side where they could see everything but were out of the lights and the Egyptian night had come on, as usual, quite quickly. From there, and with the 'music' muted they were also able to make out that the chorus of the seemingly unending song was saying something that including a repetition of 'apep, apep, apep' along with the drumbeat.

What with drugs, booze and the cool of the evening, the crowd was getting wilder, and really stomping to the beat. some were writhing in the sand. Others jumping and falling. The songs changed but little, and the underlying chant of apep, apep went on along with the beat of the drums, Kate recognised it as a subliminal message, most of those listening to the band wouldn't hear it really, but their brains would register it.

Feral meanwhile was having a wonderful time at Apep's Rave. He'd loved being with Elvira at the Bubastis Festival for Bastet, but this was even more fun. Especially as many of Apep's demons were small and rodent-like or snakes. And most of them were of varying degrees of the genre 'horrible, ugh' but also made very satisfactory squeaks if he pounced on them. Feral had never been a cat to be put off by a dreadful shape, he would chase and catch and bite whether they scuttled on 4 legs or 8 or 20, it was all the same to him. As he was well fed, he didn't need to eat them, and a sample bite had convinced him these weren't something he'd eat even if he starved to death. But chasing and swatting a scuttling thing through the air, even a bit of killing, that was something else again. He was revelling in the carnage.

But behind him out of the dark something large was looping toward him. Soundless, it crept forward and then the front end rose up…and up. And the gaping maw lined with fangs opened wide. Feral just had time to notice the shadow, and turning beheld the mighty Chaos God himself, risen up and about to strike.

Then out of the shadows leapt a dragon.

Chapter 41

Not content to stay carefully hidden by the rocky escarpment and just observe, Dawn had drawn on both her new skills at lizard-like blending of her colours and her well-practiced invisibility to creep closer to Feral. She was concerned he had got over excited, or possibly even drugged in some way, to have so completely abandoned Elvira and the others and to be behaving like, well, like a cat having his own version of a rave.

She wasn't quite quick enough to stop Apep from striking, but she hurled herself at his head and knocked him sidewise, or he surely would have sunk his fangs through Feral's skull. As it was a fang slashed a long wound down Feral's side and knocked him flying. Then the great head turned toward Dawn. The force of her collision with him had knocked her to the ground also. There was a scuffle where dragon and snake were entangled and he had cut her with his fangs, but her talons slashed gashes along his sides. He tried to get her within his coils so he could squeeze the life out of her, but she was too quick, and she stomped down on his body with one of her hind feet, raking more bloody wounds, while he bit her front leg deeply. Her tail whipped around and the spines did some more damage, and she had nearly grabbed him by the neck when he also managed to spray some of his poison over her face and neck, causing her to scream.

This brought Feral, despite his wounded side, leaping off the rock outcrop above them and landing on the reptile's neck where he clawed around at Apep's face and managed to sink one claw into a corner of the old God's eye. Giving out his own hiss of pain and outrage, the snake withdrew, fading back into the dark among the rocks. Dawn and Feral were left lying in the sand.

The band and the general noise hadn't stopped, and the crowd was still in the grip of the beat and the mind-altering substances they'd consumed, but following Dawn's cry Silver had plummeted down from his outpost, and found Feral who screamed, "Get water, he has sprayed her head with venom, we must rinse it off."

Silver immediately withdrew to where the Misfits were coming toward the scene of carnage, luckily with water bottles. They rinsed Dawn's face and eyes, and managed to get her to rinse and spit water. She was in pain, but not unconscious. Kate, Robin, Feral and Elvira said spells for healing and for relief of pain. Elvira even remembered one for counteracting poisons.

Meanwhile, Silver, Tigris and Amazon

swooped down out of the sky and wrenched the board on which the videos had been projected loose and carried it to where Dawn lay.

This totally drove the crowd, who'd never seen a live dragon, into hysterics, and they fled the scene, trampling over each other on the way out of the area.

Laying the board down beside Dawn, the other dragons carefully lifted her onto it. Lilac, Peony, and Dark Moon joined them. It was quickly decided that Lilac would be the dragon at the fourth corner of the improvised stretcher, while Dark Moon could carry both Robin and Kate. Peony would carry Elvira who was cradling Feral in her arms and saying her own spells over him. Then at Silver's count the dragons took hold of a corner each and as gently as possible, took off. As they did the dragons and their burdens all became invisible to anyone looking up.

§　§　§

Dawn lay sprawled on the deck of the dahabeeyah, blood seeping from the wounds along her sides, her eyes closed, her spines limp, her talons coated in the dried blood of the enemy.

Elvira and Feral were saying spells over her, but she appeared comatose. "Her heart, it is fainter," cried Elvira, her face traced with tears. Feral was muttering spells and had inflated himself as large as possible, but even his voice faltered as his own wounds exhausted him. Then out of the river came all the young dragons.

They gathered around Dawn, pushing Elvira and Feral aside. They each reached out and placed their taloned hands upon her, with six dragons their hands touching everywhere, their wings unfolded to make a tent over her.

Then Silver spoke, 'Dawn, you are a dragon, you were brave beyond your years to save your friend. But here me now! Dragons do not die in a fight with an insignificant ancient god, no matter how large, how poisonous. Dragons *don't die*, Dawn Rain."

Every dragon used their own talons to pierce their wrists and each talon on each hand began to drip dragon blood into her wounds, some was even carefully dribbled down her throat. Silver himself pierced his own neck in the soft place where it joined under his chin, and cradling her head, fed her his blood.

"Wake up Dawn," they all chorused. "Wake up and heal. It takes more than this to kill a dragon. Wake now and know that you are a courageous dragon, and you will not die."

And Dawn woke up, looked at these friends and smiled. "Dragons do not die," she whispered, and then she fell asleep.

"She's passed out again," cried Elvira.

"No, no, it's all right," said Peony. "She isn't unconscious now, she's sleeping, She needs to sleep."

§ § §

Early the next morning, Tigris came over to Feral, who was lying at the foot of Dawn's bed, curled around her inside her tail, which was curled around him. They both were still bloody and bandaged. Tigris gave the dragon equivalent of a hiss at Feral.

"What are you doing here? How dare you set foot on her bed, let alone curl up with her while she's unconscious. It's your fault she is so badly injured, you nasty fur ball! You could be one of Apep's demon's, you look like one!"

Feral wanted to spring for Tigris' neck and do real damage, but he knew that even at his full health and in a furious rage he could not really damage her. As he was now, he could barely raise his head.

"You...you total bitch! You don't know our history! Dawn and I go way back. I saved her life, she saved mine. And that was over a year ago. She is my friend, my sister, my FAMILY! Don't you dare come over all 'dragons together' with me. She was alone, we found each other.

"Where the friggin' hell were you then? Get out of here, you scaly reptile. If I remind you of Apep's demons, you remind me of him! Go away and let us sleep and heal."

It was probably just a coincidence that Elvira came over at that point, but she put her hand on Feral and Dawn together and spoke quietly to Tigris. "We are her family, Feral is her brother, she saved him last night. They will both live. I suggest you go away and talk to Silver, or maybe Lilac Moon, they will fill you in. You may be forgiven this time for your ignorance, but I do suggest that you stop judging people by their skins and begin to see them for who they really are. Go away, Tigris, go *now!*"

Elvira sat in the chair by the bed and stroked Feral's head and paws until he settled once more and, when he turned and embraced Dawn's tail, she felt she could also settle by them and read the book she had in her pocket. She looked over the top of it as she turned a page and smiled at the sight. Dawn would heal, so would Feral and their bond would be closer than ever. Elvira felt a wave of happiness—these two, and all the rest. This was her home.

§ § §

Two days later and Dawn was up and scoffing down a trough full of everything a dragon needs to regain strength and power, including all the elements for producing fire. Her wounds that had looked so hideous and life-threatening were almost healed, leaving just silvery shadows as scars upon her scales.

"So dragons don't die, huh?" said the familiar sardonic voice as Feral strolled over. "That's good," he added. "That's very good, because cats can die, and I would've. So thank you." He rubbed against her legs as cats do, describing a figure-eight and nearly tripping her up. She raised her head from feeding and brought it down to his level.

"You saved me once, you saved my life when I really wasn't worth saving. It made a difference. It made me begin to see things differently." She nodded as if replaying that process in her mind's eye. "So, you're my friend, and what I did was what friends do. I know that now. You and Elvira taught me that.

What happened after I, err, passed out?" she asked.

"Oh, all the dragons heard you, and they came really fast, and the entire festival broke up, and that snake god, Apep, he was injured, you really got him with the teeth and claws. But he slithered away into a dark hole. They're gone, all gone. For now."

Chapter 42

They made their way back down the Nile to Luxor, where *Heka* could almost always go so much faster sailing with the current.

"As often as I've studied maps of the Nile, and tried to get my head around it, I still find it almost impossible to accept that the Nile is flowing *from the south,* the middle of Africa, to the *north* to the Mediterranean," confessed Kate.

"I know it's confusing, being so used to thinking of maps as showing north as *up* and south as *down*, that a major river like the Nile flows north to the Mediterranean Sea," remarked Perry, who was showing them the path they had already taken to near the Aswan Dam and back to their anchorage by the side of the road in Luxor. Here they left *Heka* and made their way to the invisible door that led them directly to the entrance of their immense palace within the Egyptian Principality.

Where they found Chen Shi and Imhotep enjoying the afternoon sun in the private garden.

"Well, that accomplished most of what we'd hoped," said Robin. "Apep and his minions did arrange a 'spur of the moment' festival for the locals down in the Gebel al Silsila ruins. So we actually got a look at a number of the demons." "And I killed quite a few," interjected Feral. "Not that it made much difference, except that it drew Apep himself out of a sort of magic hole in the ground or doorway from the netherworld. Some fangs on that boy, I must say."

"Yes, you wretched cat, and they'd have killed you if it hadn't been for Dawn,"
said Elvira. "I can't say I think it was worth it."

"Oh, but it was," said Kate. "I mean, I am so very sorry that Feral and Dawn were injured, but they are okay again now, and they—well, plus the rave itself—shocked Apep into revealing himself."

"Which means he has now regained some of his form and strength which should allow him the ability to enact his wish to destroy Bastet," finished Perry.

"And how can that be called any kind of a benefit?" spat Elvira. "You have put our Goddess in danger, and for what?"

"Because," said Chauncey gently, finally coming into the conversation, "it was inevitable that it would happen sooner or later. Bastet has known that ever since she spied the difference in the fresco in Ramses the Second's tomb. It's why she needed our help."

"Plus the rave was cut short," Kailen. "And

the dragons all flying in to help save Dawn and Feral from Apep scared all the celebrants who made a run for it. So although Apep may have gained power and strength from the rave and his somewhat impromptu appearance there attacking a cat, he also must have either lost it as well, or not gained as much as he would if the rave hadn't been cut short by the participants running away in fear."

"I don't entirely understand," said Elvira, still more focussed upon keeping Feral, Dawn, Bastet and Blue safe, tucked away if necessary, than on promoting an engagement where she feared that rather than triumphing over Apep, he might triumph over them.

"Think!" instructed Imhotep, "Our Goddess, however frightened of Apep she is, according to some legends was always aboard the Sun Barge, called the *Mandjet* or the Boat of Millions of Years, with her father Ra. As the sun set, the boat they took to go into the *Duat*, the ancient Egyptian underworld, the realm of Apep, was the Night Barge, or *Mesektet*, the Boat of the Justified Dead. And one version says she morphed into a cat with a knife to protect the sun from Apep. Every night. And every night they triumphed with her help. Although she says she was not ever the 'night cat' who fought Apep, which is quite possible, since she'd already spent the day on the Sun Barge. But as it is there are only the two old gods who have awakened and taken on form and power due to belief, and they are sworn enemies.

"To keep Chaos from triumphing, Bastet must ride the *Mesektet* and challenge and triumph over Apep. When that happens, things can go back as they were—Apep will know that he will never, in this new world, defeat Bastet. Bastet will be free of her fears that he might. And as the only two ancient gods who have been called back to life, they can each get on with the life they've been given. There will be balance.

"Of course, there are many other versions where the Pharaoh and Ra ride the *Mesektet* alone, or protected by a different set of gods not including Bastet, or sometimes by Atum alone. And in reality— if we can use that word—protecting the Pharaoh and the Sun was done through a series of special incantations, or magic spells, recited by the spirits of the dead and by the priests of Ra in his temples."

§ § §

Meanwhile, Bastet had been asking her father, Ra, indeed prayed silently to the Sun God and to Osiris, most important gods of the ancient Egypt pantheon, for help and advice about this coming confrontation. She searched with all her senses for some evidence of them, but, as with all the others, there was …nothing.

It was as she'd feared, only she and the God of Chaos existed now. Try as she might to bring herself to do her duty, she could not help feeling that it was useless. Worse than useless.

The Evil One could triumph, and even today's Egypt would be ground under while she, the protector of home and hearth, of family and order, would simply be swallowed into that great poison-dripping mouth. Magic knife or no, without the concentrated power of all her fellow gods and goddesses, without the chanting of the many protective spells of the priests of Ra, she would not be able to face this creature and survive, let alone triumph.

She felt shame and anger, but must tell her friends before they also could be destroyed because she could not accomplish what they expected.

Bastet kissed the cheek of Blue, squeezed her taloned hand, and stepped forward between the huge forms of Chen Shi and Imhotep and the gathering of all the magical creatures who had come to help her.

It was hard, but she was a Goddess. "My friends, my dear ones, I cannot do what you all expect would end this battle in our favour. I am a Goddess, I am proud, but I have searched the cosmos above and below for my father, Ra, or Osiris god of the dead, or for any of the gods of ancient Egypt. Any at all. They are not here, they are deaf to my call, and as I feared it is only myself and Apep who have gathered belief enough to take form and be 'alive' once more.

"And even with your help, my lovely friends, I cannot best Apep. I cannot. It is not just a fear, but a certainty. Whatever called us from beyond history and back to the present it was not given to me to triumph over Chaos. I think it was not perhaps given to you either. But maybe it was. I just know in my essence that I am not the one who can send Chaos back into his dark realm.

"The legend that I stood in the form of a cat each night with my father Ra to overcome Apep is false. I would remember, and I do not remember. There are other stories, other legends. There must be truth in some of them, since for over four thousand years Egypt remained strong.

"As I said long ago, the Egyptians often confused the cat gods, particularly me, my brother Sekhmet, the lion god, and Mut the brindled cat who could and did attack Apep on more than one occasion with a knife, and protected not just Ra but the Tree of Life as well. It wasn't me then, it is not me now. Forgive me my friends, I haven't the power to best Apep in combat, and the other Egyptian texts of magic and protection do not mention me in the Night Boat. In fact, they often don't tell which gods were there at all.

"You must, I think, devise from what you know, and from what you are, a new strategy. This, after all, is not outside the ancient Egyptian way—stories of how the gods behaved and bested one another were many and varied. Maybe if you can take the dahabeeyah *Heka* into the underworld as the Night Barge, you will find your hero, a Cat God who can drive off Apep and convince him to leave me, Bastet, alone." And Bastet stepped back within the crowd of her friends and took refuge by Blue and Elvira.

There was a movement toward her from all the Misfits, the Fae, and the Dragons, all with pleas that she change her mind. "But you must…" "We cannot drive him away without you." "Do not be afraid, we will protect you, we will win if you are there."

"STOP!" There was silence and all movement stopped.

Feral strode through the crowd, the meteorite knife in a harness fitted to his body. "I will do as I promised before when Bastet appealed to me. She asked me to be her Paladin. She is right, she was never the cat who bested Apep, and therefore she could not do so now. But Mau did—and Mau can again."

And before their astonished eyes Feral changed. His midnight blue-black coat turned brindle, he grew to the size of a snow leopard, his fangs and claws extended, his brilliant green eyes became golden. But the grin that exposed those fangs and the look in those gold eyes were pure Feral. Feral who knew that it would be his duty, his pleasure, to inflict a number of wounds on the upstart snake in order to teach this heartless reptile with his little army of demons to go back to dozing in his dank underworld, deep in the mud of the midnight Nile. It was as if Feral had just been awaiting his moment.

Even Elvira, always wanting to keep her beloved cat safe, who worried every time he left their abode whether he would come back safely, even Elvira didn't cry out that he must not do this thing. It was clear that Feral was indeed Bastet's Paladin, the hero who was destined to teach Apep that alive, risen again he might be, but the world had changed and he had now met his match.

Chapter 43

"DECAY! Where are you, you miserable excuse for a demon. I have been attacked by monsters, I am hurt, I bleed, my eye was pierced. DECAAAY!

D K had been hiding behind a number of the other demons, all of whom were quivering with fear both of Apep and of the great black cat who had killed several of them and injured many more. Now, in fear of their own lives, they pushed him forward until he crouched, his head on the sand, before the brown serpent.

"Your Frightfulness," he managed through chattering teeth, "I am here."

"What were those creatures? We have seen nothing like them. The green thing with the wings and the teeth and the shocking fire, it is a monster sent by Bastet to kill me. I will declare war upon it, it shall be ground to dust within my coils.

"And you with your 'rave' and your posters that made me look like a great coiled dropping from some stinking animal's bowels. You *invited* these creatures from the beyond, from hell itself. You will be punished as none of my demons have been punished before. I shall hang you up by your feet and have the rest use you for target practice."

"Oh, Greatest of the Horrifying, most Powerful, Ancient and Appalling of all the Gods, I beg you to listen to the pleas of your humble servant. I did not *invite* them. I did not invite anyone. The whole idea was to have them come in their hundreds and be an audience to your greatness. But Dearest of all that is Dreadful, I never invited anything that might hurt you. Indeed, spies tell me that you hurt *them*. Oh, yes, you bear a few wounds which will quickly heal, but you inflicted serious damage upon both the black menace and the green monster.

"It can only add to the legend of your greatness, your power, your invincible ability to overcome such major terrors quickly and leave them lying in pools of their own blood.

"Stupendous One, they are in grave danger of dying slowly and horribly. Do not make the mistake of having your most faithful servant follow that path as well. For only I can make these shivering, miserable excuses for demons into the force you need to overcome Bastet and these, who were undoubtedly her servants."

"I am bleeding, you slinking excuse for a demon. And it WILL NOT stop! And it hurts. This is not the nightly fight I faced with those of the *Mesektet* boat, from those I emerged with even scores of cuts that simply healed and never hurt but in the most passing way. Now…now I am injured by that hideous creature. Green with spikes and wings, red eyes, fire, it created fire. There is nothing in our grand scheme to explain it. I want it *dead*! But first, if you want to *live*, D K, tend my wounds and make the pain stop. I order it!"

D K was no fool. In the millennia while his master slept he would often wake to check on the state of the world. He had discovered many interesting and even very tempting things — chocolate, baked potatoes, Caesar salad. But also interesting and useful things—his earphones and rap music, films and television, and now computers, but also antiseptic and bandages. It was these that he brought forth now, including a cream that dulled pain, a spray that served as a liquid bandage and stopped the bleeding and opium in various forms.

"I humbly beg you, oh Greatest of the Big Bads, to stretch out so that I may assess the damage and give you help and relief."

Apep laid himself out and was immediately relieved when the first big gash stopped bleeding and then hurting and then felt the comfort of soft bandages carefully applied around the wound and his body. This process continued along his immense length wherever there was a wound. Then D K approached with a glass of liquid and begged his master to drink.

Apep sniffed, and recoiled slightly, "That's

very strong, if it's poison…?"

"Never, Master of Malice, never. This is a potent pain removing potion. It will make you sleep, but when you wake there will be no more pain and your injuries will have healed." *I hope, oh by all that is powerful, it must be so or we are in trouble,* he thought as he held the glass so that Apep could drink the potion easily.

Chapter 44

Now that Bastet had said she could not attack Apep successfully, and Feral was to be the Cat God Mau to do that job, it was decided to lay out all they now knew about the God of Chaos before Chauncey and Imhotep and get their advice for how to make sure he would never threaten Bastet again.

That night they all, witches, fae, cat and cat goddess, sat down at an ethereally beautiful table, the cloth a beautiful green that changed colours gently like a lake reflecting the sky. Set with silver, crystal and gold and decorated with flowers of all colours from cream through gold to golden red and on to dark maroon, then lightening to amethyst and gentle pinks.

The women were all dressed in cream and gold, the men in dark green. The dragons, at a much larger but similar table all kept their own colours, except that their gold streaks and spikes shone brighter, their greens, blues, blacks, purples, all their colours, shone like jewels, their scales shimmering.

The time had come. They had done what they could to find out as much as possible about this ancient God of Chaos, the snake the ancient Egyptians had envisioned and given life to as the explanation of why the sun, whom they'd made their primary God, disappeared every evening below the western horizon only to rise again at dawn in the east. To the ancients, with all their knowledge of building and creating beauty and even of medicine and surgery, gods, a vast pantheon of gods were the answers to otherwise unanswerable questions. So much belief and so much work to placate or subdue them resulted in a society that did indeed give life to these gods.

"But why," Kate asked Chauncey, "do they attribute a set of personal traits to a certain god, and then in time add to or drop personality traits and a god becomes both good and bad, capable of wonderful deeds and of betrayals, of acts of charity and then turns upon a member of his own family?" Chauncey wished he could properly embrace his adopted daughter, a witch of incredible powers, a loving and honest young woman. Difference in size prevented this, but magic gave him the ability to envelop her in a warm feeling of love and understanding.

"Their gods' characteristics were drawn from human beings, and human beings as you know are capable of so many different personality attributes, love and hate, honesty and lies, to love someone until they believe themselves betrayed and then to vow vengeance. Their gods are similar, and as with humans, some are basically one type, honest, kind, protective, or jealous, changeable, full of rage. The difference is that as the gods took on life, they became more powerful, and capable of making changes in themselves not attributed by humans. They'd made a believable explanation for how their universe worked, but like the universe itself, it was not always within their power to control."

"So they gave themselves reasonable explanations for all the things in the world that they couldn't otherwise explain, and then these 'reasons' took on a kind of life." said Kate.

"Yes, that sounds like as good an explanation as any, and of course it gave them a feeling of control. Humans like a feeling of control."

"Everyone likes a feeling of control," commented Elowen, Queen of the Seelie Fae, sardonically. "It often comes as a great shock to find out even rulers of great lands only have a transparent gauze of such power, real only at a distance and if not looked at too closely."

"I cannot but agree with you, my old friend," said Chauncey. "But now we have two ancient gods who have come back you might say from the dead and happen to be age old enemies. And we must restore balance, because we have promised Bastet."

"I take it that this beautiful dinner, fit for royalty—and there are indeed a number of us that are royal—is also our time to hear or plan how we are going to finally do that. I know finding Apep at his rock concert was just a way of finding out for sure he was here and making him aware of another force besides Bastet that stands against him.   But my question is—now what?" said Kailen.

"Now" said Chauncey, "I have something to show you." Behind him, all along the terrace fronting the dragon wing of their beautiful palace, was a deep crimson velvet curtain.   They'd all known that something special lay behind it. Silver and Dawn now got up and each unhooked a braided rope and slide the velvet curtain back to reveal a large and beautiful boat, flat-bottomed like a Nile barge, but with great up curving prow and stern like the Sun barges depicted in the frescos of the temples and tombs.

"This is the *Mesektet*, the Night Boat Ra and Pharaoh take into the Underworld or Duat every night as the sun sets in the west," explained Chauncey. "This horizon was called the *akhet*, and was sometimes called the door that leads to the Duat."

The *Mesektet* Boat was glorious in its trappings, and its colours were of jewels— amethyst, emerald, jasper and turquoise, lapis lazuli, and everywhere the lustre of gold. There were gasps even from the dragons.

"But we thought, well, Silver said, we'd be enchanting *Heka* to become the, err, *Mesektet* boat," commented Amazon.

"We considered it, yes, but that would require both tons of magic and also most likely real physical changes. It isn't just difficult, but also could upset the balance by sending a real boat, however disguised, into the Duat. It might not be accepted by the Underworld or could otherwise fail. Plus it would be more work than 'building' this with magic, just as we've built this beautiful Egyptian palace for ourselves."

"Okay," said Perry, "but what's the rest of the plan?"

"Yes, how does this protect Bastet?" asked Elvira.

Chauncey said "The plan is simple. We will use our magic to transform some of you into the shapes and the character of the gods and goddesses who often accompanied Ra into the Underworld. You will follow the Duat underworld through the twelve doors or gates that correspond to the twelve hours of night, and you will probably meet some of the characters placed there to test the soul of the Pharaoh. You will gain access to each door by reciting the appropriate parts of the text from the book of the dead or more often just by saying the name of the guardian.

"You will also meet with Apep inside the gate of the fifth hour. He will try to come aboard to eat the Sun, destroying Pharaoh and some of the other gods and goddesses as well. I think he will have a special eye out to attack Bastet, but that is when Feral here, as Mau, will attack him with the magical meteorite knife. As Feral does that the rest of you will be chanting a special addition to the Book of the Dead that will warn him off our beloved Cat Goddess forever.

"But...but...he'll know, he'd have to!" cried Robin.

"Know what?"

"That we aren't real, not the real pharaoh, or the real Ra or Set or any of the others. He knows there's only him and his little demons and the Cat Goddess that are real now."

"Where do you think he went when he disappeared back into that blackness?" asked Chauncey.

"Err...I have no idea."

"But he did, he went back to where he always has been—in the Duat, the underworld or possibly the subterranean Nile, murky and liquid. And when this authentic replica—with some added spells to enchant it properly—of the night boat *Mesektet* that carries the Sun God and his protectors under the world every night, and you, also with the help of some spells, are guarding the Sun God/Pharaoh as Ra, he will fall into his role automatically.

"In any case, those gods aren't any more dead forever than Bastet or Apep—enough belief and manifestations of that belief over time would certainly re-animate any of these gods. Apep believes in them. He battles with them every night.

"I might add, that just as our authentic Cat Goddess has refused to risk herself in this endeavour, any of you who prefer not to take part can also ask to be excused and you will be.

"The gods and goddesses that accompanied Ra were often different in different accounts, and occasionally there were no other gods at all. Ra as Pharaoh in his ram-headed underworld form called Afu must be there however, just as he is depicted in his falcon-headed form in the Sun boat during the day. In fact, in the day, Ra and Horus are often considered one and the same, and when the pharaoh is identified as a god it is as the falcon-headed God Horus who represented kingship itself and was seen as the Son of Ra. So the Pharaoh in the Sun boat is Horus with healing and the sun and the sky under his protection. Whereas at night there are various stories of his purpose on the *Mesektet*, including to go as an ageing pharaoh and become younger as he faces each challenge, arising at dawn as the young strong pharaoh.

"But that interpretation is not of primary interest to us here. Here pharaoh's job with the help of any others on the *Mesektet* boat is to keep Apep from destroying him and the sun and ensuring that the sun rises the next morning."

"Apep will not find these changes unexpected or wrong. Nor is he attacked by a Cat wielding a knife every night either," added Perry.

"But he will be this time," snarled Feral. "I will see that he is dead."

"For a certain value of dead," murmured Chauncey, but Feral didn't hear him. "So let us sit and eat and perhaps you will choose among yourselves which of the usual guardians on the *Mesektet* you would like to be. If not, I have some ideas."

"And I will gather a few who stay here" said Imhotep, "and we will perform the rituals and recite the sayings the priests of Ra did during the night to help those in the *Mesektet* make it safely through the Duat until sunrise."

Chapter 45

At first there was some consternation amongst them, but as they ate the wonderful food the satisfaction of hunger and a selection of wines calmed them, and they began to see that this could not only work, but could in fact be fascinating and exciting without a huge element of danger. So that later, they sat around the beautiful pool as a crescent moon rose overhead, dangling their toes in the water and discussing the list of gods and goddesses and the various verses from the books of the dead that they could say as they reached each gate along their journey.

It was decided that the gods most likely to have accompanied Pharaoh as Ra or to have been already in the Duat would be Thoth, the ibis-headed god of the moon, wisdom, knowledge, art and judgment; Thoth's wife, Ma'at, goddess of balance, order, harmony, morality and the good working of the world; Hathor, sometimes depicted as a cow for her maternal aspect, but most often as a beautiful woman wearing a head-dress of cow horns and a sun disk. Along with Ma'at, Hathor was perhaps the most important goddess, being the mother and wife of the sky god Horus and the Sun god Ra, and therefore the symbolic mother of their earthly counterparts, the pharaohs. Finally Isis, with her great power that allowed her to bring her husband Osiris back to life, would be on the boat as a passenger, and that would take her to the final gate, of which she was guardian.

"So sitting here digesting our dinner and enjoying the evening light we have how many people who could become stand-ins for the gods on board the *Mesektet*?" asked Robin.

"Not counting Bastet," responded Elvira, giving the Cat Goddess a gentle hug to indicate no hard feelings.

Kate, on the other side of Bastet, squeezed her hand gently as well before saying, "There are the five Magical Misfits, which include Kailen even though he's Fae and a Prince, then the Fae Queen Elowen, and our friends Ariane and Dmitri, also Fae, and Elvira, who is also the daughter of a King of Egypt. That's four men, Kailen, Robin, Dmitri and Perry and two of them are Royal, or part Royal, Kailen and Robin. And five women, me, Maggie, Elvira, Ariane and Elowen. Elowen is a Queen, and Maggie is the consort and mother of Fae princes. And of course there is Feral as the Cat God Mau, but he is already chosen. We have plenty left to choose from for the rest.

"So if I chose" Kate continued, "Perry should be Thoth, because he is god of wisdom, art and judgment. This suits Perry perfectly, he is all those things. And Maggie should be Ma'at, because she does so often bring us back into balance and is very fond of harmony and seeing the world in good working order."

Robin chimed in. "My father, Prince Kailen, should be the Pharaoh as Ra, since he is Royal and has the natural ability to be both human and god."

"And on the *Mesektet* he joins with Osiris and takes on the head of a ram. Are you up for that, Kailen?" asked Perry. "After all, if I'm there as Thoth I'll have the head of an ibis."

"I'm quite ready to be a god king joined to the god of the underworld, thanks Perry, but I would of course be depending upon your wisdom as well as all the rest of you," replied Kailen with a small bow.

"And I could be either Anubis, the one with the dog's head, as guide through the underworld, or Heka, god of magic, ready to use my powers to protect the Pharaoh." said Robin.

"You're more suited to Heka, God of Magic, my son," replied Maggie. "And as that is the essence of who and what we and our own boat are, it allows you to call upon all of that power if needed." She was thinking that if there was any real danger then having Robin in a position to multiply his magic might be a good thing for his and their survival.

"This leaves one of the most important

goddesses--Hathor, mother and wife to gods and therefore often to the Pharaoh in his god-form. She is wise, kind, motherly and powerful. I would suggest Queen Elowen as the obvious choice," said Kate.

"You are right about the 'obvious', laughed Elowen. "But I feel I must decline the honour. I would suggest that Maggie take the place of Hathor, she is after all the mother and wife of princes and she is known for her wisdom and practicality—something a mother must have—and kindness, in addition to being a powerful witch."

Ariane and Dmitri, both Fae, also declined to become a goddess or god, both because it could be complicated for the Fae and the boat would be getting very crowded.

"That leaves us with Kate, who is if anything the most powerful witch and the one who from the start bound us all together," said Maggie. "So she is the most suitable choice for Ma'at—the one who keeps us in balance, particularly with the help of Chauncey. I think although she is young she is the perfect choice for bringing order and harmony."

"And my mother and protector, Elvira, she is a daughter of the last king of Egypt, she has helped, mothered and protected me and Dawn and other street children both in Cairo and later in Luxor. She should be Isis, who was known for her magic—she put her own husband, Osiris, back together, after his brother

Set murdered him and scattered his pieces to the four winds so he could never be alive or well again. Elvira has done that magically and psychologically for more than one person, so she is Isis." said Feral with conviction and no one would have dared dispute him.

Chapter 46

D K was as usual managing Apep's demon army, setting them in rotation on the top of the Fifth Gate to have warning if the *Mesektet* boat was seen traversing the Duat through the Fourth Hour. They'd been doing this only since the disruption of Apep's Rave, where he was injured by and injured in return both Dawn and Feral. It had been Apep's delusion that they were 'the demons of Bastet, sent to bring him a painful death'. Since then he had not sought to regain the sleep of all the ancient gods, but lay awake and plotted how to kill her.

He also drank more opium than was good for him, so that he was now essentially addicted to the powerful substance which made him even more paranoid, but (*thank all that is powerful* thought D K) also made him sluggish and un-willing to do anything active. He lay, not sleeping, but not really awake, dreaming of the perfidious Cat Goddess and what she might do to him. Occasionally, in a better mood he dreamed of what he might do to her.

"I will gnash, I will slash, I will pin her body within my coils and slowly, slowly tighten them as she screams until she can no longer breathe. Then I will cut her into very small pieces and feed them to my demon army."

For in truth he was afraid if he ate her flesh it might also kill him.

D K had tried to soothe him over and over by telling him the *Mesektet* boat had not been seen for eons because all the ancient gods were asleep or dead, and the new gods had no interest in Apep. But the paranoia exhibited now by Apep was stronger than anything D K could say or do, because by adding opioids to the other pain mixtures he'd been feeding his master as Apep healed he'd unwittingly produced a head full of paranoid fears in the ancient serpent.

"I thought he was a nutter long before this," D K confided to Slime, "but with most of us safely sleeping the sleep of a thousand years, and with the ancient gods only shadows, it didn't seem a problem. Now he is worse than he ever was, total nut job and yet so lethargic. I'm worried, what if the Cat Goddess does show up? What if Ra comes in the *Mesektet* boat after all these years? How will Apep fight against them in the state he's in. He's screaming for vengeance, but he's hardly moving. Could they have poisoned him?"

Slime and Doom howled with laughter. "You mean you don't know? You gave it to him!" choked Slime between gasps.

"I did what? I did NOT! I have never hurt our

master. Have you all gone mad?" shouted D K.

Calming down, Slime threw a skinny insectile arm around D K. "Not on purpose, then, you idiot. No, I thought you'd decided to make him docile, even helpless. He's been such a pain since he woke up. But I see now, you didn't know."

"And I still don't know," cried D K. "For Duat's sake, tell me, you monster, don't tease and laugh or I swear I'll decapitate you. Tell me!"

"It's the opium," came Doom's gloomy voice. "Someone told you it killed pain, and you gave it to him, and he's been guzzling it ever since. Because it does kill pain, but it also totally screws you up. That's what opium does after a bit, turns your body all soft and you mostly just sleep, but turns your head into a fantasy factory, full of crazy stuff."

"I...I was trying to heal him. And stop him screaming, because that was making *me* crazy. It worked so well, no pain no screaming. But then he started behaving like a raving lunatic. Opium does *that*? Oh, sandstorm. Ok, so we take it away, and he'll be fine again. He's asleep now, we'll just get it and get rid of it right away."

"Not so fast, that would probably drive him utterly mad and then kill him—and he now needs it so much that searching for it you can bet he'd kill all of us." cautioned Slime.

"Yeah, has to come down slow," muttered Doom. "Little at a time."

"Have you ever tried to keep Apep from getting what he wants?" demanded D K, collapsing into the damp sand.

"Err, no, that's been your job, you're like the Major Domo or Prime Minister, 'cause you're the smart one," said Slime.

"Only not so smart this time," said Doom.

"Who told me it was for pain? Who gave it to me?" cried D K, looking for the scapegoat. There was a rustling as the demons backed away, shaking their heads.

Only from the back there was a shuffling and several demons dragged forth a ragged and skinny one of their number even more dreadful looking than the rest.

"Dogbreath, he an addict, he brought you the stuff and you paid him so much for it that he's been totally stoned ever since," said Scumbag, Slime's brother.

"Tell me how to get him off this horrible stuff without him killing me," demanded D K taking the hapless Scumbag by the throat.

"You have to take the dose down a little at a time," gasped Scumbag. "He'll be able to tell, he'll know, but if you do it in that drink and add other powers that help take the edge off, he won't go totally into withdrawal all at once."

"Why not just do withdrawal?" asked D K.

"Because it will probably kill him, or throw him into convulsions and horrible shakes and, well, then kill him" slurred Dogbreath, shaking at the very thought of withdrawal.

"He's only been on it a few days, he can't be so totally addicted he can't get off fairly quickly," said Slime. "But you must swear to him that he is getting the maximum dose and that you don't have anymore, so you have to make it last until he is healed. Tell him it is the wounds that are causing the pain and the symptoms, like shaking and throwing up and all that, but that any more of the medicine would just kill him. Lie, D K, lie like you've never lied before."

D K turned to shaking Dogbreath, who affirmed this would be the case, which Dogbreath could swear to since he'd had to undergo withdrawal several times. Having that knowledge, D K waved the wretched demon away with his guards and said they could either kill him or just tie him up and let him go through withdrawal too. He was feeling very angry and hard done by. Apep's demons were indeed a hapless lot of toadies, with hardly a brain between them.

The next few days were not something D K ever wanted to go through again. He couldn't turn the care of Apep over to anyone else, so he went through the horrors if his master's withdrawal, and lied and lied as he reduced the dose of drug, giving what others he dared. Finally, some days later, Apep raised his great head and looked down upon his most faithful servant.

"You were right, D K, I am my old self once more. I feel a little weak, but the pain is gone, the other dreadful symptoms are gone. I am once more Apep, God of Chaos and Evil. I will have my revenge upon those who hurt me and upon the Cat Goddess who sent them. But before that I will have the first real sleep I have had to regain my physical strength."

D K breathed a deep sigh of relief, and bowing before his lord, he murmured his thankfulness to see Apep well once more and fled.

Chapter 47

That night again there was a group banquet on the huge terrace where Chauncey and all his resident dragon family could join in. There was one major difference in their previous gathering. All who'd chosen to do so were dressed as the Egyptian gods and goddesses they would become to crew the *Mesektet*.

Before that in the late afternoon, each had read up, if they needed to, on the particular god they were to become, and as part of their adoption of becoming first ancient Egyptian and later morphing to some extent into the gods, they did this in the simple garb of ordinary Egyptians. Spells had been cast by Elvira and Perry and especially Imhotep. who knew the most about what ancient Egypt had really been like, and each found in their quarters clothing that suited themselves and the period. So at dinner they all dressed as ancient Egyptian palace occupants would have dressed, the men in pleated white linen kilts and sandals of soft leather with some jewelled decoration, wearing necklaces with the hieroglyph depicting the name of the god they would become. Spells were cast so that all had shaved heads, without the necessity of actually shaving them.

The women dressed in white linen sheaths of approximately ankle length and ending below their breasts, but these were covered by the wide straps that held the dresses up. More elaborate necklaces adorned them, and they had wide cuff bracelets on their wrists as well. A few chose to wear black wigs with cones of incense on top that would melt slowly in the early evening heat. Others, including Kate and Elvira wore their own hair, held back or put up. Dinner was a prolonged affair, well into the night, while they worked out the exact rituals they would enact, and how they would each play their part in the twelve hours from sunset to sunrise as they sailed the *Mesektet* boat through the underworld.

"Keeping as close as possible to some of the less complicated rituals written in the scrolls should make Apep feel more at ease with what is happening. Although Imhotep and I and possibly some of you as well wonder if he, or any of the 'players' in this particular nightly ritual are actually aware that it takes place every night," said Chauncey. "It would make more sense if at least Apep thought of this as the first and only time this happens."

"Because otherwise why would he submit himself to being beaten every night?" asked Kate.

"Exactly. You'd think he might at least change his tactics." said Robin.

"I think," said Perry, with Bastet nodding agreement, "that it is the same every night and he knows it because that is how the ancient Egyptians 'invented' it to be. He and all the gods and goddesses were or—forgive me Bastet—are, the embodiment of human ideas about how things run. And although it appears the power of belief has given them life, and even the possibility of changing some of the aspects of these rituals, they go through them nightly with total belief that these are their 'jobs' and they do them as if they were actors in a long-running play, line for line, action by action."

"Now that does make sense to me," said Maggie. "It explains how they could do these jobs over and over, but with occasional deviations. Maybe it also explains why Apep isn't afraid of the many knife attacks he endures, maybe they are 'stage props', not real knives."

"No, dear Maggie," said Bastet, throwing an arm around her friend. "You fear too much the pain and injury. Throughout all of history I've been learning, there are many, many people who make a living fighting, and hurting or being hurt. If he knows anything, Apep is aware that he will survive to fight another night, and another. And, yes, I expect the cuts from the knives are not as painful as they would be in this reality and they heal quickly. But it's like being a gladiator, or a cage fighter…"   There were assorted gasps from the others. "Don't look so shocked, you modern people—I've had a fascinating time looking at YouTube videos since I've been here. And Sci-Fi films. And   cartoons.   Injury,   real   or   pretend, dismemberment and putting back together—it's all over your popular entertainments. Just, I should add, as it was in ancient Egypt."

"I agree," came almost simultaneously from Chauncey, Perry and Imhotep.

"The only major change we must incorporate is that Feral injures Apep badly and we produce a chant that is specifically designed to keep him from ever thinking of harming Bastet again," said Kate. "I suggest that we spend a few hours either inventing or amending a specific magical chant that we will pronounce over him while Feral chops him up as severely as possible to make sure he gets the message."

§ § §

Before dinner Chauncey said it was time for them to change into the gods and goddesses that would be on the *Mesektet* that still sat between the great dining tables and the main entrance to the dragon side of their palace.

"Referring to illustrations and ancient descriptions, I have taken the liberty of using magic to make your costumes and any extras your god or goddess carried to establish their identity. You can wear wigs, as Egyptians often did, taking them off to be cooler and more comfortable at home, or we can create appropriate hairdos for each of you, again using magic. Kate, many Egyptians were red headed, but it was not considered an appropriate hair colour for royalty or for gods. Maggie and Perry, blonds were foreigners, you will either wear wigs or we will give you a magic makeover. But to get used to the feeling of your new clothes and the additional paraphernalia I think you need to spend this evening and tomorrow wearing them.

"Tomorrow night is the big night. You will take your places in the *Mesektat* boat and by magic you and the boat will disappear just as the setting sun disappears over the horizon. You'll find yourselves at the beginning of the nightly journey that Ra, the sun, and Pharaoh take through the underworld from west to east every night, for the sun to rise in the east and Pharaoh to rise also renewed and ready for the day's events. "Tonight and tomorrow we will study the texts and memorise the order in which things will occur. You don't have to memorise the texts themselves because you will each have a—what is it you call them?"

"A script?" from Kate.

"A crib sheet!" said Robin.

"Yes to both," said Chauncey. "You can refer to these as the boat sails the underworld."

"What about Elvira?" asked Feral. "She is Isis, and therefore her place is at the last of the gates or hours."

"Elvira, what do you suggest," asked Chauncey. "You could ride the boat and only disembark to stand by the gate or *be* the gate when the time comes. Or you can be there from the beginning. Perhaps you can take a book if it seems boring?" and he winked at her.

It made her laugh with delight. In all her long life, and although she'd met by now more than a few dragons, never had she imagined that this enormous but somehow fatherly, and certainly vastly intelligent being would be urging her to take part in magical adventures and winking wickedly at her.

"I think, Grand Dragon, that I would like to study the plans this evening and tomorrow and tell you then what would suit both the situation and myself best. I will of course not do anything to put this mission in jeopardy."

They all then made for their private apartments where they found laid out for them entire sets of clothing plus jewellery and the various staffs, headdresses, and things they needed to carry to transform them into the deity they would be enacting, indeed partially becoming, for Apep's particular benefit.

§ § §

Kailen found his clothing was simple, a finely woven pleated white linen kilt that wrapped around his waist and then a cloth of gold was wrapped around his backside and split at the front.

"Like wearing an apron backward," he commented to Maggie, as she giggled while helping him with the ties that fastened them around his waist. There was the staff, a symbol of power and dominion, with a straight shaft, a crooked handle in the shape of an animal head and a forked base. It was made of very strong wood like lignum vitae and decorated with bands of lapis and gold. The animal head, attached at a 45degree angle was so abstract that they couldn't tell what it was supposed to be. In his left hand he would carry a gold ankh. Jewelled cuffs for his wrists and upper arms and several rings completed this part of his attire.

What came next was not unexpected (they had all studied pictures of what they would look like) but was still off-putting. In a large hat box was the stylised head of a ram, in this case dark green in colour, as depicted on the painting in Ramses tomb, with either a sort of black-haired mane or a modified Egyptian wig that came down over the shoulders. Under the head, which was hollow to fit over Kailen's head, wrapped in tissue, were the pieces of the 'crown' or symbols of Pharaoh as Ra— two golden horns, only roughly akin to ram's horns, and the sun disk of Ra balanced upon them.

Kailen stood holding the head and turning it in his hands, staring unhappily at it. "I...I'm not at all comfortable about putting this thing over my head, look, there are no eye holes or nostrils. This surely isn't how it's supposed to work."

Maggie came closer to embrace him and explain. "We, that is Kate, Chauncey and I, thought it would be less distressing to put this on like a Halloween costume, and then magic will fit it comfortably to your head, plus allowing normal breathing and seeing."

"Less distressing than *what!*" Kailen almost shouted.

"Well, than doing a spell that turned your actual head into this thing. We thought no one with an animal's head (except Bastet of course, who was created that way) as part of their 'god' would be comfortable with that option. So, honestly, my love, this will slip on easily, it is not stiff, it is malleable, just like a face or a head, and you will be able to see, breath and hear just as normal. Nor will it itch, be too hot or feel heavy or claustrophobic.

Plus from inside it, you won't have to see your loving partner with a head of such a distressing green that you might have been dead for weeks, as I will. You have my promise as a witch and your wife."

Kailen looked at her long and hard, and then

grinned, and popped the head over his own. It immediately settled and shaped, eyes and mouth opening and she could see the sparkle in his eyes.

"Okay, witch, you're right as usual. Only you might have explained before I opened the bloody box. Yes, yes, perfectly comfortable, not hot, feels just like my head, I'd have to look in a mirror to see that it isn't just me. Don't feel like I'm inside anything, just like myself."

Maggie was watching as the mouth of this strange green ram's head formed these words. It actually made her feel quite weird seeing her dear love suddenly transformed so entirely. To keep any of this from showing on her face, she busied herself unwrapping the stylised horns and sun disk, and once she was sure her own expression didn't give away anything but approval, she turned and fitted them carefully onto the top of the ram's head.

"Okay," she said. "You're about a foot taller now than before with that headdress on, so don't go dashing through any low doors!"

"It's dinner soon," Kailen remarked. "I'll eat okay, will I? Or, (and somehow the ram's head took on some aspect of Kailen in a teasing mood) will I have to eat grass?" The smile on the ram's face was Kailen's smile.

"Wait until you see Perry—he's Thoth," laughed Maggie.

"Hope someone has explained the whole head thing to him before he sees it then," said Kailen. "Who's helping him dress?"

Chapter 48

It was Robin who was helping Perry with his transformation into Thoth, the God of Wisdom, Art and Judgment. Thoth's appearance was that of a man from the neck down, with the head of an ibis (a large wading bird with long legs and a very long down-curved beak). Ibis lived in flocks and were considered intelligent and good at living in families.

Possibly if it has occurred to him, Robin might have tried to tease Perry a bit with his head. It was another green affair—green symbolised new life, growth and joy—and not, as Maggie had felt, the green of decaying flesh. The head had the long black beak and a rain of black feathers down his back and over his shoulders, ending in gold and red bands. Thoth also had an elaborate necklace of rows of precious stones ending in a band of gold.

Then Robin got into his red kilt, as Heka, God of Magic, and a broad collar of precious and semi-precious stones. He completed his outfit with a blue headband that supported a raised platform on which was the sculpted figure of a lion.

Heka's magic and therefore Robin's that night was many things, but above all, it was closely associated with speech and the power of the word. In the realm of Egyptian magic, actions did not necessarily speak louder than words—they were often one and the same thing. Thought, deed, image, and power were theoretically united in the concept of Heka. Robin as Heka therefore had great power to help the *Mesektet* boat and its crew through the night, and to subdue Apep, using his power to wield words like weapons. His powers increased the force of the others as they said the words from the texts that opened the gates and came up against Apep.

Heka also carried two snakes, possibly cobras, and these were magically entranced, so that although illustrations showed the god with the snakes crossed in front of him, one in each hand, Robin could carry them looped quietly around his neck or waist leaving his hands free.

"It's a good thing I don't mind snakes," he said. "And these will apparently do exactly what I want them to, which is quite reassuring."

§ § §

Meanwhile, Kate and Elvira, with Bastet to help them with just how to walk in the rather form fitting sheath dresses and anything else that might cause them problems, were joined by Maggie and all of them had a lot more fun with their goddess attire than the men had had.

For one thing, none of them were expected to wear animal heads. For another, witches, and goddesses they might be, but they were women trying on clothes and accessories together and it was fun.

Maggie as Hathor, Goddess of the Sky, Goddess of Beauty and protector of mothers and babies, wore the typical dress of a high-born woman of the time, a formfitting sheath dress in red that went from under her breasts down to just above her ankles. Her breasts were covered by the wide straps that held the dress up. Red was an unusual colour for a dress, but it was the colour of life and protection—derived from the colour of blood and the life-supporting power of fire. It was therefore commonly used for protective amulets, but for Hathor, the Goddess prayed to during childbirth, it was the appropriate colour for her dress. There were also the usual arm, ankle and wrist bands of precious stones.

Finally, Maggie's blond hair was covered with a long black Egyptian styled wig, and topped with a headdress of stylised cow horns which held a sun disk. All this was created by magic and included spells that made sure the wearer was comfortable.

"I love it," Maggie pronounced. "My figure has never looked so good, and I had no idea black hair would suit me, but it seems to, definitely". Bastet and Elvira both worked on her eye makeup, the kohl that both enhanced the eyes, and protected them from how bright everything tended to be under the Egyptian sun, and magic turned her blue eyes dark brown.

Then it was Kate's turn. As Ma'at, Goddess of Truth, Justice, Cosmic Order and Balance, she was not just a goddess, but represented the crucial concept of universal order and balance. Her white linen sheath was the twin of Maggie's red one, outlining her figure. Her black wig had a head band that supported the divine feather of truth— the one that was balanced against the dead person's heart to see if they could be admitted to the afterlife.

And Kate got wings! Beautiful gently tinted feathers that went from her shoulders down to her wrists. They represented the wings of the vulture, her sacred animal.

"A *Vulture*?" Kate had exclaimed indignantly when she had read this bit earlier. "I have to say I'm not very pleased to be having a vulture as my animal. Why, for pity's sake?"

"Because Ma'at is very important in the Hall of Judgment, where each dead person's heart is weighed on a scale against the weight of your feather of truth," explained Bastet. "So Ma'at is there overseeing the dead, just as a vulture does. If you let go of your idea of vultures as ugly birds, you will see the connection, and also that both perform very important functions in disposal of the dead."

"Ah," Kate had said. "I understand now." And when she put them on, she gently stroked the feathers.

Finally it was Elvira's turn. She was to become Isis, the origin Goddess, a virgin but wife of Osiris. And when his jealous brother Set murdered Osiris and tore his body into pieces, scattering them across Egypt, Isis searched for them, gathering all the fragments, and put him back together into a living god again.

This was why Feral had wanted her to have this part, because he said that Elvira was no one's physical mother, but she had in her lifetime taken battered and damaged people and offered them help, including him and Dawn. Isis was associated with healing and magic because of her healing of Osiris which suited Elvira. She was dressed in a red shift dress similar to Maggie's as Hathor, and also had wings like Ma'at. Her headdress was a miniature golden throne.

Elvira was a plump older woman, but upon getting into her Isis clothes, she became both slender and young, as the goddess was depicted.

"Ah, isn't magic wonderful," she said. "I feel exactly like myself, and these clothes and wings and headdress and jewellery all feel perfectly comfortable, but when I look at myself in this mirror I see the

Goddess and not myself at all."

When they gathered for dinner, everyone was laughing and applauding each other, and Chauncey, who had created the magical garments and all the extras was looking quite pleased with himself. It had been a very long time since he'd enjoyed himself so much doing something magical he'd never done before. Chauncey in fact was enjoying himself more than he had in centuries. The fantasy aspects of this adventure were all very much a reality for those taking part, particularly Bastet and probably Feral, but for Chauncey to be able to stage manage and use his magic and his power to create such things as the *Mesektet* boat and turn his friends into gods and goddesses, pleased him as much as a child with a new toy castle full of knights and horses and exciting adventures to be had.

Although now free himself of danger, his enormous size, and the very fact that he was a real dragon always limited his scope to some extent on this Earth, so this was a chance to indulge himself as well as help a good friend.

Because he hadn't told his friends his plan to accompany them through the ancient Egyptian underworld, invisible and unnoticed by any of the old gods or guards or spirits that might still be there, but actually taking part in an adventure. So that during or just after Feral's attack on Apep with the meteorite knife, he intended appear to the great God of Chaos and have the fun of scaring him witless while delivering the message which those on the boat would have recited as well—that the Goddess Bastet was strictly off limits if Apep wanted to stay alive in any form whatsoever.

It had been such a long time since Chauncey had allowed himself the pleasure of scaring any form of creature on this earth, or within this particular time-bubble, into behaving itself for all time to come.

They did discuss the actual changing from their palace garden near Karnak to the dark underbelly of some four thousand years ago. Doing it as the sun disappeared over the dessert in the west and making a precise entrance into the ancient underworld had also been Chauncey's project over the past few days. It helped immensely that the whole of this was designed around gates, since doors or gates were the embodiment of both how to go from one space-time-bubble to another and also happened to be the exact method ancient Egyptian gods and pharaohs used to traverse the 12 hours of the four-thousand-year-old underworld. Chauncey and Imhotep and Perry had all had the same enthusiasm for making this the basis of the spells that would get the *Mesektet* safely from early 21st Century Egypt seamlessly into the 4000-year-old Duat. He had no doubts it would work—they had worked it on a small model, and it went entirely smoothly.

Chapter 49

Everyone slept in the next morning, since they would be staying up all night in the *Mesektet* boat, travelling through the twelve hours of the underworld or Duat. Sitting around comfortably in the late morning having had a large breakfast, and many still sipping coffee, they listened to Chauncey explain the mission.

"You are going as gods and goddesses of Ancient Egypt aboard the *Mesektet* boat that will magically enter the Duat or underworld at the very moment the last of the sun sinks below the horizon to the west. Only Pharaoh as Ra is always there. Many scrolls and stone carvings describe different companions—sometimes he is alone, but mostly there are companions to help Pharaoh and the Priests of Ra (this night to be portrayed by those who are staying here with Imhotep to lead them) who stay up in temples throughout Egypt to chant the magic words.

"Remember, Heka, God of Magic, indeed Magic itself, is responsible for the merging of words and actions, so that when the gods do it, or as we practice magic, to say something is identical to doing it. Robin, you have that magic as Heka, but all of you as gods have it also, Robin can just reinforce its power.

"Once you are within the Duat, we have chosen

the texts that deal in the twelve hours of night as doors or gates the boat must pass safely. There are many other texts with other stories, but this is the most likely. Also, with the 'get out clause' that the word becomes the deed, so also a picture becomes the word, becomes the deed. So many texts are abbreviated, and some have different words to say at each gate. Most however believe it is sufficient for the pharaoh simply to name the guardian of the gate correctly to pass safely. It's the priests who say the longer texts."

"In fact," offered Perry, "many pharaohs are buried with this important list of names in their coffin with them, so they won't forget."

"This does not count when facing Apep, however," continued Chauncey, "and he will, as he always does, attack the boat, and you on it, to try to eat the sun. Feral, as the Cat God Mau, will in turn attack him with the sacred knife, and this will, as it always does, make Apep retreat without getting to Pharaoh or the Sun God Ra—which for these purposes are one and the same. Kailen, I hope you will have added some of your own protective magic to what we have generated to protect all of you. In fact, each of you is protected by the protections afforded those aboard the *Mesektet* boat, but I have added spells, and I want each of you to add personal spells for safety and to protect your disguises. It could potentially knock things sidewise if for instance the Goddess

Hathor is suddenly revealed as the modern Maggie Spencer. I don't know what it would do, but I prefer not to find out."

There was general nervous laughter and a few attempts at teasing as they imagined what might happen if they were stripped of their disguises. Laughing mainly because they knew Chen Shi and Imhotep with Perry's help had designed the clothes and the spells that turned them into perfect Egyptian gods. Even Maggie's wig was attached in such a way that only a contrary magic spell could dislodge it. Plus they had each been magically tinted a darker shade, and all eyes were brown. But they agreed that all of them, each with their own magical strengths, would both guard themselves and be ready to help another if there were any slip-ups.

Kate however did have a worry, "We're about to spend some twelve hours in a dark, dank, chilly underworld in very skimpy clothes. Will my warming spell work there? And what about the others? I'm honestly more concerned about that than any dangers we may face, since I know you've thought through all the dangers."

"You're warming spell, and all your spells should work just fine in the Duat," said Chauncey. "But you may have made a false assumption."

"And what is that?" asked Perry. "We don't want any unexpected surprises."

"Dark, dank and cold," said Chauncey laughing. "But have you ever heard of a reptile who would choose to spend its eternal life in a cold place? Ah, I see Maggie has it, am I right?"

"Dark dank and tropical," laughed Maggie. "I hope it's warm and not too hot, humid and hot are not favourites."

"Even humid and warm aren't great when you have to spend a whole night," remarked Kailen.

"This isn't a pleasure cruise, although it's a royal boat. But nor should you be plagued with ongoing discomfort. So I have equipped each of you, along with the clothes and your darker skin colour, with both cooling and warming spells that will keep you each at a temperature you find comfortable. But Apep finds the Duat to be a comfortable warmth for a snake. I wouldn't be surprised if you don't find the occasional tropical plant. It is after all in some ways the mirror image of the Nile."

"We've read about evil spirits and crocodiles and other things down there as well," commented Elvira.

"All of that and more, and there are so many different descriptions, we haven't a real idea of what you'll find. But take heart my dear ones, all the scrolls say that the names, words and spells are quite sufficient to quell any and all of the otherwise potentially dangerous creatures. You have all memorised the most important, and you have the scripts for all the rest."

"But we won't be speaking ancient Egyptian," said Robin.

"Again, just as I once told Kate, my own vocal cords aren't designed to speak any human language, yet here I am speaking to you. That's because magic changes my dragon speech into fluent, in this case, English. Your English will be translated in the ears of the gods, spirits, whatever you meet, into fluent ancient Egyptian."

"And while you do your night shift," Imhotep grinned (it's always a bit startling to see a full grown dragon grin, with all the teeth and the smoke that rolled a bit at the back of his mouth), "We, myself and several other dragons who have studied this period of ancient Egypt in depth, and all of your friends not on the boat, will be doing the chants and offerings that the Priests of Ra did every night while the Sun God was making his voyage under the earth."

They ate an early dinner, a buffet where they could pick and choose, because some of them were feeling a bit nervous and they only nibbled a few things or sipped soup. A few others including Robin and Kailen, ate heartily but carefully, aware that although an actual fight wasn't expected, it was as well to have the energy and they would be taking the boat into the Duat at sunset precisely and surfacing in the

East with the sunrise.

Chapter 50

As the sun sank in the west, at a little past 5pm they gathered at the great Boat of the Night, *Mesektet,* splendid in its colours of amethyst, emerald, jasper, turquoise, lapis lazuli and gold. Imhotep had explained that the boat, once prepared with them on board, would be magically transported to the Gap of Abydos in the western mountain of Manu which, with the eastern mountain of Bakhu, held up the sky in ancient Egypt.

The Misfits, now gods, took their places, Kailen in the middle as Pharaoh/Ra in his Ram-headed form, with Maggie as Hathor behind him and Perry as Thoth before him. Elvira as Isis with Feral as Mau beside her stood before Thoth at the front of the boat, guiding and keeping watch. Finally, at the back keeping guard over them all was Kate as Ma'at, her wings spread out as if to embrace them, her eyes vigilant for any trouble, her powers for order and balance ensuring that this journey would go as planned. Robin as Heka was free to move about the boat, making sure that the magical words were said and that anyone tiring would be renewed.

In the blink of an eye, their lovely garden villa disappeared and *Mesektet* was now at the Gap of Abydos ready to enter the Duat the instant the last tiny scallop of the sun disappeared behind the earth. Kate was wondering what that would be like and was sure everyone else was as well. Would it be a slow sinking below the earth and into the darkness of the Duat, or would it be as instantaneous as a moment ago when the boat left their garden and was suddenly waiting by the Gap of Abydos? She let it go, only hoping that either smells or too much ooze wouldn't be a major part of the landscape.

Kate, and the rest, were aware from their study that there are a number of descriptions of the Duat, including different countries behind each of the twelve gates, signifying the twelve hours of the night.

In the end all the different descriptions were so confusing they had to trust that the script would be essentially the same one. And if ancient Egyptian ideas of the gods and the workings of the sun didn't make a country created by magic, but by belief, then the belief in the more straight forward of the texts would have been the one most in use, and therefore the more powerful. Even if it wasn't quite that, they were workers of genuine and powerful magic and could cause changes to be made.

So they would follow their script, which involved passage through the twelve gates, each guarded by a spitfire snake before it, and the gate itself which was both a real portal with sealed doors and a goddess whose name would bring safe passage. If anything got complicated, Heka's magic should allow them to pass unharmed.

Their main objective was to meet with Apep and have Mau attack him successfully with the meteorite knife while they all chanted the magic spell that would turn him away from Bastet. The rest was essentially just getting to and from the main event.

So Kate's thoughts went, and in various ways so did all the others.

§ § §

Then the sun slipped below the horizon, and their boat was instantly in dark flowing water in a twilight world where before them was the first Gate guarded by a snake spitting fire.

The door was a pylon of stone such as stood at the main entrance of major temples, with huge wooden doors. It was daunting.

All of them gasped or cried out but Kailen. Prince of Faerie in his own right, and now Ra as the Sun God, he didn't gasp, as he was made of very stern stuff when faced with possible danger.

"That snake is huge!" said Elvira."

"You haven't seen Apep—this is just a gate guardian," said Feral coolly, "And you're Isis, you shouldn't be frightened by, well, virtually anything."

"Part of me is Isis," Elvira replied. "But I'm still here too. And I can assure you that, just as with Bastet, Isis is capable of all the human emotions, and she was as startled by this reptile as I was. You know perfectly well the old gods are full of all the emotions known to mankind, and act on them. If it weren't so, we wouldn't be here. Besides, you spawn of Sheitan, reading about these gate guardians, about the lands between the gates, all that, is quite, quite different from actually being in the thick of it."

Perry agreed, "Our boat that seemed so large, our learning and training and even the knowledge that this is just a sort of stage set—all seems a lot more dangerous now that we are actually doing it."

"Like the first time you go sky diving or bungee jumping," added Robin. "It all looks so exciting but safe on a video and there's the wonderful soaring bit you watch and imagine how it will feel to be actually flying. Then you do it and, yes, the soaring part is wonderful, but it's quite short compared to the free fall before and the jerk when you hit the ropes. This is like hoping the ropes will hold or we could sink."

At the same instant the goddess Sia appeared as a part of the gate, and when they told her the snake's name was 'Desert Protector' she instructed the snake to unlock the gate to Ra and his retinue, which allowed the door and its pivot to fold back flat against the stone pylons. The boat passed through to the First Hour part of the Duat where they watched as on a grainy black and white film Ra's enemies were being massacred.

"I hope this doesn't last an entire real hour," murmured Maggie. "Maybe you should have brought a book to read," said Kailen. "One that doesn't make you laugh," offered Robin. And it seemed that as quickly as that, they were through this first hour and on to the Gate of the Second Hour.

The guardian was called 'Swallower of Sinners' and once they named him the gate opened and the *Mesektet* boat sailed through into—a lake of fire.

"Oh hells bells and buckets of blood," cried Kate. "Do they just keep getting worse? But this can't burn the boat, or will it?"

"Of course not," said Robin slipping an arm around her. "This is essentially like a 3D film, imaginary but made to look real. See, it's not hot, and nothing and no one is being set on fire."

"We should have asked for a set of spells or names to make the hours we spend go faster, like the first one," said Perry. "A spell, of course. Robin, help me."

Together the God of Wisdom and Knowledge

and the God of Magic cobbled together a simple spell and spoke it: "Let this hour pass swiftly, warm and unharmed by fire, let us meet the next gate rapidly." Everyone spoke it and through the flames and smoke they could see they had survived the second hour were approaching the Third Gate.

The Goddess of the Gate was called Mistress of Food, and when they told her the snake guardian was 'Stinger', the gate opened on the Lake of Life, with the land full of growing crops. Kailen/Ra inhaled a special breath that brings extra life.

"Well, that's a surprise my love," murmured Maggie. "I hadn't realised that your Ra part was not exactly alive before."

"I did feel a certain lethargy," replied Kailen, "but I thought it was the sulphurous fumes that seem to be part of the air here. Apparently, it is true that when the sun sets, Ra/Pharaoh does in some sense die, and now he begins to take on new life and energy."

The Fourth Gate was without an obvious goddess within its structure and they had not been able to find the name of the Guardian who would let them pass unmolested.

"That's what I was worried about," said Kate. "A few of the Twelve don't have obvious names we can use. Robin, what does Heka have to say about this one?"

Robin laughed, "It's simple in a way, it just an

extension of the Third Gate. Here we will find the Egyptian people working in the fields, producing crops under the renewed strength of Ra and in the name of the Mistress of Food. He called out, "Open in the name of the Mistress of Food and the Cattle of Ra".

The gates opened gently and they sailed into a vista of fields and the four ethnic groups of people (called the 'Cattle of Ra'), the Levantines, Libyans, Nubians and Egyptians, planting and caring for crops.

"Something like when the Romans realised that ten months screwed up their calendar and added July, named for Julius Caesar and August for that wily old fox, Augustus Caesar, to balance their calendar." murmured Perry. "But it is certainly the most welcoming of the hours so far."

"Don't get complacent," advised Kate. "Next is the Fifth Gate and within that Hour Apep is poised and waiting to attack."

Chapter 51

Apep was better, indeed he felt entirely his old self. But he was angry and full of the desire for revenge. He was aware as one could remember some dreams that for eons each night he'd been attacked by gods aboard the *Mesektet*, cut and stabbed sometimes several, sometimes dozens of times, yet nothing had hurt particularly badly, and the next night he had always been both healed and alert and eager to battle again to kill Ra and eat the sun. He knew that recently he had been attacked by a green monster with scales and wings, biting and burning, and opening painful wounds that did not heal and that hurt like fire. He also remembered this happened when he had attacked a large black cat who had been chasing and biting some of his demon army.

He had immediately put this down to a devious plan by the Cat Goddess Bastet, the only other ancient Egyptian God awake in this modern age. He burned with the desire for revenge. When next the *Mesektet* boat came through the Fifth Gate, he would be ready to destroy not just Bastet but all who might be on board with her.

Then the night came when one of the watchers

from on top of the pylons supporting the doors passed the word. "I see it, I see the boat floating this way through the fields of the Cattle of Ra. Alert D K!" And D K flew to his master's side and delivered the tidings that finally the *Mesektet* boat was approaching and would soon enter the Gate of the Fifth Hour.

§　§　§

As their boat navigated the fourth hour, between the fields of crops being attended by the Cattle of Ra, they came within sight of the Fifth Gate, abode of the Goddess of Duration. Kate as Ma'at was charged with calling out the name of the guardian serpent that would allow the gate to open to them. She was not happy about this, it meant meeting Bastet's nemesis, Apep, and although she knew that the magical text they were following would allow them to pass through, after the Cat God Mau inflicted injuries upon Apep, she was only too aware that things could go wrong.

Particularly, she thought, *where there are literally dozens of versions of this 'story' and we have further mucked up the version we've chosen as being most likely by choosing to stock the boat with our own particular choice of gods.* Still, it was her duty as Ma'at to do her part. Standing tall in her white linen sheath with her wings spread, Kate called out the name of the guardian serpent "Flame Eyed". The gate opened and the *Mesektet* sailed through.

Within was Apep, waiting.

Elvira as Isis, her own wings spread and standing beside the brindled cat holding the sacred meteorite knife, now called Apep by the name used in this nightly ritual, "Oh, Evil of Face we have come to sail through this Fifth Hour, with the help of the Cat God Mau who will protect Ra from your wicked intentions." And in a voice only Feral could hear, she whispered, "I trust you my friend, but do not get too excited, do as Mau has done and we will go on our way. I do not wish, as Isis had to do for her dead husband, to be left gathering bits of you from this dreadful place and piecing you back together."

"Don't even concern yourself, my dearest mother, Mau will do his duty," replied Feral. Then he turned and launched himself at Apep as the great God of Chaos made his own strike toward Ra.

Apep curled some of his immense length around the prow of the *Mesektet* holding it from going forward and pulling the prow downward. Elvira held onto the railing as the deck tilted. But Feral as Mau flew through the air to land on the great snake's back near his head, and slashed down with the meteorite knife, slicing deeply into Apep's flesh. He repeated the action along down the serpent's body, leaving bloody wounds, snarling as he moved. Many people think cats don't snarl, but given sufficient cause, hissing and yowling are abandoned, and cats snarl (and in Feral's case, curse).

With his head only a few feet from Ra, Apep was overcome with pain from these multiple wounds, and turned away from the Sun God to make a strike at the Cat God Mau.

But Feral/Mau was much too nimble, and jumped to the prow of the boat where several coils of the great God of Chaos were lodged. Mau stabbed with the sharpened point of the meteorite knife, and then sliced, cutting wedges out of Apep that dropped into the dark waters. Apep uncoiled from the prow of *Mesektet* and let his wounded parts dip beneath the darkness of the Duat while his head pursued Mau, who now leapt to the mast, out of reach for the moment.

Wiping the bloody knife on a fold of furled sail, he turned to see Apep winding his way up the mast, and leapt once more, this time over the heads of the others in the boat back to where Kate stood as Ma'at with her wings once more spread.

"Assume your vulture form," demanded Feral, forgetting once again his instructions not to kill Apep, "and you can rip his head from his body."

"Feral, no!" commanded Kate. "We, rather you, as Mau, are to keep him from attacking Ra, remember? We must do this as we were taught. No one is to kill Apep. This does not happen."

"But we could!" yowled Feral. "It would solve everything. Bastet would be safe."

Perry as Thoth, God of Truth, Learning and Wisdom, who had hardly spoken, now said, "It would solve nothing, and give us an entirely new set of problems. Feral, you have allowed your real personality to overcome the part you are playing. You *must* behave as we have read Mau behaved. We cannot change the ancient histories of the gods so dramatically without the risk of changing the future of Egypt itself all along the timeline."

My stars, thought Kate. *We're half one, half the other, half ourselves and half the god we've chosen to be. We are all confused and afraid, we want to use our usual magic, but it is not as strong in this ancient time. And we are half afraid of our 'god personas' who presumably do know, yet must now do something they've never done before. All of us in a new situation with new selves, with the possible exception of Apep, the never-changing. Yet he is now about to be changed too. And we are re-writing history—which is never a good idea if you're magical and can actually change the past, present or the future. Yet it appears the Egyptians developed and wrote so many different 'stories' or books of spells and books of the history of the gods and who they were and what they did. Perhaps that's why this is possible for us. Just another small addition to the four thousand years of making and unmaking, changing and reinventing gods and a way of life based on their worship.*

She was also aware that, unlike what they were attempting to make Apep believe, in fact a number of the 'stories' or 'spells' did have Bastet attacking Apep. And she knew that most of the others knew it too, but were sticking to Bastet's own belief, and who knew but that it was the right one. Or possibly it was a case of the victor wrote the history. Whatever, the time had come.

"It is time." said Ra. And they all, including Ma'at and Isis, said the spell they'd worked out:

Apep God of Chaos, hear us! It is not and never has been the Cat Goddess Bastet who has tormented you. She is one of several cat gods, and not your tormenter. The Cat God Mau cuts you. Mau is a personification of the Sun God, Mau guards the Tree of Life which holds the secrets of eternal life and divine knowledge. See and learn—here is Mau the brindle cat who injures you nightly, never the Black Cat Goddess Bastet. Leave Bastet alone!

This ritual chant, repeated the magical three times, became the chorus that provided backing for the next and totally unexpected part of their mission.

Feral, who had been having an exciting but sometimes difficult time slashing at Apep with the magic meteorite knife, saw out of the corner of his eye a disruption of the dark waters of the Duat.

Chapter 52

The Dragon King Chen Shi was rising up out of the primordial ooze. Chauncey, his scales navy and black with gold streaks, his spikes golden-red, his wings spread slightly, and his nostrils giving off smoke and flickers of flame, loomed over the fight between Apep and Feral and the others chanting the protective spells.

"Kill him!" screamed Feral. "I can only injure him slightly, here in his kingdom we haven't the strength to make him die!"

"No, Feral," said Chauncey quietly. "You have all done your jobs here just as they should be done. Clever, brave Feral, it is not part of your task to destroy the God of Chaos. Or for me to do so now." His long neck rotated so that his giant head with its golden eyes and the flames that flickered around his nostrils showing the extent of his fangs and teeth were only a few feet from the considerably smaller head of Apep.

"In spite of what the Egyptians equated with Evil, Chaos is not bad. It brings forth innovations and change. Chaos lives within the very magic of creation.

"Apep, God of Chaos, letting you live to continue the cycle is one thing. Having you run—or slither—loose with hatred and longing to destroy the Cat Goddess Bastet is quite another. Look you now at this gathering of Gods and Goddesses. Is Bastet here? No, she is not. Who is the Cat God that wields the knife that has delivered numerous cuts this night?"

Apep was silent, whether in fear and awe, or possibly stubbornness, or because he hadn't looked closely at the brindled cat holding the knife, he said nothing.

The Dragon King let out a roar that echoed, and flames now shot out of his mouth, but passed harmlessly over Apep's head and the *Mesektet* boat.

"This is the Cat God Mau. Mau is the brindled cat that has attacked you whenever you have attempted to destroy the Tree of Life. Mau, not Bastet, fights you to a standstill when necessary. Do not attempt to push the boundaries of your endless battles to any kind of a victory.

"See, Ma'at, the Goddess of Balance, stands with the others. There also is Thoth, God of Writing and the power of the Word, and Heka, God of Magic, who enhances the power of words so they are as effective as actions. All are here tonight to protect the balance of the world, a balance which depends also upon Chaos, but Chaos within bounds. Without the nightly glorious quest through the Underworld, Ra the Sun would not rise strong and renewed each day. Ma'at as balance would not maintain the world.

"Heed my words, do not pursue the Cat Goddess Bastet of modest powers to help and heal.

She is nothing to do with you. Should I hear anything to the contrary from now until the end of time, you may be certain that I will seek you out and make you suffer for ages before I decide whether to kill you or not. Say 'yes, I understand, I will do as you tell me'."

Apep looked aghast, he turned his head this way and that looking for even one supporter, looking for a way out. But there was none. He thought upon the eons of being the Evil One. There had been a lot of satisfaction in causing fear. But then he thought upon what this huge other-worldly being had said, that Chaos brought forth change and was a part the magic of Creation.

He was the God of Chaos, and Chaos was integral to the working of the world. He could live with that. So he raised his head and in a firm voice said, "Yes, I understand, I will do as you tell me."

"That is all that anyone could ask. Thank you for your understanding." responded Chauncey. His fiery breath passed harmlessly over Apep, but in its wake, one scale of the God of Chaos turned a pale gold that showed just the bright outlines of all the colours of the rainbow. A gift, a beneficence, a promise?

Kate reached out with her winged arm to touch Chauncey. He stopped his slide back into the Duat and met her eye.

In their ability to meet mind to mind, Kate asked, "The rest don't know you're here, do they? Except Feral. And me."

"No daughter, they don't, they believe their chant is working to be-spell Apep into forgetting his grudge against Bastet, and that all is going as it should. I didn't think you would see me either, but it seems our connection is stronger even than my magic, or perhaps because you were just reprimanding Feral as I came up. But, no harm done, I know I can trust you not to reveal this."

"I won't, not if you don't wish it. But why?" queried Kate.

"Because the power here must come from you as Egyptian Gods and I, a being from another world and time, would only mess up that power. Even Apep is already forgetting. and he will not remember me."

"But you gave him a scale—a gold scale with rainbow glints—is that a reward, or what?" asked Kate.

"It is a connection, and should he ever be so foolish as to begin to have evil thoughts about Bastet, that scale will alert me, and also stop him."

"You mean kill him? But that will undo history, won't it?" asked Kate.

"No, dear girl of mine, not kill him, simply short-circuit that thinking, remove it. It's simple and will not upset history."

"And Feral? Feral will want to tell this tale, he couldn't help himself," sighed Kate

"You worry too much. Remember whose child you are —mine—and do not worry. Feral has already forgotten that he saw me, and he will prefer his tale to be of his own bravery and how he did not falter when attacking Apep.

"Now it is time to leave this gate and Apep behind and travel toward the rising of the sun. Remember, as far as ancient Egypt and all the Misfits know, there was never a dragon here." Chauncey slide soundlessly below the waters of the Duat and disappeared.

Chapter 53

They had all breathed a sigh of relief as Apep agreed that Bastet was not his enemy. He had spoken firmly but appeared hypnotised or spell-bound. It was the latter of course, their magic both as the Misfits and with Robin as Heka, the very embodiment of magic had created a spell that got through even to Apep.

And, although only Kate would remember it, Chen Shi, appearing as they were chanting the spell, reinforced its power, plus the size and other worldliness of the enormous dragon impressed the God of Chaos deeply. Chen Shi also offered Apep a truth about Chaos that Apep could accept as being much more important than waging a private war against a Cat Goddess. Ra was his enemy and his job. Cat gods were a nuisance, especially this brindled Mau. But he was too literally enchanted to be bothered with Bastet anymore, the magic had got into his blood and his heart, the organ Egyptians believed was the seat of consciousness as well as life.

§ § §

During the planning stages, they had discovered that after meeting Apep in the Fifth Hour, they had been left dangling as to the names of the rest of the gates and their goddesses and guardians. The accepted practice of calling out the name of the goddess and the guardian serpent to open the way was blocked when none of the texts they found included this important information.

"Perhaps the goddess of the gate will tell us," ventured Kate.

"Perhaps it will be so," answered   Kailen. "But it could also leave us stranded. We need something better."

Chauncey was always there as guide and helper. "I suggest Heka, as God of Magic, use that magic at the time to discover the name which will open the gate."

Robin as Heka was frankly nervous, so much apparently depended upon getting the names right. "Maybe…but maybe it is better to work out a useful name based on what we know about the gate, the hour ahead and any other information we have. I would not want to be the one to fail, not when we could be stuck in the Duat and the sun might not rise."

Chauncey had laughed gently. "My brave young mage, we have already made up a spell that never existed before to hopefully subdue Apep and stop him believing the Goddess Bastet is his enemy. I have every faith that it will do just that despite a number of texts that include her with the various Cat

Gods available to do this job. Because in this case ancient Egypt is our ally. They have left behind so many versions of spells, of gods— a god could hardly stand still for a moment before some priests grabbed him and changed his looks, his clothes, his powers.

And who knows how many lost scrolls there are that give names to the guardians of these gates? We have a few, and they don't always agree, as we know. It is a virtual certainty that amongst the lost scrolls there will be names aplenty. You don't even have to alight upon one that matches.

"Take what Heka knows of these things and trust him and his magic to give you names and attributes that will work for us.

"Personally I have no doubts about his ability. You, Robin, may be in ignorance, but when you are Haka, you will be given the knowledge you need. The ancient Egyptians were famous for their surplus of possible names and attributes for virtually everything, and that is one of the things magic is for—to see into the future or the past and pick out the right one, or at least one that will suffice."

"But, getting back to Heka, God of Magic," said Kate. "Why is he powerful or magical enough for you to trust him to come up with names or phrases or spells to get us through the remaining gates safely? Look, we've all read a lot about Egypt, Perry and me especially, and honestly, until I saw the Egyptian word for Magic was the name of our dahabeeyah I'd never heard the word, and even then didn't know there was such a god. Why does Heka get this job?"

Chauncey nodded understandingly. "Until recently Egyptologists didn't really know about him either. But in fact it was like standing on top of a large mountain and looking around for it, not realising that it was so big and you were already there on top.

"Heka was so much a part of every god's magic, so pervasive that he was not noticed as a being or god in his own right. They read of magic and spells done by or for gods and attributed it to them. Also, he had no cult or ritual worship for the most part. The ancient Egyptians knew him as the power behind all the other gods when it came to magic, so it was not necessary to mention him.

"Magic was considered the operative force in the creation of their universe, which makes Heka one of the oldest gods in Egypt, and so all pervasive that he was everywhere. If you were pregnant, you'd pray to Hathor or to Taweret, if you were worried about the crops you prayed to Min, God of Harvest. To pass your exams, you asked Thoth to help. I could go on almost infinitely, but the point is these are gods with limited magic or power to help in certain circumstances. Heka, however, is the power behind all their thrones. If we need magic, all-seeing all-knowing magic, we need Heka. As such he is perfect for receiving the knowledge of how to get you through the rest of the night and safely into the morning."

§ § §

Now the boat moved on toward the Sixth Gate. As they approached, Heka stepped forward (Robin's shape, Robin's voice, yet somehow, this was clearly Heka) and announced, "Oh Mistress of Darkness the name of your guardian is 'Destroyer', please let us pass." And the gate opened upon the Sixth Hour. Here they were faced with a daunting scene: seven jackal-headed poles were upright in the thick, muddy water and on each two men were bound, waiting, Chauncey had said, to be beheaded. Maggie objected. "These are human men it would appear, are they here just waiting for eternity or are they beheaded nightly only to find themselves here again the next night?"

"Calm yourself, Mum," said Robin. "This is a dream of sorts. They are dead already and do not suffer as we would expect."

"A DVD on permanent replay," offered Kate. "Besides we've seen worse, and I suspect there is worse to come. We must remember our jobs, and not interfere."

They moved on neither fast nor slow, but the Sixth Hour passed, and they were again approaching a gate. The Seventh Gate was the Goddess called The Shining One and Heka named the guardian 'Ikenti', at which the gate opened, and they passed through.

This was part of Osiris' dead kingdom, and it was even worse, as Kate had said. There were 20 gods holding a rope ending in four whips, four falcon heads and four human heads. The heads had expressions of great suffering. Kate put her winged arm up over her face. Maggie put her hands over her face, even Perry, as Thoth, turned his head away. But Kailen as Ra, stood erect and proud and even somehow become stronger.

"When I was a child, my dad took me to an amusement park and we went on the ghost train, it scared me to death really, but these, these are horrific," said Kate.

"But, like your ghost train, they are here every night," said Robin, "and I suspect they aren't 'real' as in alive and feeling, just as the scary things in a chamber of horrors aren't real. In any case, none of this is real in one sense, just as in another sense, it is real. Either way, just as you stopped Feral from going too far, neither can we. We must go on as it is described, or we might as well have done nothing."

"When did you get so smart?" said Kate, half laughing, half miserable at not being able to relieve suffering.

"When I met you, I think. Around about then

something happened and everything changed."

"Yes, it did, didn't it?" said Kate, looking back through time and all that had taken place. "And not all, or even most, of what has happened has been fun and games. But I wouldn't change it. So we'll keep going."

"That's my girl," said Robin kissing her hand.

"Let's get our minds back on tonight's business," Perry intervened. "This is no time for romance or reminiscing—the Eighth Gate is approaching, and we have work to do."

Chapter 54

Once more an hour had passed and *Mesektet* approached the Eighth Gate where Heka named the flaming snake as Lighter of Flames and the guardian he called Protector of His Body. The door opened and they sailed into a lake once more, but now the flaming snake was looping through the water with flames coming out of his mouth, burning things in the water.

"He is incinerating the enemies of Osiris," explained Thoth.

"Of course, you would know that," grumbled Elvira, drawing Feral in closer to her and away from any errant flames. In truth, although their god selves were in residence, their witch selves were beginning to become extremely tired of the endless hours and the sudden dangers.

"I'd often wondered" said Kate, "at the upright posture of all those gods and goddesses in the boat on the frescos. Of course, they were painted, caught in a moment of time, but here we are, maintaining our postures over what feels like an eternity, and honestly I am getting very tired and even have muscle cramps here and there."

Robin came over, being the only one except Feral who seemed free to roam the boat, "You are working with your human body, and doing witch spells. They are not nearly as powerful here. Try being the Goddess Ma'at and use her magic."

"I've done that a few times when Ma'at needed ascendency within me, but she or it is so powerful, I've been afraid to give myself over to her." admitted Kate.

Robin understood. "I know how that is, Heka is a very powerful God, and giving over my will to him was quite scary at first. But I've found that I can switch back and forth or blend myself and the god, and Heka doesn't object, doesn't fight me for dominance. Come, Kate, exhaustion is not necessary, let Ma'at help."

Maggie also called back from her position near Ra, "The power of the gods is stronger here, and our ability both to maintain ourselves and fight off anything that could cause harm to *Mesektet* or Ra is weak—but when I call upon Hathor to help, or even take over, strength and serenity and calm come to me. You must be exhausted from holding those wings out."

"I certainly am," grumbled Elvira, "but, yes, I've been fearful of giving myself or even some of myself over to Isis for fear of not getting back to myself properly. So I am sore and tired and a bit trembly."

Perry was quick to reassure them. "I have allowed a sort of sharing between myself and Thoth so

I can use his strengths and magic when and if necessary but remain myself as well. There is nothing about these gods that I can tell—or Thoth can find, and he is the God of Truth and Wisdom—that would do us harm. None of them desire to possess us, and all are here to help. So let them help."

With sighs of relief, all the others relaxed and allowed their Egyptian God or Goddess to carry the burdens and stand ready to help or fight if necessary. It was, Kate found, a vast improvement on how she'd felt before, and she could actually feel that Ma'at, Goddess of Balance, Truth, Harmony and Reciprocity, also felt more at ease and totally approved.

"It wasn't even a fear I actually knew I had, I just felt that keeping myself as myself was wiser," Kate said. "I must have been afraid she would want to take me over without ever having the actual thought."

The others nodded. Except Kailen, who had maintained his Ra persona virtually throughout, but now said. "I felt it was appropriate as Ra/Pharaoh to adopt that identity completely, and it has made the journey seem both ordinary and fascinating. But had I known the rest of you were fearful and suffering in silence, I'd have calmed you."

"So," asked Maggie, "You are truly Ra, but are you still truly Kailen?"

"Yes my love, I am also truly Kailen, your partner and Robin's father. Set those fears aside, you have not lost me in any way."

Weak with relief, Maggie was also shot through with a surge of anger and adrenaline. "Why the hell didn't you or Thoth, or even Robin tell us sooner? Did you think it was fun watching us standing like statues hour after hour?"

"Especially with our arms out supporting these damn wings," said Elvira with some vehemence.

"We didn't know," interrupted Thoth. "We thought that your stillness, like ours, was using the power of the Goddesses."

Maggie was still indignant. She turned to Robin. "You were free to go all over the boat, didn't it occur to you to ask some of us if standing stock still for hours was getting uncomfortable?"

Robin shrugged. "Ask any of us, we thought we needed to do this, me move around, helping when things were dicey with Apep or anything else. But no one, not you Goddesses or Witches, or us thought about our own comfort as such. Except that it must have been very tiring. But all our energies were focused on what new dangers might be behind each door, or under the Duat, like that fiery snake."

Maggie's anger dissipated, and her witch self would have sat down, except Hathor kept her standing, but now without discomfort.

Elvira said somewhat sadly, "Since it all went

more or less like clockwork each night, I suppose we could all have sat around drinking coffee and cold drinks with snacks and possibly playing cards, and it wouldn't have made a difference."

"Possibly we could have," said Kailen. "But I found various things happening to me as Ra/Pharoah. As we went deeper into the night, I became somewhat weaker, and as we crossed into the hours moving toward morning, as now, I have felt reinvigorated, stronger. So I suspect, imposters though we are in some ways, in others we are very much connected successfully to the beliefs and rituals of ancient Egypt. Maybe they also sat around, but I doubt it, not because there aren't any frescos or statues showing that, but because of how I, and probably all of you, felt."

Kate nodded, "Yes, even tired with my arms throbbing with holding them out hour after hour, nothing in me was crying out to sit down and have a rest. It was uncomfortable, but I never for a second felt what I was doing was useless and I might as well sit and read a book until we got to sunrise."

Chapter 55

While they'd been talking the boat continued steadily toward the Ninth Gate. Robin was confused, as this Gate seemed to have different symbolism. Here stood Horus and Set. However, Heka's magic told him the name of the Gate Goddess was Foremost, and the name of the Guardian was Fowler.

Having said these, the gate opened and the boat sailed through, but within were carved and painted statues of the nine gods of the Ennead: Atum, Shu, Tefnut, Geb, Nut, Osiris, Isis, Nephthys, and Set. In the story The Contendings of Horus and Set these nine gods decided whether Set or Horus should rule.

Perry spoke up as they sailed along between these statues, "These nine gods, called the Great Ennead, are from another Egyptian myth that has little to do with our journey through the night. It's my guess that the juxtaposition of the Ninth Gate and the appearance of Horus and Set at the entrance has given us this panoply of nine gods of the Ennead, in which they form the tribunal to determine who, Horus or Set, is to have the throne of Egypt. So either it is a long-ago mix-up of two important foundation stories, or just possibly a recent one for this night only, where somehow, as we come closer to the dawn, the reality of this night and the mythological status of it have become mixed.

"In any case," said Kate, "it appears that the story of Horus and Set is not as important here as our own guiding of the *Mesektet* through until we reach the sunrise, since this is a tableau and not something with any life in it."

"And now as we come to the Tenth Gate," said Kailen, "we will once more face Apep, but thanks to our brave Cat God Mau, and some protective soldiers, we will find him helpless in chains so he cannot harm Ra."

Which, once Heka had called out the name of the Goddess of the Portal (Piercing of Voice) and the Guardian Snake (Great Embracer), proved to be the truth. Apep, bound as he was, managed to say "I will remember that the Cat Goddess Bastet is not my enemy. I have sworn it."

Their boat sailed on, and all of them felt the increase of strength and energy coming from the knowledge that they had accomplished the task of freeing Bastet from future threats, and that only two more gates stood between them and delivering the Sun God once more to Egypt, where the sun would rise, and their work would be done.

Now they approached the Eleventh Gate where the Goddess was called "Mysterious of Approaches and the Guardian's name was Meeyuty (a pronunciation of Meow).

Elvira laughed, "That is the perfect name, as almost always a cat approaches mysteriously, one second there is no cat, then there is one. Is it not so, Feral?" she said, tickling him behind the ears.

"Oh, yeah, there are special courses in it," grumbled Feral, still in his brindled coat as Mau.

"Well they certainly work, I've never seen a cat enter a room unless it intends for everyone to see it," said Kate. "Whereas many times there has suddenly been a cat in a room and no one has seen it enter." Which caused a lot of smiles.

"But now, the final Gate, where Isis stands," said Elvira, who was also Isis. "I have no idea how to do it, to transfer myself from here to stand at the Twelfth Gate. Does anyone know?"

"In the same way as our boat was instantaneously transferred from our garden in the Egyptian Principality to the Gap of Abydos," said Ra.

"And I will be at the Twelfth Gate with the goddess Nephthys. But *Mesektet* will pass through, and I will be left behind— or do I automatically reappear on the boat?"

Heka laughed. "You do, right at the prow as before. It is amusing that the name of the Guardian is 'Cat'. And the sun will appear over the horizon."

§ § §

It happened just that way. Just as the sun rose, as suddenly as they had left they were back, still in their *Mesektet* boat, in the garden of the villa where Chauncey and Imhotep and their various friends, including their dragons, waited to greet them and hug them and exclaim over how glad they were to see them back safe and what a wonderful thing they had accomplished.

"Although," said Bastet, "there were times when the night seemed endless. But Imhotep kept us informed when anything important happened. I am so grateful to you all for the spell that convinced Apep that he no longer holds a grudge against me, Bastet, as he had believed for so long."

Epilogue

After the hugs and the congratulations, and the shedding of ancient Egyptian identities (including Feral returning from brindle to black) they sat down at tables for various sizes of creature loaded with an excellent choice of breakfasts. But having loaded their plates, quite a bit of wandering around took place as the crew of the *Mesektet* were approached by those who had stayed at home.

Having eaten his fill, Feral went to sit in Kate's lap, since Elvira had taken her place at a piano and was playing a medley of songs old and new. After a bit, Feral turned over in his sleep and displayed his tummy to the enchanted Kate. She knew his reputation, and that included being very picky about who he would consort with, and very much that he wouldn't relax like this on any lap except Elvira's. Until now. She felt absurdly honoured.

Bastet came to sit beside her and watched Feral with eyes that glowed with pride and love. "If this were a different era, he would be a god in his own right," she said.

Kate couldn't help laughing softly, "He certainly has all the characteristics— massive ego, balanced with genuine kindness, help for the helpless, fearless, loyal and with a charisma that mingles charm with ruthlessness. I am beyond honoured that he should choose to relax as he is with me, because he is not known for easily letting down his guard."

Bastet laughed and laughed, "Perhaps he is Feral, perhaps he is Pharaoh." Which woke the sleeping Feral, and he stretched, then, seeing that he was in the presence of the most important Cat Goddess of Egypt, he sat up and bowed his head.

Still slightly out of it, he turned to find himself not with Elvira but in Kate's lap. He gave a start, and then, remembering, he bowed his head to her too, but jumped down. Here he stood, quickly assessing the day and of being in the presence of Bastet.

"My Lady," he said. "I did my best for you, I acted as Mau and cut and cut the God of Chaos. Then I would have ended him if I could but was brought to my senses and proceeded as Mau. We all heard him say 'I will remember that the Cat Goddess Bastet is not my enemy. I have sworn it'. My Sovereign Goddess, you are free and need not fear ever again."

Then he turned, looking, "Where is the meteorite knife? I cannot have lost it. It must be returned."

"It's all right my Paladin," said Bastet. "The knife is with Kailen and Perry. They will clean it and make sure it is perfect for return to the museum."

"And I will take it there," announced Feral, in a voice that brooked no argument. But Bastet and Elvira both knew him well, and Elvira scooped him up, bowing to Bastet as she did so, and carried him away, murmuring "Of course you will, you scamp. But you will need and accept help. No arguing!" (as he opened his mouth to protest).

They moved away and Kate laughed softly, "He will do it, and accept help, and he will feel justified."

"If he ever learns to cooperate with a little less arguing, he could rule a world. I've met gods who didn't have half the guts and intelligence he has," said Bastet. "Ah, well, it would have to be another world though. Still, he is a cat worthy to be my Paladin." And Bastet too walked away, having accepted a hug and a small bow from Kate.

Kate made her way over toward Chauncey who was surrounded by his children and some of the grown dragons from the Principality. She watched as he singled out various of them for a special comment, praise or a bit of conversation. They all were clearly happy to be near him, and more relaxed than she'd ever seen them when together. She watched as he spoke to Silver, the two Rivers and Dawn. There was Dawn, the one they'd been scared for (and scared of), looking radiant as an accepted member of the group, Silver's spy dragons. There were the Moon Dragons, the Misfits special friends. They looked so relaxed and unworried.

We helped to do that, we set them free and now they are freely mixing with magical folk of all sorts, and for this moment at least without a care in the world.

She felt a warm glow as Dawn came over to present her front foot and say, "Come walk with me. Our father wants you here with us, we were both outsiders, and now we are both part of his family."

"But I am not a dragon," said Kate half in jest.

"But you have a dragon's heart," replied Dawn. "And we are sisters, and daughters of Chen Shi. How amazing and lovely that is, don't you think?" And Kate agreed wholeheartedly.

She went to stand beside him as she often did, her hand on his front foot, surrounded by other dragons of different sizes and colours, and she felt again the wonder of it, that this was a life with purpose, excitement, love, danger, and always new things to discover.

"You are doing what I expect you often do, aren't you?" asked Chen Shi.

"I have been mulling over what you said to Feral that brought him to his senses. The thing is, I could sense that it had a most amazing effect on Apep as well. My knowledge of chaos theory is almost nil, but what you said also struck a chord in me. I may have it wrong however and have been waiting to talk to you.

"What was it I said, Daughter?"

"You told Feral and Apep, 'In spite of what the Egyptians equated with Evil, Chaos is not bad. It brings forth innovations and change. Chaos lives within the very magic of creation.'"

"And so it does," rumbled Chauncey. "It is why Apep was the first god, aside from Atum, and it may be that they are mirror images of each other, because Atum created and maintains, but he created from chaos, and there is the connection.

"Every planet in this solar system is the result of chaos and of chance—asteroids crashing together to form larger bodies, Jupiter rampaging through the new planets, destroying and building, and now protecting this Earth. Then, for this small time in this small corner of the universe, there is quiet and the creation of order of a kind, and out of this springs life and all that we have. But it is only from your viewpoint that all follows an orderly path, step back and back again and you will see this as just a breathing space between chaotic periods. Or take a few flowers, they grow, they flower, they are pollinated, and seeds fall and become flowers in their turn. But all the time there are also 'accidents' that produce different flowers, or different plants. Creation on large and small scales depends upon Chaos. It is the mixing spoon that stirs the ingredients and changes them. Neither good nor bad, just different, a good change for some, perhaps a deadly change for others. You humans look around and want stability on your Earth with only relatively small changes. From a dragon's point of view it is a much more volatile place. Without Apep there would have been no ancient Egypt, and without this form of Egypt the whole world would have followed a different course. Good or bad? It simply depends upon your point of view."

"So Chaos does really live within the very magic of creation?" asked Kate.

"Scientists of all varieties and certainly astrophysicists, say that. And anyone who really watches how things happen must at least guess that is what happens." Chauncey's smile was infectious, and Kate certainly knew he believed it.

Kate, too, could sense that it was true. *Harmony out of Chaos,* she thought, looking with love at the beauty of their gardens, the tables with food and drink, the people of so many different species with their different sizes, shapes and colours who were her friends, and more than friends. *This is where I stand if only for a nano-second of universal time, but this is my point of view, and I cherish it.*

THE END

AUTHOR'S NOTE

Just like my characters, I have tried to search out the 'real' ancient Egyptian history of their gods and goddesses to do my best to make this fantasy coincide as much as possible to theirs.

The Egyptians at the time were doing much the same it seems. There are so many conflicting stories and religious texts and histories. So, understandably, if a scribe was missing a bit of connecting 'stuff' in his story he either left it out, made it up or filched it from another version. And so have I. But I have done my best to fit my fantasy into their fantasy as well as I could.

The meteorite knife is real. It was found in King Tut's wrappings, placed right over his heart. Egyptologists were excited because smelting iron was very rare in Egypt at the time, and they hadn't the skill to produce iron as expertly worked as this knife. It is still one of the great treasures ever found and it is thought it was a bridal gift to a previous pharaoh from a Mitanni king. It is possible they knew the origin was from a meteorite, since also among the wrappings were small beads of meteorite iron, crudely worked, and referred to as 'stars'. Whereas the knife blade was clearly of expert workmanship.

And having introduced the cat Feral in Chen Shi's Children, he has become a major character and fan favourite (and one of my favourites). So naturally he has a big part to play in this book devoted to saving the Cat Goddess Bastet from the God of Chaos.

Thank you for reading this book, and I hope you enjoyed it. Independent writers depend upon reviews on Amazon or mentions on FaceBook and word of mouth to spread the word. If you do, I will appreciate it very much.

ABOUT THE AUTHOR

What makes a writer? A childhood full of books, discovery of L Space* a land without end. The need to disappear into that land to remain sane within my extremely dysfunctional family (books can be escape hatches, transport to faraway places and fortified castles). A working career that involved research and writing. Ultimately good friends who 'saw' who I really was, then urged and prodded and provided emotional support when I finally started to write fiction.

That was my journey, and it continues with the surprising discovery that my fictional characters take on a life of their own, and therein lies the secret of how one book has become four books and may in time (if I am granted the time) become more books.

*L-Space is what the great Sir Terry Pratchett dubbed Libraries – they are fantastical and endless sources of knowledge, pleasure and escape.

Reviews

THE DRAGONS OF WYVERN HALL

Heart stopping action, inventive magic, and a super plot in this ingenious first novel by Nancy Wolff! Terry Pratchett fans will rejoice!

Imaginative Page-turner with Engaging Characters ...full of ingenuity and imagination and kept me reading even when I should have been going to sleep. I can't wait to see what they get up to in the next book.

I laughed out loud, cried out loud, and cheered out loud. What more can you ask of a book? And a first book, at that. I will be holding my breath until I can read the sequel. I'm a far cry from a young adult, but it struck a chord and took me back to some of my favorite reads.

Fabulous story! ...the characters become much loved friends in no time.

It's not often that one book can span the generations. I enjoyed the book very much. I purchased one for a granddaughter aged 14 who raved over it.

Dragons, magic and common sense - a winning combination. A jolly romp of good versus evil with a few twists and turns along the way. I will certainly read the next one when it comes out.

A Classic in The Making. A magical novel that winds its way into your heart and becomes part of its landscape forever.

A WEDDING IN VENICE

You just can't miss reading "A Wedding in Venice" if you read "The Dragons of Wyvern Hall". Her characters are so well developed that I could almost reach out and touch them, and I surely cheered them on.

Superb! I loved it, the characterisation is amazing and you can relate to all of them. I can't wait to read.the next book!

The Perfect Escapade and Escape The author has an extraordinary ability to take well-known landmarks, both real and mythological and inhabit them in ways never done before. Her approach to treasures of our childhood allows us to revisit them as places altered with maturity and thus ever surprising. I loved hanging out with this motley crew again, and relished the beautiful landscapes Ms Wolff conjures so vividly. It indeed became an "escape" from these troubled times for me. Thank you so much, Nancy. Keep on!

CHEN SHI'S CHILDREN

A 'fantastic read in every sense of the word. This story expands on so many things in the previous two books - The Dragons of Wyvern Hall and A Wedding in Venice - and takes us on an exciting adventure full of suspense and wonder by turns. Wonderful!

Well worth the wait for this wonderful book. just love the detail Nancy puts in her books. This is enchanting, happy, sad, humorous, witty, and beautiful. Each individual has such a full character and background and all their adventures take you to fascinating places across the world and magical places too. Plus the cream on the top are the nods and winks to Sir Terry Pratchett.

The third instalment, but hopefully not the last. Movie please.
Or a miniseries. Nancy Wolff's describes the Dragons as if she has seen them with her own two normal eyes instead of her mind's one. Just as the Dragon Principalities. Not to mention Egypt! I've read the last chapters in one night, I was so curious to know how it would end.

Printed in Great Britain
by Amazon